FEB 1 7 2021

# THE
# UNCOLLECTED
# STORIES
# OF

# ALLAN GURGANUS

ALSO BY ALLAN GURGANUS

*Decoy: A Novella*

*Local Souls*

*The Practical Heart: Four Novellas*

*Plays Well with Others*

*White People*

*Blessed Assurance: A Moral Tale*

*Oldest Living Confederate Widow Tells All: A Novel*

# THE UNCOLLECTED

 STORIES OF

# ALLAN GURGANUS

LIVERIGHT PUBLISHING CORPORATION

A DIVISION OF W. W. NORTON & COMPANY

*Independent Publishers Since 1923*

Earlier versions of some stories have appeared in magazines or as limited edition chapbooks. "My Heart Is a Snake Farm" and "He's at the Office" and "The Wish for a Good Young Country Doctor" were seen in *The New Yorker*. *Harper's* published "Fourteen Feet of Water in My House." "The Mortician Confesses" was in *Granta*. "Fetch" appeared in *Tin House*. *The Virginia Quarterly Review* printed "The Deluxe $19.95 Walking Tour of Historic Falls (NC) —Light Lunch Inclusive." "Unassisted Human Flight" appeared in *The Sewanee Review*. "A Fool for Christmas" became a limited edition chapbook printed by Horse and Buggy Press in association with the Duke University Libraries, distributed by Duke University Press.

For information about permission to reproduce selections from this book, write to Permissions, Liveright Publishing Corporation, a division of W. W. Norton & Company, Inc., 500 Fifth Avenue, New York, NY 10110

For information about special discounts for bulk purchases, please contact W. W. Norton Special Sales at specialsales@wwnorton.com or 800-233-4830

Manufacturing by Lake Book Manufacturing
Book design by Brooke Koven
Production manager: Anna Oler

Library of Congress Cataloging-in-Publication Data

Names: Gurganus, Allan, 1947– author.
Title: The uncollected stories of Allan Gurganus / Allan Gurganus.
Description: First edition. | New York, NY : Liveright Publishing Corporation, a division of W. W. Norton & Company, [2021]
Identifiers: LCCN 2020029010 | ISBN 9780871403780 (hardcover) | ISBN 9781631498763 (epub)
Classification: LCC PS3557.U814 A6 2021 | DDC 813/.54—dc23
LC record available at https://lccn.loc.gov/2020029010

Liveright Publishing Corporation, 500 Fifth Avenue, New York, N.Y. 10110
www.wwnorton.com

W. W. Norton & Company Ltd., 15 Carlisle Street, London W1D 3BS

1 2 3 4 5 6 7 8 9 0

TO JANE HOLDING

*whose company makes even the unendurable*
*worthwhile,*
*and who heard these tales first.*

There is another world, but it is in this one.

—PATRICK WHITE

# CONTENTS

# ACKNOWLEDGMENTS

I've been blessed with many amazing teachers. I owe them everything. Some of these are: Ethel Morris Gurganus (aka "Mother"), Daisy Thorp, Grace Paley, John Cheever, Stanley Elkin, John Irving, John L'Heureux, Paul Nagano, Elizabeth Spencer, Bill Park, James Zito, Paul Taylor, Bessie Schonberg, David Rubin, Danny Kaiser, Connie Brothers, Elisabeth Sifton, Hobson Pittman, Cynthia Thorp, Diane Disney, Catherine Walker, Mildred Teague, Lula Brantley Simmons, Ada Spencer Hobbs, Jackie Cook. And Margaret Lewis, who taught me to read and write.

I am indebted to my inspiring editor, Bob Weil. Amanda Urban has humanely represented my fiction and me for decades. I thank Chase Culler for tech help and moral support.

# THE
# UNCOLLECTED
# STORIES
# OF

# ALLAN GURGANUS

# THE WISH FOR A GOOD YOUNG
# COUNTRY DOCTOR

M OST KIDS lose or break their toys. I curated mine.
　　Sure, I've lived long enough to earn this Santa beard.
But some of what pleased me as a boy still does. Who can resist
smooth objects, ideally miniaturized, made only to be funny,
colorful, and touched?

　　The master's thesis became my first book: *Hand-Wrought
Iowa-Illinois Farm Toys 1880–1920.* In 1976 the University of
Iowa renamed an existing history-literature program "America Studies." It drafted me and other merry hippie researchers.
The school issued us small monthly checks to go gather "folk
manifestations." We plundered far-flung Salvation Army thrifts
and rural junk shops. We hunted the simple tools and dolls our
essays over-interpreted. Such start-up treasures helped form
my folk collection, one not-unknown today.

Hand-wrought nineteenth century artifacts were criminally cheap then. "Midwesterners don't know what they have . . . **had**," we Easterners gloated after country raids.

Prior to radio, before television, savage winters spent indoors made many German-Americans excellent woodcarvers. Unable to afford child-whimsies (even from the Sears catalogue), a farmer just whittled his brood's amusements. Those things sure lasted! Here we have a horse-drawn farm cart toy-scaled for one specific kid. You can still feel the dad's February yearning for warm weather, for October's wheat crop. You can sense this carver's love for the mismatched horses hand-portrayed and for his boy, born to inherit Dobbin, Paint, and the family acreage.

These days, I'm sometimes interviewed about my collection. Lazier reporters ask me to name my single most valuable purchase. It was actually a gift. I divide my career into two rough phases: "Toy" and "Post-Childish Things." And this—hung right over my rolltop desk—still marks the turning point.

Until moving there on scholarship, I had not known the Middle West. New Englanders are sometimes called emotionally frozen. Southerners? considered armed traditionalist hotheads. I soon learned Midwesterners have flukes, too. They're simply better at hiding. Everything. They practice Nordic shunning. They know you can kill your neighbor's soul simply by ignoring it.

Even now there is a town in Illinois that chose to name itself Preemption.

*    *    *

We cheerful Ivy youngsters, lured to Iowa City, were given five twenties a month to go spend on outsider art. Our professor joked this was: "ethnographic colonialism within one's native land." He'd been born in Rome, and his standing room lectures inspired; he was callous in the pan-gender bedding of his students—yet sensitive to how all empires fall. He'd grown up amid artistic beauty broken to bits but left in place.

We set off that Friday full of caffeine and an acquisitive sleekness that sometimes passed for sexy. Wearing thrift-shop moose-motif sweaters, driving borrowed jalopies, we were cerebral hucksters out to plunder the second-flight antique shops of eastern Iowa, western Illinois. The odder our finds, the brainier we felt. Uncover some hand-wrought gimcrack, write an article about it, read that aloud in class then seek publication in some journal suitably obscure. Our Roman professor stressed the long view, advising us: "Sapete sempre che voi siete stranieri . . . in un paese molto più strano." And, this being a state school, he immediately translated: " 'Always know you are strangers . . . in a land far stranger.' "

That day I'd already spent eighty of my allotted hundred. The haul so far? —One rural mailbox, made in a 1946 shop-class and shaped like—not one or two but three Scotty terriers, two white, the middle one black, whose conjoined mouths accepted letters, parcels. —One pink chintz hostess smock edged with so much 1940s ric-a-rac it looked all but Aztec.

And, best, my hands-down ironic iconic Find of the Week, one handsomely lettered five-foot sign explaining, "You've Got To Be A Football Hero To Get Along with the Beautiful Girls. —THEREFORE, GO TECH!"

This kind of joke was then thought 'smart.' And no one lived more enslaved to fashionable smartness than a hyper-educated boy of twenty-six with his twenty-nine-inch waist and, so

Mother always hinted, a colossal IQ. I look back on him with a curatorial mixture of pride, amusement and pity. I think he condescended to the very loot he intended to praise and save. (But surely that problem's built into taking a graduate degree in "self-taught artists"!) And yet, the kid was a student, thereby admitting he had a little something left to learn.

We'd clocked our many country-miles that long Friday's 'picking.' Classmates were now bound back to Iowa City in a borrowed Ford wagon; I followed in my overloaded Jeep. We stopped for gas and bathrooms. Then the others waved good-bye. Though tired and hungry, I still felt greedy for one more twenty-dollar prize. Proud as I was of my football pep-squad board, I knew I'd not yet found this outing's "it." I imagined discovering, in every dairy barn I passed, some primitive oil portrait done of Lincoln when yet a beardless state legislator here.

Looking back on my start-up self, I at least feel stirred by all the lit-up detective attention. Peculiar to the Young, this expectation of discovery. I miss such crazed daily belief! Maybe I knew even then that the word *belief* springs from the German for *beloved*.

My friends swore they'd save me a stool at Hamburg Inn No. 1. The Blue Plate Special, this being Friday, was surely fried fish. Sunset offered a limitless salmon-orange. In one farmyard, a tractor-tire on its side—painted white—had been filled with soil then white geraniums. Dusk now turned these all the colors of a campfire. Tidied fields shadowed toward something sinister. And should that huge a rooster be crowing right at sundown? In my corduroys' pocket, just the two tens left. I'd had my fun but, as I sped through a pretty little town called La Verne, just as its Propane Gas Works and beauty parlor (itchily called LuAnn's House o Hair) reverted to corn-green countryside, my Jeep banked a curve. I spied one abandoned grocery-gas-station. And against an eventide inked Disney red-green-gold, one colonial sign dangled. Its girlish freehand promised:

*Theodosia's Antiques*
(REAL AND IMAGINED)
*Only Thing Reasonable Here?*
*Our Prices*

"Well, hell. *Some*body's thinking," I said aloud.

I aimed my Jeep toward an unlit store that, up-close, looked out-of-business. I'd already popped my clutch to find reverse when I flicked on headlights, then high-beams, then braked. At eleven hundred hours? that cigar-store Indian thing bent in the window? with jewelry all over it? appeared either some dressmaker's dummy or a possible human being. Oosh, it'd definitely moved. Was she crookbacked or polychromed? Then I noticed: her parking-lot showed no tire tracks since yesterday's big rainstorm. Did she walk to work or sleep, bat-like, inverted among her junk?

"Evening." I smiled through door-chimes' sweet-and-sour tinkling. "You must be the eponymous The-o—"

"Her*self*." I warranted one courtly bitter nod.

Caught hovering at her window, worried this might seem invitational, the owner must've made a fast crab-like retreat to one high stool. The climb still had her panting. She hovered behind one outmoded silver cash-register that itself appeared a costly toy, circa 1923.

What had bent her so? Fever, birth-defect? Her spine showed the exact angle of an opened-safety-pin; the clasp, her hooded face. Body angles were reflected in the immense vitrine where she presided. (Most good antique stores offer one such holy-of-holies throne-bench. From there the owner presides over what little she can bear to study all day between visitors.)

But Theodosia, weighing under ninety pounds, seemed to wear her best stuff. A county's worth of brooch timepieces burdened the chest otherwise concave. Thirty watches pinned there, ladies' ones, some clockfaces visible, others locketed away, a few on pulleys allowing easy consulting, quick return. Various metals glinted across her front like bogus German military decorations.

Our professor gave us extra credit for what he called "five-finger discounts." He'd assigned us Abbie Hoffman's 1971 *Steal This Book*. (But someone had alerted the student store's floorwalkers. They stood guard, making us feel grouchy and bourgeois paying retail.) I could never swipe a single trinket from owners of these funky last-chance shops. Each proprietor seemed a local maverick who—lacking the will to leave Mother's cooking or some awful high school marriage—had settled for wearing the whimsical bowler hat indoors, had settled for hours with cast-off oddments at a dead town's farthest edge.

Day's last stop, I quickly scanned, nose wrinkling. I sometimes imagined I could smell the hidden treasure. Where was "it"? I knew my Jeep-load would bring hoots in Monday's class. But such rough-cut items felt too coarse to be the masterwork I always sought. Maybe it lurked within reach of this "it" girl, Theodosia. (Her given name? or one created by a novel-reading farm daughter, hoping to at least sound classier?)

I noted how her thin hair, un-dyed, showed as many metal colors as her watches. She'd yanked hair then pinned that handful any old way behind. Her backbone might've been cruelly bowed, but deep-set eyes gleamed my way briar-sharp. Theodosia seemed one of those maimed or homely people who—feeling themselves un-improvable—make a militant point of glaring you down. Seated on-high, she flaunted her un-assets as a form of deficit flirting.

Being twenty-six, I still likely looked my best. (I remained ignorant of face-value, even while trading on the bargains it brought. You only really notice your looks once you've lost them). Now, barging toward the poorest-lit corner of her two-roomed shop, I felt "it," hiding. Ballroom chairs stacked to the ceiling. Narrow pathways corkscrewed tributes to her bent spine. Theodosia offered no chat, none of other clerks' jolly prying: "So, where you folks say you're *from*? You with the Depression Glass convention in Moline, betcha." Nothing past her alum glaze, her arms crossed over six pounds of locket clocks.

"Hope I'm not keeping you open right at closing time?" I risked, to no response.

Things here did look finer than most shops' out this way. And—a good sign—her place smelled, not of euphemizing potpourri, but of the proper musk peculiar to some dry attic's last few centuries. And yet Theo's major Gothic grandfather clock lacked one finial; three beautiful nineteenth century pumpkin-colored paisley shawls had been moth-dessert decades back. Nothing displayed justified full snootiness. I did stop before a pile of the 1860s *Harper's Weeklies*. Hating knowing that **she** knew—I stood scouting for Winslow Homer's war illustrations. Nothing.

Her voice scratched me from a room away. "The **toys** are in that half-timbered neo-Tudor sideboard to your right, you."

I asked stale air before me, "How'd you know?"

"You're wearing the red. You toy people, cutthroat bunch, ofttimes wear the faded tin-toy reds in your reindeer sweater. Me, with so little else to do here, I've got it pretty much down to a system. Can identify all migrating birds, boy-o. I get three of you a day in here."

I doubted that but felt on notice.

"Thanks," I said, for spite.

Theodosia's toys proved familiar, overpriced, missing wheels, made in Munich or New York circa 1915 just before war claimed all such metal. —I found nothing local, handmade or heartfelt enough for my advanced urban taste.

Last thing, headed for the Jeep, I, feeling as irked as stubborn, did squat before the clear vitrine and—through that, incidentally—noted her gold ballet slippers. Four minutes' silence hadn't thawed her. She still emitted the nunnish hauteur of some impoverished old countess out of Chekhov. Theodosia seemed to want me to despise her; she was certainly getting her way.

"Hope I'm not holding up your evening plans, right here at six and all, ma'am," so ran me in faux-farmboy mode. She just clicked like a time-bomb with brooch-clocks dragging down her blouse. In lieu of visible breasts, metals' differing weights tugged starched fabric in ways uneven.

It was only now—as I squatted before glass, peering over Grover Cleveland campaign buttons and crystal bulldog inkwells—I felt observed from floor-level. Beside her white shin, bruised along its central bone, one face—a force—stared back at me. This head-and-shoulders portrait rested on the floor. He must've been my age. Dark-eyes over a beginner's goatee; he'd posed fastened in a black tie and high starched collar. His face was handsome if both blank and sad, hound-earnest.

"So what'd be his story?" My index finger touched cold glass. I felt then in the knots of my stiff neck and impressionable groin, a collector's sense that he might be today's "it."

Silent, she studied her fingernails. Sales technique? Witch-orneriness? Both.

"*I asked*: Tell me about this sweet guy in the painting nearest your left foot?" She kept fussing with an imagined hangnail. Why did her not answering mount up so? Unlike the last three shops, no radio played Champaign-Urbana's classical FM. No noise out here past wind crossing her roof or the odd twist of carved wood popping in her far room. I felt foolish at the din my voice made in a building chockablock with clock-ticks of all sizes (her chest, a knitting-class of those).

But I kept gazing through this glass box at one young gent's melancholy message of a face. . . . Maybe he looked a bit like me—and being painted actual-size, given all the glass between us—became some sort of mirror? Maybe all bright young men, seriously questing at twenty-six, look a bit alike.

The picture tipped half out of its 1850s rosewood frame. Canvas showed its age, some flaking. The oil-paint execution seemed able, even affectionate, if Midwesternly conventional; his background, solid black. But what held me was the boy's expression. Not just an invitation, almost a plea for help. I felt first **approached** then nearly **summoned**. Didn't understand quite **what** I'd found, but seeing him, I recognized some caliber of longing or emergency. The sole way I'd find out? Theodosia, on her high stool, fussing with one index nail.

"Just want information, lady! But, why'm I even **both**ering you? As if you knew the slightest thing **about** him!" This is how one avid story-'picker,' holding only twenty bucks, challenges another.

## II.

LOCKETS' TICKING seemed the Geiger-counter minefield guarding her. Sunset, gold as egg-yolk, now scored with value many otherwise half-worthless things. Pot-lids, cuff links, rims of chipped Venetian claret glasses. She snorted finally: amused at *anybody's* thinking Theodosia might not keep total-narrative-lock on every celluloid buttonhook in here.

As her small mouth twisted tighter, as bone wrists drew nearer her waist, I thought I saw some bored amusement light her eyes' fierce dots. (Since she belonged to my grandmother's flapper generation, I'd maybe gauged her partly right: Such ladies were most charming when provoked. Women in love with standards, their own or just some marked-down tradition's.) When Theodosia's voice at last emerged, it sounded adenoidal, dry, so 'local,' I felt disappointed.

"You look to be one those ones I get in here from the grad school over to Iowa City. Printmaking department's pretty good, they say. But why would anybody waste time doing prints when you could just *paint*? Yeah, real 'artistes,' you kids! You all look alike. Come out here huntin' somethin' for nothin'. You'll get *nothin'* for nothin' in here, however well-off you like to think you look, son. From the parking-lot, I knew ye. Expensive haircut wanting to play like it just grew wild that way. Wearing clothes the people in New York City wore three years back. Ooh yeah, nosing out this far from Moline, hoping and trick us natives. One of you's forever taking me aside, trying and get the *real* scoop. You'd probably make a funny story out of me, my shop, this poor boy painted here."

Now some test would be required. Proof I was not just another trust-fund tinhorn, condescending.

*     *     *

And as I leaned nearer glass, I saw Theodosia smirking over secrets she felt enriched only by withholding. I 'read' her bony chest. Most clocks clamped there told roughly the same time (within fifty minutes). —But, scouted from left to right, four rows, top to bottom, her system started coming clearer: we begin with austere Federal design, chaste and 'classical,' till Ionic geometry blossomed, enlarging to certain manufactured over-elaborations of the 1850s, sprouting roses and leaves and fat gilt tendrils of prosperity, till this stylized itself toward a silver Nouveau calla lily then onward toward a watch mitered with onyx swallows and the chopped fan-lines of the Eastlake moment, slimming square again into industrial edginess as a Deco locket put end-punctuation to time's weird progression across a pigeon-chest otherwise un-notable.

"So," I tilted up and spoke over the glass. "You've set yourself chronological, eh? 'Chrono' equals clocks. 'Logical' is . . . well, logical. Makes a certain 'mount of sense, I guess. So, you've come to work today dressed clock-logical as '1830 through 1930'?"

She gave her hardest look. "WRONG. 183-4 to 193-4! — Even so, for a town the size of La Verne, you're at least the first today to 'get' my latest attempt. I try things. They sometimes go unnoticed. Anyways, you're close enough for **graduate** work."

I laughed. She coughed—her laughter's substitute. I absorbed one lateral rake from her poisoned eyes and inwardly admitted, "I think I'm a little in love here. . . ."

**Is there ever anything except intelligence?**


Then, as my own eyes sought some moment's added heat from hers (she was a woman, I was a man), her piping oboe voice conceded in a hurry half-mechanical, "**About** this picture you're s'dead-set to blunder into the story of: Around 1849, no, **in** 1849,

June fourth to be more clock-logical"—she paused for the nod too quickly won from me—"a sailor named Sanders Woolsey came home to La Verne from his eight-month voyage to the Far East. Sandy's ship, *The John Gray*, brought back tea, Canton ware, and ginger. He'd sailed into Chicago (then a going port, thanks to their dredging Canada's waterways). You can imagine the meal his mother and sisters fixed, his first night home. Baked chicken, be my guess. And Sandy most-like so full of tales: monkeys, the pagodas, what have you. They ate that dinner at their farm three miles due east more toward Matherville. And it was Sandy Woolsey who pretty well ruined us out-this-way. Was Sandy brought us cholera. Real contagious stuff, ooh yeah. His poor mother and sisters would be dead in six days, along with most of three households, their nearest neighbors. Two those homes still stand, back by the propane distributor-ship you passed but never noticed. A new doctor'd just arrived in town. Boy so recent to practicing medicine, he had price tags still strung on his best surgical tools . . . —You think I'm exaggerating what-all I got in here, do ye? Think I made up that about his tools?"

"No, so far, I trust you. You clearly know your stuff. And, seeing how packed your place is (I mean with excellent things), your having proof of the man's having lived around here wouldn't be a shock. So the fellow in this picture isn't the sailor but the new town doctor, right? My only question is whether you'll need to stand up to run fetch that doctor's bag, or have you maybe got it tucked somewhere even closer?"

"Look harder at me, son. I've never 'run' toward (or, comes to that, 'from') anything in my whole life spent here. However, you're not **totally** stupid. . . ."

She bent, first with a broken-backed degree of inconvenience then with visible pain. (Now I knew: she would never let me see her actually **walk**.) From beneath the cash-register (her abacus eyes steadily tallying me), Theodosia lifted a cardboard box intended for canned green beans. From it she hoisted a goodly leather satchel. Brown, it was bigger than the doctors' black bags seen in movies and pharmaceutical ads. Clanking it atop her glass-counter, she expertly opened its silver latch. Her eyes never abandoning mine, she now slid toward me one small saw.

Ash-wood handle, a fine blue Sheffield blade. Amputation-worthy, that heavy to the touch. And suspended from its cutting-edge, one price-tag still dangled from string. "Dollar-fifty," she read aloud. "*Then*."

This implement she whisked from me and shoved back—as the satchel dropped to the flooring just beneath her stool. As she rushed right on, "Doctor's name was Frederick Markus Petrie, since you asked. He'd just turned thirty. Had been in town less than three weeks when Ordinary Seaman 'Sandy' Woolsey, twenty-one, brought sickness home out here to us. Morning after the Woolsey ladies' homecoming feast, their boy begged to stay in bed till nine. By noon admitted he was pretty sickly, had to ask for help when they seen how sick he'd been most everywhere. First the sailor's older sisters tried treating him. They were proud girls, skilled in home arts. Glad, I guess, to finally lay eyes on a boy who'd been far away so long. Sandy was a beauty, people admitted, platinum hair. Better-looking than his spinster sisters, who could've used such beauty in a town harsh as La Verne . . . then.

"Before the Civil War I guess we were even a more backward little place, being out this far from Kewanee. And just the idea of a local boy getting to sail clear to China and back without being drowned, well, a certain kind of fame must've hooked onto that fellow. And hadn't he brought his mother, to dress up her plain farm mantel, one of those ivory carvings with little worlds inside other little worlds and all shaped from one hunk of tusk? I have that in back, though it's not cheap. . . ."

"I've seen plenty of those. I can live without touching that. Please, go on. . . ."

Now we seemed in this together. Sunset's last pink light squandered itself along the edge of everything glass, serious evening drawing down hard around us. Darkness mostly had us now. Opening a box of kitchen matches, Theodosia lit one candle.

### III.

"PRETTY SOON, 'a little feverish' turns more toward 'diarrhea.' Till their bringing another basin becomes, 'Maybe too much for us. Send for Doc Eaton.' But old Eaton, he'd just retired, see? And there was only that recent graduate, so new he yet boarded with Hester Brinsley, and was still out looking for some rental of his own.

"They say the eldest Woolsey girl, which'd be Dorothea, found the boy-doctor out this way having just paid his first month's rent on a little house about the size of this, not an eighth of a mile back toward the Coal Valley turnoff. Dorothea rushes in, says, 'We've got something. At home, we tried and take care of it, but Sandy's having something bad to where we . . .' and fainted. She had rushed out here so fast, see. The horse, a nag, was lathered. So there stands our young Doctor Markus Petrie. He'd best get prepared. And him not even all-the-way unpacked. And having to replace old Doc Eaton that everybody loved. (Because Eaton'd do everything you wanted and never tell another living soul about it.) Girls in trouble used to troop out here on the train clear from Chicago, stay in Hester Brinsley's pretty rooms, and she'd look in on them for the day before and after; till they appeared strong enough to climb back on that train alone. (Most of them arrived and left alone, poor souls.) But Eaton always managed to keep such 'helpings' quiet. (Eaton did his li'l operations right at Brinsley's boardinghouse after dark, leaving his buggy out of sight in Hester's barn, we heard, with her getting a little cut, so to speak, out of every lost child. What **wouldn't** a Brinsley do for a dollar?)

"But Eaton had lately grown too shaky to even fake acting able, being so up in years. And here's this new boy, Petrie. They'd advised all the young fellows graduating from State Med School, boys should grow facial hair that'd make a kid look older, so's people would trust him more. Important, trust. Anyways, young Petrie, mustache and silly new goatee, helps the sailor's sister rise up, he ties her horse behind his new-leased phaeton and a rental bay from Brinsley's stable. (They were big around here then. But you know, not a one's left?) Petrie walks in and here is the Woolseys' parlor strewn with fine red and gold silks that Sandy's just brought home, cloth still tossed everywhere, and . . . no, I **don't** have those in back since somebody-careless left them in direct sun and they pretty much fell to pieces. But Petrie goes in the room and there are basins set all-round the iron bed and the poor mother, burning up herself, is working hard, washing a naked boy, who's embarrassed and, you can see he knows it, losing his life at both ends. . . . This going to be too much for you?"

"Nothing is too much for me. **Yet**, I mean. And this? is the. . . . ahm. . . . portrait of that very doctor, you say?"

"Didn't. Say. Getting to that. But answer me this, you think you're so smart. How did young Markus Petrie **know** it was cholera and from halfway 'cross the room? Hmmn?"

I shook my head one sideways swipe. (Never contradict/ upstage your teller. Besides, I hadn't a clue.)

"Because *in* the bowls, mixing bowls, pans pressed into service to spare the home's one good mattress, the doctor saw 'rice stool.'"

"Which *is* . . ."

"Which is where the person has already been so emptied of food that nothing but what's clear is left to come out and, here's the cholera part: it's only clear broth but with little white bits of dissolving intestines that *look* like rice . . . and float just like cooking rice."

"A trip home from the Orient bringing rice-stools."

"'At's it. But, of course, what happened, the sailor was already near-to-dead and his sister and mother went soon after, then the two neighboring farms downhill of their groundwater and all that scrubbing and suds the brave Woolsey women loosed on that poor boy's leavings, they let seep into the soil, and stream downhill. —Back in Chicago, the disease was going wild, folks falling over by the hundreds and hundreds. Back then nobody knew the word *bacteria*. Pasteur hardly being a professor yet, if my dates are right. Their sad idea of 'cure'? Mustard plasters, hot as you could stand, then 'bleed' the patient to calm him good. No, up Chicago-way? the panic got so bad, town-fathers felt sure they were now non-electable, so they eventually voted to pump in drinking water, not from that little latrine Chicago River downtown, but bring it in from clear cold Lake Michigan. Officials were that desperate and, for once, the bigwigs got it right. But *they* had money, city ways and lots of things to try up the direction Chicago. But out here? here our folks, well, we only had just Petrie.

"That young doctor was so new among us he'd not made arrangements to get his laundry done. And yet already Markus was giving us whatever we were going to get of hope. He'd have to trust himself now to take care of every local who'd soon come down with it. And all of us were strangers to him, all. Looking after even those mortally sick people you love, that is hard enough. (I should know, believe me.) But to get some address in writing that's on a street you don't know how to find, even in a town as tiny as La Verne, and to walk in there and discover another whole family puking and voiding in plain view and down with it already, and even the kids giving you that look like, 'This is all? this here's *it*?' See, that's what got the town to thinking, see.

"They were so grateful there was somebody *to* call. He turned up at the hardware store and asked for rope to use for quarantining homes and the owner gave him for free a coil of orange rope that looked so new and city-made no customers would touch it, and Petrie kept that in his buggy and wrapped it round many a home's front door. That orange struck fear in folks. But when he did turn up, Markus was also a fine looker. You see him here, with a deep voice too, sober and polite and right out of an accredited Illinois school, well, it reassured. Little beard, such dark eyes. Likely kind to his mother. And with a plain way that out this far means real skill. No wonder the worship started! Even old Doc Eaton couldn't have got such a sudden following. It'd taken Eaton years, but he grew on you. We already knew *him*. They did, I mean. (For, ancient as I must look to a boy your age, this went on it'll be seventy-odd years even 'fore *my* time.) Old Eaton, see, people still tipped every hat to him downtown. Hadn't he delivered most the folks in sight? But they knew about his serving those family-way city girls, about certain other mistakes he'd buried. Plus there was a little drug habit he got into real bad at the end. Strange, somebody like that waiting so late to find a vice. Like some delayed vacation for him to retire into. Eaton, being that old, man couldn't travel, so he went right into a pretty red-lacquered letterbox, oh, I've got it in back, the case where Doc kept his opium-products. Old Eaton soon drifted into falling asleep while standing there mid-operation, hands'd fly up all of a sudden palsied, so the mayor and a committee had sent, just in time, for Petrie fresh-as-paint out of university. Fourth in his class, too.

"But even if Doc Petrie had come during a normal healthy season around here, he still woulda been quite a standout. I mean, unmarried. To this day, that's rare here. Keeps you off from the wedded pairs. (*I* should know.) Fine-looking boy, as still shows here, if in a darker than Swedish kind of way, but that would be romantic to all these braided towheaded girls for miles hereabouts. It was that everybody liked his quiet manner, long legs. Just felt flattered, being watched over by a public servant, but from a good family, you know?

"He kept asking locals to please please just call him 'Mark'; but 'Doctor' was a godly word by then. And those folks of ours that **hadn't** come down yet with the cholera? instead of hiding from Doctor Petrie, they took to bringing him fresh-dug beets from out their gardens and sending their slimmest daughters over with the food. Matchmaking! and here it was the middle of our terrible epidemic year. I guess it was superstition. Because the more folks got sick, the healthier and taller did that boy look. He'd turn up at church and, my mother's mother told me, they clapped. Doctor Petrie, white shirt, black tie, black suit like you see here, he walked into the Lutheran chapel and the whole place, choir and sour-puss preacher and all, applauded. Organist held a chord. . . . Made him stay away, of course. Man never set foot in there again. And he'd only come into their sanctuary hoping to maybe find a little support from On High, a little quiet, relief from farm folks that were turning gray and

then becoming a puddle at both ends. See, that's what the cholera bug does to you, I guess. *Liquefies*. Gets its energy by turning the host creature to a liquid it can then ride on to the next
host and the next. It's awful 'catching,' I guess. And the doctor
was soon the only person brave or fool enough to duck under
the quarantine ropes, ignoring warning signs he himself had
nailed to doors of those farmhouses worst hit.

"And him introducing himself as 'just *Mark*, please.' Fat chance.

"Locals were real glad Doc Petrie was up on the techniques
of 1849 from our best state school. Taxpayer money well-spent.
But, listen, there **were** no techniques except don't wash your
ricey basins in the river where the poisons will drift, which is
exactly what they went out and did, poor fools. And too soon the
Mengers and the Hurleys, then the Hopwoods and the Mortensens, they all come down with it. 'Come down,' you hear me?
Going back like this, I fall right into my grandmother's voice.
—Now, after such-like buildup, you might think there's not
much of a story to the rest of it. But what's mainly inter-resting
is such madness as grew all up around **him** during the worst
part of our plague. All La Verne left enough bread puddings
and busheled fruit outside his house to where he couldn't open
the front door of a morning. Had to go out around the back to
see what gifts had him so locked in. Doc kept busy, writing off
for help, him so new to the practice and here he'd landed out
here in this throwback sickness. But most other doctors elsewhere had their own hands full. Still Petrie made newspaper
suggestions that the *Bugle* printed and passed along. He listed
dos and don'ts, most of them a scared boy's purest guesswork.
Things to do. Mainly meant to keep folks' panic down. And,
at the end, he added how important it was that people stick by
each other through the worst. The doctor wrote how civilization depends on nobody going untended.

"And then Petrie 'strongly suggested' that families gather into bands of five to ten to assure no matter how bad it got, somebody'd stay put and tend those left alive. And local tribes, especially those whose farmland adjoined, they went along with him on this. And oh but that sure saved many a local. Later, they gave Doc Petrie all the credit. His idea: The 'Health Alliances' they were called, and that still holds. Nowadays they're mainly used for tornado-watch and swapping Christmas gifts. Community granges-like, but they're still called the Petrie Alliances.

"Was a real warm June that June, which was bad for spreading the cholera, but good, you know, for how stuff grows in soil this black. Young girls brought him masses of zinnias and they got into his house and folks heard-tell that more than one threw herself at him. What *he* did, who knows? And yet you kind of hope he at least tried something with a few of our better-looking ones that *were* spunky. They weren't all peaches, trust me. I remember some these ones from when they'd oldened up later. And they had never been an inch better looks-wise, be my guess.

"But young Markus Petrie would buggy home exhausted, not even expecting to get much sleep before somebody else was there pounding on his door like they owned it, which they thought they did. And here he'd just turned up at his rental house (barely furnished, the bed and two chairs being about it) to find some young girl, lovesick for a hero, leaning on the rail of his front stoop, wrapping one curl around her finger. Like it was noon on any healthy Sunday! Didn't care how late it was, or how he smelled after all that ugly work for strangers. He would maybe nod and go into the house and just start washing up in that terrible way they had to around something as catching as that. You'd pour carbolic acid right *on* your hands, to burn the infection off. He'd had no more sleep than a cat-nod, and for weeks. Kept going anyhow, like only some boy that young even could. On med school graduation day three weeks earlier, he'd said his vows about helping anyone, regardless, hadn't he? Well. But Petrie must've at least con*sid*ered turning tail and running anywhere else. **Had** to've. 'Cause the world is made for a fine dashing doctor with so strong a back and eyes this size. And La Verne, Illinois, couldn't have been such a prize assignment anyways. Here poor young Doc Markus, hoping to just be 'Mark' at least on weekends, had walked into this full-blown sickness brought by some local sailor come clear inland from China! The luck.

"Some said Petrie would be home in his rental. It still stands back two blocks on your left if now with a sun-porch and an aboveground pool behind, and while Doc was standing there, hurting his hands with acid, working by kerosene lamp, washing up, and shucking off his pants and throwing hot water and soap even over his good shoes, with him standing there alone wearing nothing but his shirttails, more girls would come in. Folks swear that for weeks about then there were virgins turning up at all hours the night. And their parents right aware of where the daughters'd gone dressed in which white frock and what for at this ungodly hour. Guess I can still hear them: 'Now, daughter, don't you be letting that Grace Cunningham, who everybody at the school for some reason thinks hung the moon, get a jump on Doc ahead of you. Why, Sister, when this is over, after all he's done to help our county and setting up the Alliances, he can stand for governor, sure. They say Boss Brinsley alone gave him two hundred-dollar gold-pieces when their spoiled littlest girl pulled through. But brush back your hair off your face, why don't you. Show those features. Grace Cunningham is not a patch on anybody pretty as you.' Oh, but it was a pagan time, 1849. Could've been the bubonic in Poland around 231 AD.

"Now, **this**." And again she awkwardly angled off the stool, finally scooping up the painting and clamping its lower edge against the glass-counter between us. "This portrait of Petrie came to me, it'd be just five weeks back. Been hanging up in the public library on the Square since our town fathers commissioned his portrait, 18 and 50. For a while, during the sickness, it seemed like folks could trust just one fellow only—especially a 'new person,' as they'd say. 'Doc is **new**,' they'd say, like he was store-bought-clean and still unused as some of the gear in his bag here."

Theodosia finally placed into my hands the unframed oil painting. His image was pulling away from the old yellow pine stretchers still marked as from a shop in Cedar Rapids. I could finally study his face held inches before mine, a face shown when only four years my senior.

"They kept telling him, 'We just trust you, Doc.' Like offering a contract. See, that's where magic gets next to you—when you're so scared it'll be you next. To see a houseful of loved ones die like that, all spilling like some hogs with the pox, and telling their last secrets just to have those told to **somebody**. And here's Petrie, finer-looking than any preacher in buggying-distance and with a deeper voice. People felt like med school must charge up a fellow's battery with good health!

"This painting, see, was done from a daguerreotype they got his mother to send. Talented local lady painted it, one Miss Beech, a teacher who'd gone to his church the few times he set foot in there before they applauded him off. Those stories about the girls, I thought you'd like that part. Just crazy enough to be true. Instead of keeping their daughters off from a man soaked through with it at day's end . . . poorer farmers dropped off girls in Easter pinafores for a boy already such a hero, they were betting on his free ride clear to Springfield as governor some few years down the pike. And their own girl on his arm. Good fortune, that. But he'd not yet got anyone in or near La Verne to let him be just 'Mark,' which I bet is how his mother called him.

"Well, one day 'bout four weeks into the worst of it, he was out at the Brinsleys' again (mighty demanding, Brinsleys), and their little daughter they thought he'd saved and had paid him so good for saving, she was down and looking but poorly again. Petrie bends over her asleep, and shakes his head and says to her rich parents, 'I just don't like her *color.*' And instead of agreeing or mumbling thanks, instead, both the Brinsleys point. Just point at him, saying, 'What? —*Her* color? Pot comin' in here callin' our dear little kettle black!' Folks claim he walked toward a mirror was hanging in her room, and when he saw it plain, him already sweating bad, they say young Markus threw up across their new rose wallpaper, like he'd been waiting the permission of others' noticing. Boy must've guessed already. Maybe it was his going back on the little Brinsley girl's health one week after her recovery had given other folks such hope. But Petrie apologized for making a mess and he at once excused himself and stepped into the hall so's he could buggy home, clean up. At their fine front door with stained glass cut in it, those Brinsleys gave him mighty wide berth and wouldn't shake Petrie's acid-black hand as thanks. Oh no, not now. His mistake was ever letting people *see* him sick. Especially Brinsleys, born talking, every one.

"Soon people said as how a native son so fine as Sandy Woolsey could **not** have brought all this much badness down on us. No, more likely Petrie had. Look at your calendar. Didn't it all turn up about a week or two after this standoffish young doctor did? And aren't you always reading in the papers about certain firemen that set the fires themselves so they'll get the headlines and bonuses? Well? Local rumor added as how young Markus Petrie's own case of the cholera—what with his having been around those many others—his **degree** of sick, it had to run you twelve to fifty times worse, way more potent than others'. Some said his ran up to seventy-five times more catching! And that's why they one-by-one stopped leaving food, and now the girls were nowhere to be seen. And even the dying quit sending for Petrie. Which meant, since he lived out here most of three miles from town and so alone, not anybody knew what-all exactly was happening to him. Might could be getting stronger? or going down toward worse? Did he have sufficient food, so forth, what with his being a bachelor and all? Well, let's say the interest in him tapered right off. And even as the number of cases did  People said more than ever that he'd been the agent of it, spreading it amongst us, then trying to take credit for being so kind. 'New here,' after all, and, in the end, what'd we really **know** about strangers? Coming in here like a rooster among our fine local white hens and turning girls' heads.

"Finally, with no word, no sight of him, about ten days in, they found his horse broken loose and chewing the neighbor-lady's dahlias. That's when our mayor that'd helped hire Petrie, he organized 'a fact-finding expedition,' the local paper called it. And they went in to check how he was faring, after all. One of the wives'd packed a few sandwiches as a false reason for their visit. Petrie had at least put together the Health Alliances, etc. You had to give the boy that. They found him in the back room.

"He'd tied himself into his own bed with the last of that orange rope, hog-tied himself owing to the shakes maybe. Or could-be just to keep himself from rushing off in search of others, at the end. All La Verne had hoped for a good young country doctor, and maybe that was his last wish, too.

"He'd tied himself not so much to keep from going for anybody's help. (Because who could **help**, once it **had** you?) No, more because, even if you've lived your life alone, you want to at least perish within the sight-and-sound of other folks. Don't you? And, even as by-myself as *I* still live here in La Verne that counts me somewhat odd, I know I hope to at least end **up** in earshot of company. (Of course, maybe that's just me.)

"So, once the local sick either started improving or went real quick to white ash on the pyres they'd put out past the fairground to contain it, once farm folks' worst fear ended, and they'd unpinned his Petrie Alliances newspaper rules off kitchen walls, they did what they'll always do when they've forsaken somebody who dies helping them, someone they failed to honor at all while still alive. Why, a sacrificed doctor looked different, now their own health was back. Boss Brinsley's pet-daughter recovered, after all. And the child, if no one else did, recalled as how Doctor Handsome's house-calls had saved her. So the Brinsleys held a late ceremony and put up oil-portrait money and, in two months, why, they'd made a hero out of our abandoned Frederick Markus Petrie, MD. Hung his painted picture in the library. And he became the new-here country doctor, the boy that'd singlehanded saved most of 1849's La Verne! . . . is who-all's face you got aholdt of there, young man."

## IV.

IT'D GROWN SO DARK—even with her candle guttering—
I had to clutch his picture nearer. Canvas all but touched my
nose. So I sniffed it then, front and back. My fingers knew his
paint was lightly flaking. And yet—even with its crackly over-
all-ness—his face would continue looking that civic, if just as
sad. The photographic image that inspired this painting had
been taken earlier (maybe during graduation?). But young
Petrie's features already seemed to diagnose some complex fate
ahead. And yet, his eyes looked half-willing to accept whatever
medieval beliefs awaited modern-medicine out here in these
wheat fields.

"But," I asked a little too loud, "who authorized taking his
portrait down? After, what? a-hundred-and-twenty-odd years,
why would your town park him out here with you with orders
to sell?"

"*'Cause nobody remembers him anymore!* Nobody but me and
the daughter of the youngest of those Mortensens he saved. And
even she claimed the library just couldn't 'keep' him, since that
last remodel made the place be real 'contemporary.' They redid
La Verne's downtown library, put in round skylights, plants big
as trees. The young hotshot librarian phoned. Calls me 'Teddy'
(which is all they've ever thought to call me hereabouts). She
explains how, in the middle of their new yellow walls and mirrors, young Petrie here, he sure looks 'kinda gloomy.' Her very
words, son. Besides, his picture needs some restoration, crusty,
it was not 'clean enough.' So, well, here he is, on consignment-
like. 'For whatever he brings.' *Brings!*

"Funny, I'm out here near the little house Doc paid his first
two months' rent on. They've shipped him right back to his old

neighborhood where he hardly even got unpacked. But, what does it smell like? 'Cause I admire you thought to nose that out. See, *my* sense of smell, I lost most of it during the tempera- tures I had from childhood scarlet fever. Was six months old, just so much cartilage. Those fever spikes rolled through me, messed me up pretty good, as you can see. So, not too much of a sniffer left. One sense shy of a load. My mind's okay but I'd have enjoyed it, too, I think. Smell is one thing I've missed in m' life. Well, *one* the ones."

"Miss?" I held it near my nose again. "The picture and *Petrie*, I guess, smell of tar and . . . maybe day-old bacon-grease likely cooked over a wood fire. Smells of dust and maybe oil paint's linseed oil. But, too, of, I swear, Bactine! Funny, there's really something medicinal about it. Though this was surely painted months after they buried him."

"*Burned* him, you mean. And all those odors still *in* there, hunh? You don't say." Theodosia finally fell silent. Slouching as if exhausted by some marathon.

Then I risked it. Told her I didn't suppose she'd willingly part with him, even considering his slightly flaking-condition. But I did vow, hand in air, no caretaker would ever hold on to him longer or be surer to never let Markus and his story get lost the next time around.

I admitted, "Stupidly I bought some comical junk earlier, whole Jeepful. But stuff outside for class was to make others laugh. Not really for me. This'd be *mine*. So, but all I have is twenty dollars cash. . . . But if you'll trust me to send you a per- sonal check, it won't bounce, I swear. . . ."

"Now you know his story, don't you?"

I nodded.

"And, after my giving you that? You figure I could take a penny for him? Why, that'd be like . . . like sellin' some other . . .

human. —No, it's yours. *He* is. Was hoping you might notice when you come in here hunting just toys. Toys aren't the half of it. They're the way we want it to be, not how things turn out. And, well, you found him. But your smelling it's what put you over the top, boy. Made me know you'd guard him pretty good. Might could, you'll someday even remember to talk about him. La Verne never deserved our fine young Petrie here. Did not deserve him, alive or dead."

I stared at his picture, then again at the lady armored in cricket-clicking watches. "You *saw* him," she nodded. "Most my customers come ringing through that door like elephants-herds hunting Depression glass. Right name for the stuff, the way it gets *me* down. —Take him. In La Verne, if we act too kind or smart or interested in much, they'll make us pay. And pay. And pay. Yeah, take him quick. 'Fore I need to hold him back behind this counter with me. *Get*, or else I'll change my mind, boy. —And not to worry . . . I've saved enough to where in six months, no more winters for Theodosia, who tends to fall on ice. Moving to San Diego, seventy-two degrees, year-round, they tell me. Now, skedaddle. Don't let me be going back on this. Get him finally clear of us. Misery loves company but help me not be selfish at the end! Said, *Go!*"


So I lifted it and, flinching through her door chimes, yelled my thanks and ran him to the Jeep. Felt like hostage-rescue. With his frame propped in my passenger seat, I snapped the safety-belt across him at a kindly angle that'd leave his dark eyes free.

And, only then, round midnight, in a Jeep full of junk from earlier, we achieved escape velocity. Night country smelled of growing corn. Seemed I was saving him from the town he'd saved then paid for saving. With both our faces aiming west, that Jeep held steady at eighty-five. Once we passed the Iowa line, we had moonlight all the way.

## V.

THEODOSIA'S LIKELY DEAD. Even with San Diego's warming help, she'd be up on to a hundred. (And yet I can picture her, infirm if cogent, stretched out on a terrace, wearing wing-sunglasses, telling tales to some tattooed young candy-striper. Theodosia, far happier out West overlooking the Pacific, with nothing left to peddle though plenty still to tell.)

Till that night, toys had been my specialty. Since childhood, actually. But once I started guarding Petrie's image, I somehow put aside childish things. The homemade treasures that've attracted me since? They're more about work than play. They are what my small collection is best-known for.

It now boasts six hundred and ten portraits of anonymous working American citizens (1710–1937). They are all shown on-the-job in their aprons or welding goggles, shown manning their forges, minding their pharmacies, curating their pyramids of wholesale pumpkins. Some of these are masterpieces. Most were painted by artists as unknown as their subjects. —Art? Yes, I consider it art, if only of the *folk* kind.

His portrait still presides over my desk here. Even a hundred and seventy-some years after he died alone, the boy-doctor's presence feels half-healing. Seems we've recognized and befriended each other across time. How do I know that it's a sort of love? —Because it's daily.

Money-wise, of course, he's far from this collection's most valuable item. But, in case of fire, I'd save him first.

Five decades into our cohabitation I found a better frame for him. And last summer—when even this new one split from radiator-heat—I was trying to mend it when an old calling card slid out from under the wooden stretcher. Some librarian's fine penmanship attested:

> *Dr. Frederick M. Petrie, b. 1820–d. 1849,*
> *saved town, Cholera. Caught it.*

Since he is from the nineteenth century, I'd never thought to Google him before. But, what first came alive on-screen? His original full-page La Verne *Bugle* proposal for surviving a plague. Those neighborhood organizations he helped found are still in use. His bulletins are yet considered models of improvised public health. So now, I can give good young Petrie the last word.

*Fulfilling the duties assigned by fellow-citizens in acknowledgment of the Epidemic Cholera now being so sadly among us, I, the Committee's newest member, submit the following report, June 11, 18 and 49. Grateful that, after being somewhat modified, it was unanimously adopted. To wit:*

*In consideration of our being presently uneasily visited by The Cholera, I recommend to my neighbors the following program intended as defensive and preparatory:*

*—Please undertake a strict course of temperance and regularity in diet, drink and exercise. I urge on you, friends, the spare use of meats, vegetables and fruit, and more particularly if the bowels be to any degree disordered, avoid fresh*

*pork, spiritous liquors, green corn, cucumbers and melons, excessive fatigue, wet and night exposure. Insure your keeping comfortably clothed especially during sleep.*

*—Should any sickness of the stomach occur while the disease be locally prevailing, consider it a commencement that may easily be cured, but if neglected might kill infants and our elderly.*

*—Go to bed between blankets and be pretty warmly covered. This course has, in other communities, proved sufficient to heal in almost all cases when commenced in time. Attention: Latest medical beliefs now question bleeding's value.*

*—Be assured my new town-and-farm-friends, all such steps, if efficiently administered early, prevent death in most known cases.*

*So try resting easy, please.*

*The singular symptom likeliest to undo us is an interfering terror.*

*—I further observe, with Committee support, that our La Verne citizens will be exposed to less danger by calmly remaining in their homes, than by flying from them. I therefore urge families, in groups of five or ten, to take care in securing Good Help, to regularly visit each other, attending to each other's arising needs. Friends will, in their hour of need, stand fast, not flee.*

*—Stay we must, however strong be our sinful urge to solely save ourselves. Certainly our very notion of Civilization depends on our group-determination that not one among us, even the most solitary and least loved, go left untended.*

*In this and all things, looking toward our healthier future, I remain your most respectful new neighbor,*

*Frederick Markus Petrie, M.D.*

*—Mark*

# THE MORTICIAN CONFESSES

RALEIGH—A former funeral home employee charged with having sex with a body he was transporting pleaded guilty Wednesday after a psychiatrist testified that the man had sexual problems and that the incident probably was an isolated one.

Superior Court Judge Davis Cashwell sentenced John Bill Whitehead, 60, of Falls, NC, to two years in prison, then suspended the sentence and placed him on five years' probation. Cashwell also ordered Whitehead to serve 30 days in the county jail, to undergo a psychiatric evaluation and to complete 100 hours of community service.

"There is not a single thing I can possibly do to make it hurt any less," the judge said before handing down the sentence.

Whitehead, a thin man with carefully combed brown hair and thick glasses, said nothing during the proceedings other than answering "Yes sir" or "No sir" to Cashwell in a near-whisper.

On Feb. 22, Person County sheriff's deputies said they found Whitehead in a funeral home station wagon several hundred yards off US 401 in Tuscarora County. Occupying the vehicle with Whitehead was the body of a 40-year-old woman he had picked up at Dorothea Dix Mental Hospital and was supposed to deliver to Nowell-Johnstone funeral home of Falls.

"There was a man kneeling over what appeared to be a stretcher in the back of the hearse and covering up a body with a funeral home blanket," County Assistant District Attorney Howard Chalmers told the judge. "They noticed that his pants were in disarray and his zipper was found, I'm afraid, down."

Whitehead told deputies that the cot "became loose and was rocking back and forth," and he had gone into the back of the vehicle to secure the body. He later admitted that he had sex with said body, Chalmers said.

The victim, Deborah Jo Hartman, had spent most of her life in state institutions and was transferred to Dix for treatment of a heart condition. The mother, Donna Coleman Hartman, said her daughter had the mental capacity of a three-year-old child. When Deborah Jo died, she weighed 72 pounds and stood less than five feet tall.

The victim's family and others in the courtroom shook their heads and muttered when Attorney Ryland R. Smith, also of Falls, claimed that he had no reason to think that Whitehead had done anything similar in the past.

"I believe this was a spontaneous, isolated event and not a pattern," Smith affirmed.

He described Whitehead as "non-assertive, timid and compliant." He said that at the age of 38 Whitehead had an inflammation of the spinal cord that paralyzed him briefly from the waist down. Since then, Whitehead had had "impaired sexual function" and "limited sexual activity," Whitehead's lawyer said.

Smith claimed Whitehead may have been seeking a sexual encounter with a person or "non-threatening object."

The prosecutor said he was satisfied with the suspended sentence. If Whitehead had been given the standard two-years for the charge, he likely would have been released after serving only two months and would not be on supervised probation. What he will do for his 100 hours' community service has yet to be determined.

Whitehead, who worked at the funeral home for 17 years and was terminated shortly after the incident, chose not to speak in court.

His attorney stated, "This case is one that from the very beginning had sadness written all over it for everyone involved. This ranks up there," Smith elaborated. "This moment on 401 South, in the dark of the night, hurt this woman's family deeply, it hurt Mr. Whitehead's family, and it hurt Mr. Whitehead himself. This was an awful night, but he has owned up to it."

—Patty Hobgood-Thorp, Staff Writer,
the *News & Observer*, Raleigh, North Carolina.

## I.

DEPUTY SHERIFF Wade Watson Cutcheon, Jr., fifty-seven: his unedited tape-recorded testimony, taken at the County Courthouse, Falls, NC, 5:37 a.m., February 20, four hours after apprehending suspect Whitehead.

A person thinks he's seen pretty much everything. Babies we all are, when it comes right down to it. We have not got clue number one, now, do we?

Betty? I will talk it all out. Please trim the rougher stuff and make it to sound official, okay, honey? I feel so lucky, knowing that my own beloved wife is the finest legal secretary in Tuscarora County. Helps steady me, knowing it's you my voice is first going to.

Okay, so me and Rocky get a call saying Mrs. Wembley's greenhouse is being broke into. Again. The call comes every few weeks in cold weather, anonymous, and we guessed who'd made it. But you got to check things out or folks will eat your ass alive if somebody really does steal fifteen hundred geranium seedlings.

I always use the five-battery flashlight you gave me, Betty. Shined it into the greenhouse (locked up tight as a tick, of course). I remember light scooting over all those baby plants. Little did I know what that good beam'd have to clamp onto not nine, ten minutes later. There was most of a moon out, everything in it looking orderly at present. Eleven forty-nine, we're talking.

So we was coming down old 401 South, snacking on your

own excellent cheese straws. Rocky having finally quit smoking, we've been keeping the baggie in our cruiser's (clean)
ashtray. Some kind of good eating. I remember we'd just
got serious about the upcoming Police Benevolent Barbeque
Fundraiser at the firehouse—how many trestle tables we'd
be needing—when Rocky says, "Wait one, Wade, bud. Now,
who'd be having a funeral at the edge of Old Man Martin's
peanut field on to midnight with it being a February this
cold?" Of course, in any town where folks call the police to
check their geraniums, a hearse misparked after the witching
hour is bound to draw a second glance. There'd been some
drug smuggling over in Castalia. Private airstrips in tobacco
fields, leather knapsacks still tainted with white powder. FBI
got into it. A local deputy found three apple-red BMW 730s,
keys, everything, abandoned in one ditch. Sure snagged him
quite some glory. So . . .

We pulled the cruiser over—and I played my five-battery
wand across the hearse bumper and read Nowell-Johnstone's
Mortuary Needs gold-lettered crest: at least the funeral home
was local. Some comfort. According to procedure, we split
up and approached from opposite sides of said vehicle aforementioned. My light showed me a single set of tiny (probably
human) shoe prints, leading from the driver's door to the rig's
tailgate, tracks crawling right on up in there as unto the grave
itself. Honey? My small hairs knew before I did.

Long, black limo-wagoneer, waxed, moonlight soft-soaped
all over and aimed at an angle like it'd been run off the road or
had car trouble. Strange thing: if the hearse had been parked
correct, we might not have noticed.

"Lookee," Rocky goes. That's when I saw some crawling and
scrambling in the back. First it appeared to be one large, weird,
busy animal. A full moon lit separate parts of it, all moving like

a pale bug, rowboat-sized, with maybe too many legs hooked on it and struggling to get upright off its back. Yuck. Moon kept making everything prettier and so, I reckon, creepier.

Our lights caught a face behind the car window, a pair of eyeglasses. Blinking, it was. Flat-white, and under the blue-green of the hearse's tinted glass, it looked like drowning, mouth opening, mouth closing. What seemed to be a man, looked to be kneeling, over what appeared to be a stretcher, in the back of what was sure as hell a hearse. The man was trying to cover the body with a blue blanket. I stopped cold. Even my flashlight tried to look the other way. Babies we all are, when it comes right down to it. We think we know decency, but we ain't got the first idea of it, now, do we?

I recognized the thick spectacles. Hadn't I known John Bill Whitehead all my life? In school, had he not been considered book-smart, if doughy and kind of a runt? Hadn't I given him a twenty-dollar tip after he'd done everybody so nice at Momma's funeral and her looking so "natural," plus fifteen for old maid Aunt Mary that won't a real aunt but we called her that?

Yes.

"What you got ahold of back there, John Bill?" Rock hollered, jolly, not knowing what a mouthful he'd done asked. Our lights held Whitehead's specs, glaring. Such a yanking up of breeches. Such wrestling, Jacob and his angel.

I think it was Rocky went around, opened the back of the hearse-wagon. Out spilled Whitehead, white as the wax on your fig preserves. Kept fumbling with his belt buckle and zipper, with more manhood than you might expect from somebody so outwardly wimpish.

Maybe if he'd just buttoned his black suit coat over the problem area, we wouldn't have thought too much about it. Maybe I

am wrong. Her being completely naked—I mean, the corpse—
was, I'd say, prominent among our first early-warning tip-offs.

Here it was, late February, quite the cold snap. In moonlight,
our breath showed plain, cut through by flashlight crossbeams.
A little fog was rising off the peanut field like the stubble peaks,
Betty, on your lemon meringue pie: like little witnesses watching. We had to help hold John Bill up some, none too sure on
his legs. Never what you'd call a big man nor a gruff one. This
off-duty mortician just whispered: "Everything under control, boys. Routine matter, really, everything covered, boys. I
should know what I'm doing here, but can't thank you enough,
boys, everything cov—" Then Rocky's light found much that
wasn't . . . covered.

It looked to be a child, spread-eagled, not real secretly: a
girl-child. That much even Sherlock's Dr. Watson could have
picked up at a glance. Only when we'd seen it was a girl-one did
we understand about certain shapes we'd spied earlier, flung up
on his shoulders. I ain't going to say Whitehead was a-pushing
into her like shoving a wheelbarrow, with the handles of her
legs to guide him, but something like that under oath, in
however crowded a courtroom—is what I'm going to have to
spill. SohelpmeGod.

Whitehead tried explaining how the straps had slackened
and she'd come a-loose. Due to speed bumps. Out here? Rocky,
always a joker but with that gentle streak you find in most men
his size, laughed. "She's probably come a-loose okay, John Bill."
Babies we all are, when you get right down to it. We think we
know decency and what local folks will do to other locals, but
the majority of us good Christians ain't got hint number one
concerning what goes on "behind closed doors," now, do we? It
was only about then, my fast-typing Betty, that I begun to glom
on to the full extent of it.

*If* Mrs. Wembley—at least we think it was her—had not phoned in that anonymous tip as how somebody was busting into her glass geranium house; *if* we hadn't then swung over to 401 South instead of our usual route past Millie's Diner (it being so late that even Millie would likely be closed), Rock and me might not have noticed how crookedy that hearse was parked at a dead-end road where the high school kids like to go to smooch (but usually earlier). It wasn't that original or clever a spot for John Bill to pick, not a whole hearse. And then we might not have caught him with the poor little Hartman girl.

Whitehead kept trying to block the open tailgate with his body, arms out and fingers spread to make for a better screen. But we had viewed enough to where it seemed we'd best go on and check further.

I go, "Stand aside, John Bill. Look at you—and a family man!" It was then he drew both hands up over his face. It was only then I noticed the white rubber gloves. Those scared me the worst so far: on hands way bigger and stronger than all the rest of him combined, rubber pale as roots. They forced me to step back one. If it hadn't been for them gloves, and the lowered zipper he'd had such a hard time drawing up (**because** of those slippery rubber gloves?), the man might have got away with it for another seventeen years, and at the best white funeral home in Falls, too.

"John Bill," I said in a style that was stern but human, like a law officer but one who'd known him coming and going all these years. "John Bill . . . **why?**"

Here, way off the record, I need to say that Rocky acted inappropriate. It was nerves, I believe. Referring to Whitehead's heavyset wife—and with John Bill being such a jumpy, bent soda-straw of a man, not much taller than five-four would be my guess—Rocky says: "What, Doris holding out on ye?"

That wasn't funny for anybody concerned (little Hartman girl least of all) and Rocky soon regretted it, hearing the lack of response. But I want to cite it, not to get poor Rock in trouble, just to show how mixed up and end-over-end we were, all of us. Sex after death. It's not something you bump into with the frequency of, say, Saturday jaywalking downtown. Lordbepraised.

"Well, sir," I told John Bill, "I reckon we need to see . . . the condition of the . . . of her . . . of the accessory. . . ."

I was righter than I knew.

When Rocky lifted one handle of the stretcher, John Bill grabbed the other, maybe thinking if he cooperated we wouldn't tell? And up to that point, I got to admit I was considering not—telling.

Because I didn't rightly know how to. Words never were my strongest suit. Betty, you know what I can do and what I can't. But, hey, a person needs college to explain this mess. Needs medical school.

In my mind I test-phrased it: "Guess what? You know that mousy John Bill Whitehead who has the rock-thick specs, and is one-third the size of his nice but humongous wife, and with a high-school daughter who's just been tapped into Honor Society? Well . . . and you know the Hartmans' Mongolian idiot child who has lived longer than anyone expected and has been in mental homes except for Christmas and Easter, when her folks dress her up like a doll in frills the color of bad cakes and punish everybody local by bringing her to church (at her age, twenty-five or forty, still carrying that same blue stuffed toy, long-since too old to wash)? You know how her folks just spite everybody who criticizes them for not keeping her at home and doing and caring for her and ruining their lives because they slipped up and had a child too late in life and there won't enough left in either of them to make a whole person? Well . . . and you'll never guess what."

No, I could not bring myself to even put these two unlikely characters in one sentence, much less stuff them in a single midnight hearse.

But here was the other odd part. Odd, past its being so late, and past its being a girl I'd never seen but on major holidays and only then in pinafores, and even past its being a body naked as day. Maybe oddest of all, atop the pile of oddness already heaped up, was—I've got to say: the beauty of her.

"What a body!" Rocky sighed, then caught himself, giggled but sounded punished. See, it made me know: beauty is odd, always. Odd like death—and near-about as surprising. Once you come to know how to see both death *and* beauty, why, they start fetching up pretty much everywhere. Betty, don't be going thinking I've flipped. This is how it reached your Wade out yonder. (Feel free to trim all this before submitting.) But, out beside a field whose crop was moonlit fog, it was the beauty of her body that first made Rocky and me look at each other, and then look across it, and then look it over, and then check back with each other before turning shoulder-to-shoulder and staring afresh at John Bill. It was an ideal, miniature midgety body. Freeze-dried perfect, like a small, white, naked old-timey statue. I think it was Debbie Jo's unexpected below-the-neck perfectness that told us we had not a lick of choice except to turn poor John Bill Whitehead in. I felt my stomach fist all up. Babies we each are, when it comes right down to it, and not having idea number one as to what-all some folks'll try when nobody alive is around. Not the first hint do we got, nor do we want it, either, right?

But Rocky and me both understood: we both could almost imagine it. Sure, we'd just seen the deed in progress. Which was rough. But imagining was even rougher. Know why? Because, that puts you into it. Her. Her coolish ankles mashed up humid near your ears. Sorry, Betty.

Our lights were aimed down on one pert chest. Strange, but her tiny nipples drew to my mind my favorite boyhood candy, Neccos, little purple discs with a nice mediciny taste. The flashlight then found her small reddish pubic brush, and her legs as tapered and strong, if a little more bowed, than Sonja Henie's. Of course, Rock and me are Veterans of Foreign Wars members, him from 'Nam, me from that overlooked Korean expeditionary mistake. But us two strong fellows studied each the other and knew; and then spun around and, as if trained in this at the Smithfield Police Academy Refresher Weekend Law Enforcement Seminar, both vomited.

The orange from certain recent cheese straws made our act a mite more dramatic—out there in the blue mud and the brown fog and the clear moon. It was only then, I believe, that John Bill gauged our seriousness, once he'd seen us upchuck (or heard us, because, mercifully, we both aimed our lights elsewhere, though Rocky couldn't resist, once it was over, from doing a quick check on his—only human).

A trained professional, I at least scanned my watch throughout. It was 12:07 a.m. when we first seen the bad parallel park that hearse had made, as if "the Moleman" (as we used to call weak-eyed John Bill at school) had been barely able to resist stopping. Maybe he drove slower and slower till, four miles from surrendering her to Nowell-Johnstone's funeral parlor, John Bill saw this muddy moonlit road and temptation activated his turn signal.

At 12:09 our flashlights first found the facts I'd rather not have lodged into this oh-so-local brain (too much for somebody like me with a big heart but just a high-school education).

At 12:11 we got John Bill, refastening his own unzipped lower body, off of her and out of there. My clipboard report states plain how both officer Rockford Suggs II and yours truly "Retched, copious, 12:14." Which must mean it was about 12:13 sharp when we started understanding, to the full extent of the law, what had gone on.

By then we'd seen her body, the opened crotch just perfect, and we knew that in some small, un-law-abiding, ugly yet beauty-loving part of us, we too, on looking at her (the face still covered), felt a teensy bit of, if not desire, then . . . imagination. Yoosch!

Forgive me, Betty?

And John Bill, cleaning those big smudgy eyeglasses (God knows where they'd been) on his shirttail without even needing to yank it out, and Rocky noting (with a little help from his three-battery flashlight—gift of **his** wife, but not near so good as the one you gave me) that just a bit of the said shirttail was pooching forth out through the quickly shut, snaggletoothed zipper of John Bill's black pants. Well, plainly, some deed from yours truly was now required. It'd already been tough. I mean, haven't I known Whitehead for as long as I've been knowing I am alive on earth? Yes. So . . .

Yours truly was forced to approach the cruiser, take up the handset, and risk reporting it. But in what language? Whose? In my head, I can sometimes imagine giving a sermon or a solid public speech. It's only when my mouth opens do I hear a piss-poor used-car's carburetor coughing. Still, here goes, thought I. In some way, your Wade already knew his life was

changing. I hope I never have another case like this. I reck-
oned I would never again enter Bob Melton's Barbeque without getting pointed out by somebody's toothpick as the man
that caught the undertaker doing an undertaking not exactly
family-authorized.

"Twelve-eighteen and over, Edna?"

"Read you, Smoky. How many geraniums did that pot-
smuggling gang swipe from a certain selfish Wembley woman,
not to name names on air, ha, over?"

"Edna, tonight we got us something a little differ'nt. I need
the rules and regs, need chapter and verse, on somebody's trying to . . . no, somebody managing right well, seems-like, to
have sexual congress, Edna, with, Edna?—with a corpse, Edna."

"Who *is* this?"

"It's just me, it's Officer Cutcheon. It's me, Wade, dummy.
I mean it. Look it up, the law, because I need a citation, I need
to be official, because I am feeling so damn harem-scarab
out here."

Edna goes, "You that drunk, Wade? You should have Millie
pour you all-black coffee. But Millie closed early on account of
her stepdaughter's birthday. So you just hightail it back here
quick, hear me? You do that, I swear I ain't going to write this
up and ruin you boys' next fitness reports."

Then I had to tell her everything. And the second I said, "An
employee of Nowell-Johnstone's Mortuary Needs," Edna goes,
"It's John Bill Whitehead."

I swallowed hard once.

"I knew it," she gloated. Edna does that. She gloats. "It is that
John Bill, ain't it, Wade? Because, just before Mother's funeral,
he had me in for the viewing. And . . . I don't like to announce
this on the air, Wade, but it was something—about Momma's
mouth. I can't say it. But, in some way, I've known. Whoever

he's got out there at the edge of a dark peanut field—I believe Mr. Martin put in peanuts last year?—I swear to you, Wade, it ain't his first. Who **has** he jumped?"

"The little Hartman girl."

There was a pause. It may be the first time I ever did (or will) hear a decent, blinky, gulping, human pause from veteran police dispatcher Edna so-called "Mouth City" McCabe.

She recovered, though. No surprise. Finally went: "The child is thirty-eight if she's a day. IQ of a collie, they claim." Then I could hear Edna inhale a full one-third of her Camel at a gulp. "Still, you know, Wade? It's something about his pickin' a person that slow: like he knew that even if Debbie Jo woke up, she *still* couldn't squeal on him. It's something even way nastier 'bout that. Me, I can abide anything but a sneak. Ten-four, over and out. Bring the scuzz in wearing cuffs, leg irons—hop him up the front center courthouse steps, and don't let him pull a windbreaker or nothing over his bald ole head. I got to get off this line, boy. I got people to talk to, Smoky. I got people to wake. But first . . . you know what this is, Wade?"

"Nome."

"This is History."

"Well, I reckon."

"Wade? I'm three years from retirement. So I best to thank you now, because you finally brought me one that's . . . well, this un's **national**, Wade. Love you to pieces. Overandout."

Edna had mentioned her dead mother's mouth. She'd said nothing more. Edna never spelled out what she meant by "it was something about Momma's mouth." But I rushed in and imagined how, if you know a person real good, and especially if you've been with them during their hard dying (is there any other kind?), and you've seen them wheeled out of the hospital room and you've known them through and through, and then you turn up at the home for the viewing not two days later and you can just tell from the look of them, from some relaxing of the face, some tightening, some twist or angle of the closed eyes, that something extra has got hold of them. As if Death ain't enough! I mean, something besides embalming. I mean, before embalming. I mean, a more familiar type of embalming, easier to administer, harder to detect.

Somebody like me yelled, "What'd you do to my momma and Aunt Mary, you?" And before I knew it, I had Moleman flung up against his own hearse. Did. I had that John Bill pretty much by the throat and him suspended mostly across the roof of it, pointy black shoes dangling—the guy weighs that little.

"Look, ah, Wade?" Rocky was behind me rapping on my shoulder like a door.

"Oh, sorry," I said. "But, Rock, did John Bill lay out any of your people?" I let the undertaker settle back on his feet.

"Only my brother, my kid brother that drowned, the pretty one that we . . ." I heard how Rocky, a little slower, got my drift.

"Why, you little . . ."

I had to hold Rocky back.

Edna being always on the job, it's in less than eighty seconds we commence to hear the sirens growing more and more out our way. Why she sent the fire department is not clear, beyond her owing several fellows there a favor.

I hated that. I didn't want others looking at the Hartman child. Not yet. Or, as far as that goes, studying myself either. I leaned forward, pulled at the blue blanket part-covering Deborah Jo's face, planned to ease it down, cover her whole slender body. In such a high-octane moon, her amazing little carcass shone white as a lit forty-watt white bulb. But soon as I tugged at the blanket, oops, her whole face was exposed. Rocky's light was trained right on it, with me hunkered not twelve inches above the thing. Its eyes were opened, see. I just kept staring down at her. Her face had this look—with its extra lids and the little mouth curled up at either end. "Poor thing," I said. "Poor pretty little thing." I never knew where beauty could seep up from. Then I heard Whitehead, behind me, whimpering, "No," like I was planning to cross-examine her. "Leave her be." His voice hoarse, him without an overcoat, and it fifteen degrees out there.

Now, with sirens building, Rocky, suddenly too interested, leaned closer to the mortician and whispered, "Ain't it *cold*, John Bill?" (I figured Rock meant Whitehead's lack of muffler or coat.)

"Only at first," the mortician answered, voice gone all soft and mothy.

"Oh," thought I. "Uh-oh," thought I.

## II.

BY 12:40 we've got Whitehead secured in holding cell number four. By 12:43 we have United Press International on the phone asking about hotel accommodation and Edna referring them all to her late husband's aunt's three-room boardinghouse.

Our jail's cell-side hall is lit by green-glass hanging lamps. Like the kind you see over pool tables. Cells are mercifully cut off from any busyness out front. One swinging portholed door (left over from the chief's last kitchen remodeling) muffles tonight's miked TV question-askers. I've never before seen such flashbulb blaze, what us bass fishermen call "a feeding frenzy." Never, except on live TV.

I am right glad to hang back here. I sit studying John Bill—"suicide watch," him stripped of belt, his good black Parker fountain pen, two shoestrings, one skinny black tie. (Most prison suicides happen in the first three hours of incarceration, for what it's worth.)

I feel like half a fugitive myself. I just know that future strangers will come right up to me on the street and grill me about tonight for as long as I live. Betty, I remember your hints about retirement and how nice Florida is. And for the first time ever, I consider not living—in Falls, I mean.

From the public waiting-room, I hear a blabbering of words in Yankee accents: "Outrage," "Final taboo," "Some people just sure are sickies."

Out yonder, we already had us the Raleigh *News & Observer*, the Greensboro *News & Record*, *Rocky Mount Evening Telegram* and, of course, late but finally here, despite needing all of forty seconds to stroll across Main Street, our own *Falls Herald Traveler*. Plus, double-parked out front on Courthouse Square, with nobody bothering about its being illegal, CNN, with two ferry-sized trailers spiked with antennas enough to supervise the next moon walk.

Concerning TV, and being on it or not, it's strictly Us and Them. Your National Power seems measured by how often you get on there. Or stay off it, by choice. Our Edna sure feels qualified. She's earned the title "dispatcher" hands down. (You want to tell "Mouth City" only your good news.) Her married daughters—all four—arrived by 3:30 a.m., toting garment bags containing Edna's five best Sunday dresses, plus a portable hair-burner. By 4:45 (huddled in that unlikely beauty parlor, cell number one), they'd done major home improvements to Edna's entire head and girdled person.

By now, out there, holding forth behind a flannel board

commandeered from the Second Baptist's Sunday School and made into a map with an X marking the "Hearse Locale (Actual [presumed] Sexual Act Crime Scene)," police spokeswoman Edna McCabe is part Welcome-Wagon hostess, part cold-front weather anchorwoman, part sweet ole apron-lady Aunt Bea. "Any further clarifications, coffee, doughnuts, required, boys? Because, given the gravity of all this mess, you got you instant access, I mean, whatever. . . ." Suddenly, chain-smoking, chain-talking, chain-charming Edna perches out yonder high behind the bailiff's desk, hair sprayed half-stiff as a cycle-patrolman's helmet, acting as prim as bossy in her suit all Jackie-pink. Our Edna is already sounding at least . . . semi-national.

Meantime, back here in shadow, in this guarded quiet, I'm still hunched outside our body snatcher's holding pen. I keep gaping in at John Bill Whitehead—the homely, blinky, half-blind mortician, a mild town-joke till now. Suddenly he's Falls' most famous native since the oldest living Confederate soldier died here (possible homicide). There is so much I long to ask him, I become tongue-tied. Only jokes dawn on me, rude, crude salesman-type jokes: "Did you, as a gent, let *her* go first? That it?" Stupid things. But my questions are real ones. What had scared me? Guessing . . . if I let myself, I might know some of why he did it.

All this tonight unseals all these possibilities: The way I see it, sex desire is surely the most living part of being alive, right? But to think of it in, actually inside, **the dead**: that put me off a week's feed and religion. What kind of God lets this stuff happen, then arranges it so's I'll be the one who comes upon it whilst on duty and holding that caliber of flashlight!

Dead folks? In my line of work, I see them biweekly, and battered besides. You try, but you never do get accustomed. You can't be vaccinated against the slow Novocain shock that comes from glimpsing Old Death ever new again. How casual it stuns you! like the jolt of seeing "skin," what boys here call "full-out beaver." Your mouth goes cotton. Without asking, your breath signs on for time-and-a-half. "Aha" and "Uh-oh" blend. Your legs feel lead. I used to make out Death to be a man. Poppa Time, ragged beard, bad sandals, that sickle and an attitude problem. But now, after seeing Debbie Jo, Death means Female. And that's what's shaking me. Death can screw us pretty much anytime she chooses. Astride, she can bear down on us, hard, and that, I reckon, I've long known. But now I have to consider a new possibility. You know, screwing her **back**.

Maybe I'm making no sense here.

I keep scanning John Bill Whitehead. But I never ask him anything. That'd seem **rude**. He just smiles, a milky smile, blinking out at me. Still has no idea.

"You thirsty? How's it going?" I say, to be nice. Somebody has to.


Folks hereabout have always known which single thing to remark about a tragedy over coffee at Millie's Diner downtown. It's like they vote on just one line per disaster, a show of hands, then stick with that.

Till now, it's always run maybe: *At least there were no children involved, that's one thing.*

Or: *It would've been worse if he hadn't already lived seventy-nine years and had him a full life. Still, it was a rough exit.* (This about gentle Cyril Mangum, whose Chevy pickup hit a 160-pound whitetail stag that was tossed into the air, came back down through the windshield and seven of whose ten-point antlers stabbed poor Mangum right there in the cab in his safety-belt.) *If just this single time he'd left the seat-belt flap*

*unfastened, why, even as we speak, he might be out playing golf.*
*Loved him some golf, our Cyril.*

And now, salted back here, safe from the world press, I wonder: What will we say about John Bill and his little victim girlfriend?

Does poor Falls, North Carolina, get more than its fair share of this grim stuff? Or is it that we're all so bored, so far from Action Central, we just remember it longer?

And how will Whitehead ever explain his motive? If he ever does, I want to be there. I bet no local act's ever likely to breed more rumors or sadness or more of this strange building excitement. Just wait till every citizen of Falls who's buried a lady loved-one out of Nowell-Johnstone's hears about this over breakfast, then starts making mind-pictures that cannot be erased.

I'm slumped here, elbows on knees, big chin propped in either palm, remembering how school-smart we'd always figured weak John Bill to be. The principal's secretary told my sister that Whitehead was the only one for years with near a genius IQ. He was a couple of grades in front of me at school, from a family of dirt-poor mill-workers. He was always considered good at pinning up hall bulletin boards: TRAFFIC SAFETY WEEK SAVES LIVES; PLANET OF THE WEEK. Polite but panicky-acting, unable to take the slightest joke, while wearing glasses thick as the bottoms of Coca-Cola bottles when there *were* glass Coke bottles. His science fair project—a working model of the solar system, one hooked to bicycle pedals—had him sitting at the center of these tinfoil moons and worlds, little feet cranking, smiling, watching what he made spin and orbit around him.

My thought's a jumble. I sure need sleep. You probably hear that in my tone. It only just happened. But, Betty, hon? Already I suspect I know who's waiting for me in my very next dream.

There, on ice, ahead, she is, so white. It feels like a date, a blind date, prearranged. I am scared of it, yet part of me looks forward. Like an appointment made for me the second I got born.

I didn't choose this.

I'm looking in at Whitehead. I get a little case the shakes. He sits on the metal bunk not four feet away, grinning through the bars, combing his hair, just so, with both wrists still cuffed. His white rubber gloves make his hands seem like ten separate condoms. His pointy shoes can't even reach the floor, keep swinging, swinging.

"One thing, Wade," he says, half-smiling. "Don't tell my wife?"

"Pardner, it's past that now. You hear the noise out-front? Those are just the ones that know so far, buddy."

He stops his combing. I feel sorry for him. But when I recollect my own lady kin, and the folded cash money I slipped him to honor what-all he'd done on their behalf, and with them being female and buck-naked and not bad-looking for their age and state, and all too trusting and so dead and totally alone with him, I want to reach in through the bars, slap him, maybe bang his head against the concrete wall.

"Rocky, pal?" I holler. "Care to come on back in here, spell me, please? 'Cause I'm starting to see things. All this brings up stuff a person'd rather keep . . ."

"Buried?"

"Buried."

I'm in pretty much total agreement. Rocky scuffles towards me from the blinking flash of the media-type carnival out yonder. But as he moves nearer, I see that the boy is weaving. Dragging like somebody drunk or older, maybe both. Young Rockford, a nice-looking, lanky fellow, doesn't act happy to leave the distracting reporters. He's coming through light and shade from the low green lamps. Me, I rise to offer him my chair. It's only now I see that this fine, rosy boy I've known all his life—excepting his Marine years—is crying. Rocky stands before me, his veiny hands a heavy load at either side of him. And he's sobbing like some kid too tired to know why he's cranky and can't admit to wanting sleep. Deputy Rockford Suggs II keeps on, right in front of Whitehead. Rock's nose is running, his eyes a sudden mess. Even John Bill quits swinging his legs. It's the guiltiest I've seen him act so far. First real guilt I've seen out of him.

I hug Rocky, in plain view of our town's overnight celebrity corpse-screwer. I hug Rocky and hear myself say, not knowing how I know, "Whole thing makes you think of 'Nam, don't it?"

I feel the boy nod against me.

Rock speaks into my shoulder, arms up hard around me. "Along the road into villages. They'd be wearing those black pajamas, some still under pointed straw hats. And'd be not a mark on them. Women no bigger than our kids here. But dead. We saw them all over. Some sitting up, like still expecting something." And he sobs now. "Why did we **do** that?" Rocky asks.

A bit, in my way, I cry with him.

It's while I'm patting Rock and him pretty much boo-hooing, glad no reporter will pry or know, I look back through the bars. At Whitehead. He is zooed like he deserves, I guess. But he's weeping too, snuffling, and, with his rubber gloves, wiping his face. Tears for him will always be a turn-on. Tears'll always be a part of it—babies we all are. When it comes right down to it, we think we know decency and what local folks will do for other locals, but we ain't got clue number one as to what-all lurks in any human heart, much less lower-down especially, now, do we? Ever?

\* \* \*

Betty, hon, please tidy this up to sounding semi-official. Keep things from seeming just personal.

As to the question: Guilty or not guilty?

I am forced to say: Guilty. If anybody is. Guilty of anything. Whitehead, over the Hartman girl, allowing himself to: I've got to say, yeah, guilty as charged. But there's more to it. . . .

So, "The End." Only, when is it, the end? If a live man, put in charge of a dead girl, can manage to fall in love with her and believe he's fallen hard enough to try stuff without notarized family permission, then dear Lord, God, the possibilities.

I just don't have the experience to judge any of this with.

Well, tonight one thing's for sure: Deputy Wade Watson Cutcheon here has plainly earned his week's paycheck. And now I'm heading home. To catch what helpful winks I can, and dream whatever scary dreams a person must.

I swear, dear Betty: the longer I live, the more of nothing, bigger percentage of nothing, do I firmly know.

Except, of course, a single saving fact.

*I love my wife.*

# HE'S AT THE OFFICE

TILL THE JAPANESE BOMBED Pearl Harbor, most American men wore hats to work. What happened? Did our guys—suddenly scouting overhead for worse Sunday raids—come to fear their hat brims' interference? My unsuspecting father wore his till yesterday. He owned three. A gray, a brown, and the summer straw one. Its striped rayon band could only have been woven in America in the 1940s.

Last month, I lured him from his self-imposed office hours for a walk around our block. My ailing father insisted on bringing his briefcase. "You never know," he said. We soon passed a huge young man, creaking in black leather. He carried a guitar case. The kid's pierced ears and eyebrows flashed more silver than some bait shops sell. His jeans, half down, exposed hat racks of white hip bone; the haircut arched high over jug ears.

He kept scouting Father's shoes. Long before fashion joined him, Dad favored an under-evolved antique form of orthopedic Doc Martens. These impressed a punk now scanning Dad's Sherman tank of a cowhide briefcase with its chromium corner braces. The camel-hair overcoat was cut to resemble some boxy-backed 1947 Packard. And, of course, up top sat "the gray."

Pointing to it all, the boy smiled. "Way bad look on you, guy."

My father, seeking interpretation, stared at me. I simply shook my head no. I could not explain Dad to himself in terms of tidal fashion trends. All I said was, "I think he likes you."

Dad's face folded. "Uh-oh."


Once a year, Mom told brother and me how much the war had darkened her young husband; he'd enlisted with three other boys from Falls. He alone came back alive with all his limbs. "Before that," she smiled, "your father was funnier, funny. And smart. Great dancer. You can't blame mustard gas, not this go-round. It's more what Dick saw. He was lighting a cigarette for Paul, his best friend, when a Nazi sniper—half a mile away—vaporized Paul's head. Your father came home and he was all business. Obedient. Just facts mattered. Before, he'd been mischievous and talkative, even strange. He was always playing around with words. Very entertaining. Eyelashes out to here. For years, I figured that in time he'd come back to being whole. But since June of '45 it's been All Work and No Play Makes Jack.

"On our fifth anniversary I hired an overnight sitter for you two. He and I drove to a famous Asheville inn. It had the state's best restaurant, candlelight, a real string quartet. I'd made myself a green crushed-velvet dress. I was twenty-eight and never in my whole life have I ever looked better. You just know it. Dick recognized some man who'd bought two adding machines from his firm. Dick invited him to join us. Then I saw how much Integrity Office Supplier was going to have to mean to him. And us.

"So, don't be too hard on him. Your father feeds us, saves for you boys' college. Dick pays our taxes. Dick has no secrets. He got hurt but he's not hurting anyone." Brother and I gave each other a look Mom recognized and understood but refused to return.

The office seemed to tap some part of him that was either off-limits to us or simply did not otherwise exist. My brother and I griped he'd never attended our Little League games. He missed the father-son Cub Scout banquet; it conflicted with a major envelope convention in Newport News. Mother neutrally said he loved us as much as he could. She always was a wry, energetic person—all that wasted goodwill. Even as kids, we knew not to blame her.

By the end, my father was a fifty-two-year veteran of Integrity Office Supplier, Unlimited. An early riser, six days a week he shaved and gargled. Mom sealed his single sandwich into its Tupperware jacket; this fit accidentally yet exactly within the lid compartment of his durable briefcase. Dad would set the hat in place, nod in our general direction, and hurry off. If he had been General Eisenhower saving the Western world or Dr. Salk sparing children polio, okay. But yellow Eagle pencils? Utility paperweights in park-bench green?

Ignored, Mom turned the spare room into her sewing studio. Economizing needlessly, she stayed busy stitching all our school clothes, cowboy motifs galore. For a while, each shirt pocket bristled with Mom-designed embroidered cacti. But Simplicity patterns were never going to engage a mind complex as hers. Soon she was spending mornings playing vicious duplicate bridge. Our toothbrush glasses briefly broke out in rashes of red hearts, black clubs. Mom's new pals were society ladies respectful of her brainy speed, her offhand wit; she never bothered introducing them to her husband. She laughed more now. She started wearing rouge.

We lived a short distance from both our school and his wholesale office. Dad sometimes left the Plymouth parked all night outside the workplace, his desk lamp the last one burning on the whole third floor. Integrity's president, passing headquarters late, always fell for it. "Dick, what do you *do* up there all night, son?" My father's shrug became his finest boast. The raises kept pace; Integrity Office Supplier was considered quite a comer. And R. Richard Markham, Sr.—handsome as a collar ad, a hat ad, forever at the office—was the heir apparent.

No other schoolboys had sturdier pastel subject dividers, more clip-in see-through three-ring pen caddies. The night before school started, Dad would be up late at our kitchen table, swilling coffee, "getting you boys set." Zippered leather cases, English slide rules, folders more suitable for treaties than book reports (*Skipper, a Dog of the Pyrenees,* by Marjorie Hopgood Purling). Our notebooks soon proved too heavy to carry far; we secretly stripped them, swapping gear for lunch box treats more exotic than Mom's hard-boiled eggs and Sun-Maid raisin packs.

## II.

TWENTY YEARS AGO, Dad's Integrity Office Supplier got bought out by a German firm. The business's vitality proved somewhat hobbled by computers' onslaught. "A fad," my father called computers in 1976. "Let others retool. We'll stand firm with our yellow legals, erasers, Parker ink, fountain pens. Don't worry, our regulars'll come back. True vision always lets you act kind in the end, boys. Remember."

Yeah, right.

My father postponed his retirement. Mom encouraged that and felt relieved; she could not image him at home all day. As Integrity's market share dwindled, Dad spent more time at the office, as if to compensate with his own body for the course of modern life.

His secretary, the admired Miss Green, had once been what Pop called "something of a bombshell." (He stuck with a Second World War terminology. Like the hat, it had served him too well to ever leave behind.)

Still favoring shoulder pads, dressed in unyielding woolen Joan Crawford solids, Green wore an auburn pageboy that looked burned by decades of ungrateful dyes. She kicked off her shoes beneath her desk, revealing feet that told the tale of high heels' worthless weekday brutality. She'd quit college to tend an ailing mother, who proved demanding, then immortal. Brother and I teased Mom: poor Green appeared to worship her longtime boss, a guy whose face was as smooth and wedged and classic as his headgear. Into Dick Markham's blunted constancy she read actual "moods."

He still viewed Green, now past sixty, as a promising virginal girl. Their small offices adjoined. Integrity's flagship headquarters remained enameled a flavorless mint green, unaltered for five decades. The dark Mission coatrack was made by Limbert—quite a good piece. One ashtray—upright, floor model, brushed chromium—proved the size and shape of some landlocked torpedo. Moored to walls, dented metal shelves. A

series of khaki filing cabinets seemed banished to one shaming little closet. Dad's office might've been decorated by a firm
called Edward Hopper & Sam Spade, Unlimited.

For more than half a century, he walked in each day at
seven-oh-nine sharp, as Miss Green forever said, "Morning, Mr.
Markham. I left your appointments written on your desk pad,
can I get you your coffee? Is now good, sir?"

And Dad said, "Yes, why, thanks, Miss Green, how's your
mother, don't mind if I do."


Four years ago, I received a panicked phone call: "You the junior
to a guy about eighty, guy in a hat?"

"Probably." I was working at home; I pressed my computer's
"save" button. This, I sensed, might take a while.

"Mister, your dad thinks we're camped out in his office
and he's been banging against our door. He's convinced we've
evicted his files and what he calls his Green. 'What have you
done with young Green?' Get down here ASAP. Get him out of
our hair or it's 911 in three minutes, swear to God."

From my car, I phoned home. Mom must have been off
somewhere playing bridge with the mayor's blond wife and
his blond ex-wife; they'd sensibly become excellent friends.
Mother, overlooked by Dad for years, had continued finding
what she called "certain outlets."

When I arrived, Dad was still heaving himself against an
office door, dead-bolt-locked from within. Since its upper panel
was frosted glass, I could make out the colored clothes of three
or four people pressing from their side. They'd used masking
tape to cross-hatch the glass, as if bracing for a hurricane. The
old man held his briefcase, wore his gray hat, the tan boxy coat.

"Dad?" He stopped with a mechanical cartoon verve,

jumped my way, and smiled so hard it warmed my heart and scared me witless. My father had never acted so glad to see me—not when I graduated summa cum laude, not at my wedding, not after the birth of my son—and I felt joy in the presence of such joy from him.

"Reinforcements. Good man. We've got quite a hostage situation here. Let's put our shoulders to it, shall we?"

"Dad?" I grabbed the padded shoulders of his overcoat. These crumpled to reveal a man far sketchier hiding in there somewhere—a guy only twenty years from a hundred, after all.

"Dad? Dad. We have a good-news bad-news setup here today. It's this. You found the right building, Dad. Wrong floor."

I led him back to the clattering, oil-smelling elevator. I thought to return, tap on the barricaded door, explain. But, in time, hey, they'd peek, they'd figure out the coast was clear. That they hadn't recognized him, after his fifty-two years of long days in this very building, said something. New people, everywhere.

I saw at once that Miss Green had been crying. Her face was caked with so much powder it looked like calamine. "Little mix-up," I said.

"Mr. Markham? We got three calls about those gum erasers." She faked her normal tone. "I think they're putting sawdust in them these days, sir. They leave skid marks, apparently. I put the information on your desk. With your day's appointments. Like your coffee? Like it now? Sir?"

I hung his hat on the hat tree; I slid his coat onto one wooden Deco hanger that could, at any flea market today, bring fifty-five dollars easy, two tones of wood, inlaid.

I wanted to have a heart-to-heart with my father. But I felt so disoriented. Then I overheard him already returning his calls. As usual he ignored me. And, within this radically altered gravitational field, that seemed a good sign. I sneaked back to Miss Green's desk and admitted, "We'll need to call his doctor. I want him seen today, Miss Green. He was up on four, trying to get into that new headhunting service. He told them his name. Mom was out. So they, clever, looked him up, found his junior, and phoned me to come help."

She sat forward, strenuously feigning surprise. She looked rigid, chained to this metal desk by both gnarled feet. "How long has he been like this?" I somehow knew to ask.

Green appeared ecstatic, then relieved, then, suddenly, happily, tears came pouring down—small tears, lopsided amounts, mascaraed grit. She blinked up at me with a spaniel's gratitude. In mere seconds, she confessed Dad's years-long caving-in. She hinted she was passing on the task. My turn.

Miss Green now whispered certain of his mistakes. There were forgotten parking tickets by the dozen. There was his attempt to purchase a lake house on land already flooded for a dam. Quietly, she admitted years of covering.

From her purse, she lifted a page covered in Dad's stern Germanic cursive. Blue ink fought to stay between red lines.

"I found this one last week." Green's voice seemed steadied by the joy of having told. "I fear this is about the worst to-date we've been."

I read the note:

If they say "hot enough for you?" it means recent weather. "Yes indeed" still a good comeback. Order forms pink. Requisition yellow. Miss Green's birthday June 12. She work with you fifty-one years. Is still unmarried. Mother now dead, since '76, so stop asking about Mother, health of. Your home address, 712 Marigold Street: Left at Oak, can always walk there. After last week, never go near car again.

Unfair to others. Take second left at biggest tree. Your new Butchers' name is Al. Wife: Betty. Sons: Matthew and Dick Junior. Grandson Richie (your name with a III added on it). List of credit cards, licnse below in case you lose wallet agn, you big dope. Put copies somewhere safe, 3 places, write down, hide many: You are 80, yes, eighty.

And yet, as we now eavesdropped, Dick Markham dealt with a complaining customer. He sounded practiced, jokey, conversant, exact.

"Dad, you have an unexpected doctor's appointment." I handed him his hat. I'd phoned our family physician from Miss Green's extension.

For once, they were ready for us. The nurses kept calling him by name, smiling, overinsistent. I could see they'd always liked him. In a town this small, they'd maybe heard about his trouble earlier today.

As Dad got ushered in for tests, he glowered accusations back at me as if I had just dragged him to some Nazi medical experiment. He finally reemerged, scarily pale, pressing a bit of gauze into the crook of his bare arm, its long veins the exact blue of Parker's washable ink. They directed him toward the lobby bathroom. They gave him a cup for his urine specimen. He held it before him with two hands like some magi's treasure.

His hat, briefcase, and overcoat remained behind, resting on one orange plastic chair. Toward these I could display a permissible tenderness. I lightly set my hand upon each item. Call it superstition. I now lifted the hat and sniffed it. It smelled like Dad. It smelled like rope. Physical intimacy had never been a possibility. My brother and I, half drunk, once tried to picture the improbable, the sexual conjunction of our parents. Brother said, "Well, he probably pretends he's at the office, unsealing her like a good manila envelope that requires a rubber stamp—legible, yes, keep it legible, *legible*, now speed-mail!"

I had flipped through all four stale magazines before I saw the nurses peeking from their crudely cut window. "He has been quite a while, Mr. Markham. Going on thirty minutes."

"Shall I?" I rose and knocked. No answer. "Would you come stand behind me?" Cowardly, I signaled to a veteran nurse.

The door proved unlocked. I opened it. I saw one old man aimed the other way and trembling with hesitation. Before him, a white toilet, a white sink, a white enamel trash can, the three aligned—each its own invitation. In one hand, the old man held an empty specimen cup. In the other hand, his dick.

Turning my way, grateful, unashamed to be caught sobbing, he asked, "Which one, son? Fill which one?"

### III.

FORCIBLY RETIRED, Father lived at home in his pajamas. Mom made him wear slippers and the silk robe to help with his morale. But the poor guy literally "hung his head with shame." That phrase took on new meaning now that his routine and dignity proved so reduced. Dad's mopey presence clogged every outlet she'd perfected to avoid him. The two of them were driving each other crazy.

Lacking the cash for live-in help, she was forced to cut way back on her bridge games and female company. She lost ten pounds—it showed first in her neck and face—and then she gave up rouge. You could see Mom missed her fancy friends. I soon pitied her nearly as much as I pitied him—no, more.

At least he allowed himself to sometimes be distracted. She couldn't forget the things he couldn't remember.

Mom kept urging him to dress as if for work. She said they needed to go to the zoo. She had to get out and "do" something. One morning, she was trying to force Dad into his dress pants when he struck her. She fell right over the back of an armchair. The whole left side of her head stayed a rubber-stamp pad's blue-black for one whole week. Odd, this made it easier for both of them to stay home. Now two people hung their heads in shame.

At a window overlooking the busy one-way street, Dad spent hours staring out. On window glass, his forehead left a persistent oval of human oil. His pajama knees pressed against the radiator. He silently second-guessed parallel parkers. He studied westerly-moving traffic. Sometimes he'd stand guard there mornings and afternoons. Did he await some detained patriotic parade? I pictured poor Green on one of its passing floats—hoisting his coffee mug and a black office-phone carved big as the Maltese Falcon. She'd be waving him back down to street level, reality, use.

One December morning, Mom—library book in lap, trying to reinterest herself in Daphne du Maurier, in anything—smelled something scorching. Like Campbell's mushroom soup left far too long on simmer. Twice she checked their stove and toaster-oven. Finally, around his nap time, she pulled Dad away from the radiator: his shins had cooked.

"Didn't it hurt you, Dick? Darling, didn't you *feel* anything?"

Next morning at six-thirty, I got her call. Mom's husky tone sounded too jolly for the hour. She described bandaging both legs. "As you kids say, I don't think this is really working for us. Might be beyond me. Integrity's fleabag insurance won't provide him the care he needs. We have just enough to go on living here as usual. Now, maybe it'll shock you to find me weak or, worse, disloyal. But would you consider someday checking out a nice facility in driving distance? Even if it uses up our savings. Your father is the love of my life—one per customer. I hate getting any more afraid of him!"

I said I'd phone all the good local places.

She went on, "Your dad's been home from the office—what, seven months? Most men look forward to their leisure years. When I think of everything Dick gave Integrity and how little he's getting back . . . I'm not strong enough to **keep** him but I can't bear to **put** him anywhere. —Still, at this rate, all I'll want for Christmas is a nice white padded cell for two."

I wished my mother belonged to our generation, where women work. She could've done anything. He still refused to dress; she focused on the sight of his pajamas. My folks now argued with the energy of newlyweds; then she felt ashamed of herself and he forgot to do whatever he'd just promised.

On Christmas Eve, she was determined to put up a tree for him. But Dad, somehow frightened by the ladder and all the unfamiliar boxes, got her into such a lethal headlock she had to scream for help. Now neighbors were involved. Now people I barely knew interrupted my office work, insisting, "Something's got to be done. It took three of us to pull him off of her. Old guy's still strong as a horse. It's getting dangerous over there. He could escape."

Sometimes, at two in the morning, she'd find him standing in their closet, wearing his pj's and the season's correct hat. He'd be looking at his business suits. The right hand would be filing, "walking," back and forth across creased pant legs, as if seeking the . . . exact . . . right . . . pair . . . for . . . the office . . . today.

\*    \*    \*

I tried to keep Miss Green informed. She'd sold her duplex and moved into our town's most stylish old-age home. When she swept downstairs to greet me, I didn't recognize her. "God, you look fifteen years younger." I checked her smile for hints of a possible lift.

She just laughed, giving her torso one mild shimmy. "Look, Ma. No shoulder pads."

Her forties hairdo with its banked rolled edges had softened into pretty little curls around her face. She'd let its color go her natural silvery blond. Green gave me a slow look. If I didn't know her better, I'd have sworn she was flirting.

She appeared shorter in flats. I now understood: her toes had been so mangled by wearing those Quonset-huts of high heels, ones she'd probably owned since age eighteen. Her feet had grown, but she'd stayed true to the old shoes, part of some illusion she felt my dad required.

Others in the lobby perked at her fond greeting; I saw she'd already become the belle of this place. She let me inventory her updated charms.

"No." She smiled. "It's that I tried to keep it all somewhat familiar for him. How I looked and everything. We got to where Mr. Markham found any change a kind of danger, so . . . I mean, it wasn't as if a dozen other suitors were beating down my door. What with Mother being moody and sick that long. And so, day-to-day, well . . ." She shrugged.

## IV.

NOW, IN MY LIFE I've had very few inspired ideas. Much of me, like Pop, is helplessly a company man. So forgive my boasting of this one, okay?

Leaving Miss Green's, I stopped by a huge Salvation Army store. It's the best around. Over the years, I've found a few fine Federal side chairs and many a great tweed jacket. Browsing the used-furniture rooms, I wandered beneath a cardboard placard hand-lettered "The World of Early American." Duck decoys and mantel clocks. Ladder-back deacon's chairs rested knee to knee, like sad and separate families.

I chanced to notice a homeless man, asleep, a toothless white fellow. His overcoat looked filthy. His belongings were bunched around him in six rubber-banded shoeboxes. His feet, in paint-stained shoes, rested on an ordinary school administrator's putty-colored desk. The plaque overhead explained "The Wonderful World of Work." His setting? a hand-me-down waiting room still waiting. Business furniture sat parlored gray-green as any Irish wake. There was something about this old guy's midday snoring in so safe a make-work cubicle.

Mom now used her sewing room just for those few overnight third cousins willing to endure its lumpy foldout couch. The place had become a catchall, cold storage, since about 1970. We waited for Dad's longest nap of the day. Then, in a crazed burst of energy, we cleared her lair, purging it of boxes, photo albums, his-and-hers unused exercise machines. I paint-rolled its walls in record time, the ugliest latex junior-high-school green that Sherwin-Williams sells (there's still quite a range). The Salvation Army delivers: within two days, I had arranged this new-used junk to resemble Integrity's workspace, familiarly anonymous. A metal desk nuzzled one wall—the window wasted behind. Three green file cabinets made a glum herd. One swivel wooden chair rode squeaky casters. The hat rack antlered upright over a dented tin wastebasket. The ashtray looked big enough to serve an entire cancer ward. One wire shelf was labeled "In"; its larger mate promised a more optimistic "Out." I stuffed desk drawers with bottled Parker ink, cheap fountain pens, yellow legal pads, six dozen paper clips. I'd bought a big black rotary phone, and Mom got him his own line.

Against her wishes, I'd saved most of Dad's old account ledgers. Yellowed already, they could've come from a barrister's desk in some Dickens novel. I scattered "1959–62." In one corner I piled all Dad's boxed records, back taxes, Christmas cards from customers. The man saved everything.

The evening before we planned introducing him to his new quarters, I disarranged things a bit. I tossed a dozen pages on the floor near his chair. I left the desk lamp lit all night. It gave this small room a strange hot smell, overworked. The lamp was made of a nubbly brown metal (recast war surplus?), its red button indicating "on." Black meant "off."

That morning I was there to help him dress. Mom made us a hearty oatmeal breakfast, packed his lunch, and snapped the Tupperware insert into his briefcase.

"And where am *I* going?" he asked us in a dead voice.

"To the office," I said. "Where *else* do you go this time of day?"

He appeared sour, puffy, skeptical. Soon as I could, I glanced at Mom. This was not going to be as easy as we'd hoped.

I got Dad's coat and hat. He looked pale and dubious. He would never believe in this new space if I simply squired him down the hall to it. So, after handing him his case, I led Dad back along our corridor and out onto the street.

Some of the old-timers, recognizing him, called, "Looking good, Mr. Markham," or "Cold enough for you?" Arm in arm, we nodded past them.

My grammar school had been one block from his office. Forty years back, we'd set out on foot like this together. The nearer Dad drew to Integrity, the livelier he became; the closer I got to school, the more withdrawn I acted. But today I kept up a mindless over-plentiful patter. My tone neither cheered nor deflected him. One block before his office building, I swerved back down an alley toward the house. As we approached, I saw that Mom had been imaginative enough to leave our front door wide open. She'd removed a bird print that had hung in our foyer hall, unloved forever. A mere shape, it still always marked this as our hall, our home.

"Here we are!" I threw open his office door. I took his hat and placed it on its hook. I helped free him from his coat. Just as his face locked—bored, then irked, and finally enraged at our deception—the phone rang. From where I stood—half in the office, half in the hall—I could see Mom holding the kitchen's white extension.

My father paused—since when had a company president answered incoming calls?—but, flushed, he finally reached for it himself. "Dick?" Mom said. "You'll hate me, I'm getting so absentminded. But you did take your lunch along today, right? I mean, go check. Be patient with me, okay?" Phone cradled between head and shoulder, he lifted his briefcase and snapped it open—his efficiency still water-clear, and scary. Dad then said to the receiver, "Lunch is definitely here, per usual. But, honey, what have I told you about personal calls at the office?"

Then I saw him bend to pick up scattered pages. I saw him touch one yellow legal pad and start to square all desktop pens at sharp right angles. As he pulled the desk chair two inches forward, I slowly shut his door behind me. Then Mother and I, hidden in the kitchen, held each other and, not expecting it, cried, if very, very silently.

When we peeked in two hours later, he was filing.


Every morning, Sundays included, Dad walked to the office. Even our ruse of hiking him around the block was relaxed. Mom simply set a straw hat atop him (after Labor Day, she knew to switch to the gray). With his packed lunch, he would stride nine paces from the kitchen table, step in, and pull the door shut, muttering complaints of overwork, no rest ever.

Dad spent a lot of time on the phone. Were his old colleagues and clients humoring him? Long-distance directory-assistance charges constituted a large part of his monthly bill. But he "came home" for supper with the weary sense of blurred accomplishment we recalled from olden times.

Once, having dinner with them, I asked Dad how he was faring. He sighed. "Well, July is peak for getting their school supplies ordered. So the pressure's sure on. My heart's not what it was, heart's not completely in it lately, I admit. They downsized Green. Terrible loss to me. With its being crunch season, I get a certain shortness of breath. Suppliers aren't where they were, the gear is often second-rate, little of it any longer American-made. But you keep going, because it's what you know and because your clients count on you. I may be beat, but, hey—it's still a job."

"Aha," I said.

Mom received a call on her own line. It was from some kindergarten owner. Dad—plundering his old red address book—had somehow made himself a go-between, arranging sales, but working freelance now. He appeared to be doing it unsalaried, not for whole school systems but for small local outfits like day-care centers. This teacher had to let Mom know that he'd sent too much of the paste. No invoice with it, a pallet of free jarred white school paste waiting out under the swing sets. Whom to thank?

Once, I tiptoed in and saw a long list of figures he kept meaning to add up. I noticed that, in his desperate daily fight to keep his desktop clear, he'd placed seven separate five-inch piles of papers at evened intervals along the far wall. I found such ankle-level filing sad till I slowly recognized a pattern—oh yeah, the "Pile System." It was my own technique for maintaining provisional emergency order, and one that I now re-judged to be quite sane.

Inked directly into the wooden bottom of his top desk drawer was this:

Check Green's sick leave—too long. Nazis lost. Double enter all new receipts, nincompoop. Yes, you . . . eighty-one. Woman roommate: Betty.

Mom felt safe holding bridge parties at the house again, telling friends that Dad was in there writing letters and doing paper-work, and who could say he wasn't? Mom could now shop or attend master-point tournaments at good driving-distance hotels. In her own little kitchen-corner office, she entered bridge chat rooms, e-mailing game-theory arcana to well-known French and Russian players. She'd regained some weight and her face was fuller, and prettier for that. She bought herself a bottle-green velvet suit. "It's just a cheap Chanel knockoff, but these ol' legs still ain't that bad, hmm?" She looked more rested than I'd seen her in a year or two.

I cut a mail slot in Dad's office door, and around eleven Mom would slip in the day's *Wall Street Journal*. You'd hear him fall on it like a zoo animal, fed.

V.

SINCE DAD TRIED to break down the headhunters' door I hadn't dared go on vacation. But Mother encouraged me to take my family to Hawaii. She laughed. "Go ahead, enjoy yourself, for Pete's sake. Everything is under control. I'm playing what friends swear is my best bridge ever, and Dick's sure working good long hours again. By now I should know the drill, hunh?"

I was just getting into my bathing suit when the hotel phone rang. I could see my wife and son down there on the white beach.

"Honey? Me. There's news about your father."

Mom's voice sounded vexed but contained. Her businesslike tone seemed assigned. It let me understand.

"When?"

"This afternoon around six-thirty our time. Maybe it happened earlier, I don't know. I found him. First I convinced myself he was just asleep. But I guess, even earlier, I knew."

I stood here against glass, on holiday. I pictured my father facedown at his desk. The tie still perfectly knotted, his hat yet safe on its hook. I imagined Dad's head at rest atop those forty pages of figures he kept meaning to add up.

I told Mom I was sorry; I said we'd fly right back.

"Oh no, please," she said. "I've put everything off till next week. It's just us now. Why hurry? And, son? along with the bad news, I think there's something good. —He died at the office."

# UNASSISTED HUMAN FLIGHT

MY FIRST NIGHT as cub-reporter and they send me to a four-hour County Sewage Hearing. I call that hazing. *You* try distilling lively prose from Waste Water Issues.

To be safe, I wore my best blue thrift-shop blazer. But when I afterwards approached the Mayor, he clammed up. I asked one question but he heard: I lacked a brogue of sufficient Dixie humidity. He sensed this newbie knew nothing yet of hog prices, hurricane damage, proof the Presbyterian pastor kept an open tab at Discount Adult Art. Having been assigned a town of 6,000, I found its every citizen obsessed with one thing only: the other 5,999.

And after five years' reporting here? I talk slower, think faster, scratch anywhere. The blazer? long-since replaced with denim work-clothes. People here now know my name because I know theirs. And today, with regret, I leave Falls. . . .

This must be my last *Herald Traveler* column. Our editor has spent years slashing my discursive if clarion copy. He's presently vacationing at Myrtle Beach. Mel has finally agreed to let me "go long." He left one urgent Post-it, "If need be, cut the issue's 'Classifieds.' But 'Recent Arrests' and the Hardee's ads are sacred, got it?"

I've been summoned to Richmond's big-league paper from this noble farm team. Let me thank you, reader, for your patience in watching a boy from Akron come to consciousness in stark civic view. You have been patient as my accent lost its harder corners. Consonants now sound Midwestern. The South is all nougat vowel.

This much I have learned from Falls, NC: Whatever story the *Herald* sent me out to cover, was never the one locals tried telling me instead.

—Today's column finally gives the people what they want. This is the tale Falls has pleaded for these five years: a secret "miracle" too-long-ignored. My last seven weeks have been taken up with the sad facts of the Mahon family drowning. If the reader is tired of this tragic event, imagine how Falls' feature writer feels. In brief, the Mahons, farmers long established in our county, inherited a motorboat. It arrived at night and the father and mother and five children decided to take said craft for a test spin in their farm's biggest irrigation pond. The eldest son had brought his pistol. He intended to fire off a traditional New Year's Eve round overhead. Somehow the gun discharged into the bottom of the fiberglass boat. No one was hurt but bullets shattered the craft's underside. This would have meant nothing if any of the Mahons could swim. Shortly after the pistol fired, their motor stalled and, out that far on water after midnight, the thing slowly sank. Since the nearest neighbors live three miles away, no shouts were heard. Come morning, only a boat trailer hinted what had happened. The Mahon drowning seemed the last tale I would tell here. Then the one printed below took me—after the dredging misery of the Mahon deaths—to heights un-guessed.

This morning I and my cat (named "Inkjet," enemy of sparrows, five years chunkier) head north, leaving behind the story I feel proudest of. It proved my hardest interview to land but the easiest to remember.

## HOW HIS TALE RECRUITED ME

A SHORT OLD WHITE MAN hoisted one thrashing catfish. It hung alongside him nearly half his length, black as motor oil. I photographed these two.

"You think this fish is something? Know who your paper keeps missing? 'Miracle Boy.' Not even my catch here can touch him. Imagine a local human flying. Thirty-odd years back one naked boy 'flew' most of a mile. No fake wings. No helium or nothing. The sky someway took him in, then coughed him back down alive. I swear.

"Your editor made you drive clear out here, son. Why? To report my hooking this forty-four-pounder. (True, my wife did phone the paper. And, sure, this creature fought me something fierce for almost twenty-six minutes. The wife camcorded every single second. And she **will** show you, if I don't walk you clear back to your pickup.)

"But you need to be writing about the strangest thing ever

happened this far down Rodgers Road. The boy that survived his flying? He's up around forty now. Still paying taxes, still pulling for 'State.' He could tell you it. But you'll likely have to trick him. Usually Larry won't talk about it. Can't, maybe.

"One naked twin, about age eight? *he* drowned. Was the second brother flew into the sky. It's the sky-one is still alive. 'Miracle Boy' stayed airborne whole minutes. (Wish Annie'd filmed *that*.) His name is Larry A. Winstead. The twin that died? now, that one was 'Barry.' Barry went under. But Larry? went up. —Don't stare like I'm a senile. Phone him, son. (—No, Annie. Our boy-reporter does *not* need your whole film of me landing this monster. . . . Maybe just the *high*light reel.)"

Since then, Larry-Winstead-flight-facts reached me almost monthly. But I admit to feeling ever-more-skeptical. Features editors on papers this small must be gluttons for local color. (Didn't I offer that hard-hitting two-part-series regarding the history of our Pun'kin Festival?) —But un-winged human air travel? For a documentarian like me, without supporting footage or some talkative surviving Icarus, that sounded hard to ever verify.

Still, flight info kept finding me. Into the paper's downtown office walked a recent bride's brisk mother. She'd come to retrieve wedding-photos from our paper's Society Editor (me also). This lady was unusual in seeming pleased with my nuptial coverage. She had even sent me a monogrammed note and some folding money.

A prosperous farmer's wife, she attends the society church in town. Being upwardly mobile might show in her preference for four-inch heels. This day she sported pearls, a lace collar, one small hat that clamped. While dictating her address for mailing purposes, she mentioned Rodgers Road. This somehow recalled to her a certain unique neighbor. She said she still owed me a favor. She admitted she'd gotten emotional when my wedding coverage mentioned bridesmaids' peau de soie. In the *Herald Traveler*, famous for typos, I'd also spelled it right. So, indebted, this lady started in the middle, saying a nude child had been jerked up into quite a wind, like the one that took Dorothy clear to Oz, and did I even know? Had my advanced degree in journalism left me too sophisticated to recognize an act of God?

"Now that you covered my Stacey's wedding so nicely, why not write **him** up? People enjoy topics like close calls during famous storms. But, past that, young man, picture a boy being held midair while getting to look down on all of Tuscarora County. And afterwards, it really improved young Larry. You see, I attended second grade with him, before. And he was . . . I won't say sneaky-mean but . . . he **would** torture frogs and three of our weaker girls. Get them into corners, et cetera. He tickled one till she, well, dampened herself. No names. But nowadays there's just something extra about Larry Winstead. Changed for the better. It's lasted, too. There's a thing when you see him you'll know, son. Larry is like . . . maybe a man you always lived near but who never once let on he'd maybe saved his whole platoon then won the Silver Star? Like that. Strong.

"I reside on his same road and pay attention. And, for instance, Larry vegetable-gardens to give most of it away. Not just excess August zucchini, either. Headed the Cub Scouts, and, let's see, coaches Pee Wee Football. I even know people he has lent thousands of dollars, but once they skip out on him? Larry still speaks to them, in church, at stores. He is a fellow very little bothers. An overqualified reporter like you, from

'away,' you might well find Larry and his wife 'a little bit'"—
she looked around then whispered—"'country.'"

"But Duke Power values him. We hear Larry's their opera-
tional brain for this whole end the state. Don't let his being quiet
fool you. Most people talk better than they write. First get him
telling it, then you do the write-up. Being so bright and bushy-
tailed, you'll someway force Larry to go on-record. 'In his own
words' type thing. It'll be like pulling teeth. But you'll end up
with your biggest prizewinner. Just make sure you spend three-
four hours with him. Over-educated people like you make too
many appointments. Which keeps them feeling important but
wears 'em out early. But Larry? Not someone who ever hurries,
Larry. Lives right on Rodgers near where wind took him up.
The child flew nude. Neighbors still swear he landed on his feet
like a bird would.'"

She made me look him up. I now see that—like his famous
storm—I started circling Larry long before I found him. Why
has it taken almost four years to bother tracing him? I just didn't
believe the thing really happened—unassisted human flight.
But, maybe this very delay strengthened me into the writer-
interviewer-detective needed for landing such a tale?

Now I can finally depart Falls with a clear conscience. For
years I've been here, listening so hard I couldn't hear. The best
true stories? they are the most unlikely. I learned that here
in Falls.

## STALKING OUR SUBJECT

SURPRISING TO FIND Larry's home and work numbers right
online. Friends spoke of him as being hermit-shy, at least about

his most unexplainable incident. So, exactly one year ago, I sent him a first respectful text; it named those ten character-witnesses most stubbornly urging me to finally get on-record his aerial adventure. Three weeks later, no response.

While awaiting a reaction from Lawrence Alston Winstead, electrical engineer, I did my own due diligence. Being a recent grad of Carolina's J-school, I have classical training. I love facts.

—I am not like some of these guys who'll try and sneak in layers of ticky-tack frosting without admitting such spun-fluff is plain ole "Fiction." I so worship unvarnished "Nonfiction," I've grown downright anti-novelistic. Who needs make-believe—given a world constructed so weirdly as ours? I now believe the girders of the mysterious are what really hold us all in place. Those provide limitless horror stories plus surging daily poetry. But first I had to know the likelihood of wind's taking up any object heavy as some tree-climbing country boy aged eight.

I queried "children carried off by cyclones but staying alive." I discovered that L. Frank Baum, bard of the prairie, heard tales of actual kids riding in houses borne heavenward then returned. He gave his Dorothy a last name acknowledging easement with her own storm: "Gale." I found that, in South Dakota in July 1955, a nine-year-old girl plus the pony she rode both got hoisted by wind but survived, wounded only by major subsequent hail.

I phoned the National Hurricane Service down along our NC coast at Nags Head. I figured I would make an appointment then drive that pretty ocean-side road on the company dime. I called a few days prior to Christmas. An office-party sounded ongoing. I heard secretarial shrieks and carols played upon what seemed a skilled amateur accordion. (I had never thought of meteorologists as party animals but, being not quite twenty-six myself, I admit I am always learning!)

The fellow that answered said, well, if I was a real reporter he might take just one official question; he explained being off-duty and drinking eggnog, though steeped in decades' savage storm experience. "I'll turn sixty-five this June," he bragged and confessed. First he sounded mellow then moderately drunk. But his love of terrible weather flung a certain sea-dog's salt into his tone and authority. Was Child Flight possible? I asked.

"Sir, not unusual for youngsters weighing less than eighty pounds to be carried aloft by winds exceeding a hundred miles per hour. (I'm told the kids that fight it often come out worst.) Soon as an infant gets sucked into the sky, I'd say trust becomes essential. Think about it. If winds can uproot silos, homes, bridges, winds'll sure shift kids from spot to spot, as an oversight. Hardest part of any ride comes as it ends, of course. Like life, buddy, getting up and started's easy, right? It's your coming down's the killer. I wonder how retirement will feel. Oh well, here's to the luck of fools and children, Merry Christmas!" Click.

Now I'd somewhat affirmed the likelihood of child air-time. I turned to our own paper's coverage of that fatal tornado. It'd happened thirty-three years ago tomorrow!

The *Herald Traveler* does not keep microfilm, we keep the papers. With those stacked at our warehouse and consulted most often for the making of rodent nests, it took me hours to find the actual piece. Newsprint had darkened to a hue between manila-envelope and Cuban cigar. "Emma Hague" read the original byline.

Now deceased, then an unmarried lady well up into her sixties, Emma was, aside from me, the *Herald Traveler*'s best local "color" artist, ever.

Some say her style sounds dated but Hague's legwork never fails to still check out. She attended Smith College, did well, but came right home. That happens. She lived with an argumentative grandfather and so—locals claim—she never minded being called out to fires, etc., at all hours, fearless apparently. True, her storm-item opens with one of that era's typical hokey human interest-grabbers. My best J-school professor once discredited this as a "little did they know" lede:

At exactly noon on Saturday September the fifth, severe weather had been widely predicted and yet residents of a small mobile home park named Whispering Pines Camp went about their midday errands undeterred. Maybe autumn's warm spell gave a false sense of security. Though trailer parks are lately known hereabouts as "tornado magnets," nobody among that Saturday's resident car-waxers, yard-sitters or bike-riders paid the skies much attention.

Winds up to one hundred and sixty mph (with swirling gusts in excess) came suddenly, survivors claim. A tempest, swirling clockwise, instantly dismantled three-fifths of the park's metal and plywood domiciles.

Pets lost to violent updrafts included cats and especially chickens. "It was more a howl than the train-sound folks tell you to expect," one elderly resident confided. She asked that her name go unlisted to avoid alarming her distant children. "Then my bone china went to powder and yet, look at me, bruised but left in my same rocker."

Eight-year-old twins, Larry and Barry Winstead, were "swimming" in a four-foot blue rubber bathing-pool beside their mother's rental trailer. The mother, Amanda, 32, Merchant Mart's Fabric Department Manager, worked inside at her sewing machine, making clothes to order. It being so warm, the twins' water games remained innocent of any bathing apparel. One section of the family trailer landed directly on top of Barry. He would suffer contusions to the head (then likely drowned). Brother Larry, however, would meet a fate far different.

Sheriff Walter Pate soon after coined the phrase now enjoying wider usage, "Our 'Miracle Boy.'" Larry himself seemed unimpressed and, on later hearing this epithet, asked, "Our the **what?**"

Weighing but fifty-five pounds, young Winstead found himself somehow carried aloft by a massive wind surge. Witnesses claim that, when forty feet up, he fell from one "shelf of wind." But Larry was somehow caught by a second plateau of force and thereby saved. The storm dropped temperatures into the forties. Shortly afterwards, Winstead was unaccountably found at a location over one-quarter of a mile away. Versions differ as to how Larry arrived there. "Flew," Belinda Hobgood, 22, attested. "I saw him do it. Like some pink angel without the wings. Larry was so far up, didn't look big as a minute." The child himself, if physically unharmed, seemed understandably numb and could explain but little when. . . .

But, no, instead of quoting the *Herald Traveler*'s first version over thirty years out-of-date, I prefer to go with an older-wiser Larry alert in the here-and-now.

And yet I'd find extracting one F5 storm memory from the grown Larry involved an eleven-month communal campaign. By the end it had lassoed into my acquaintance a fond posse of former strangers. —Even while strategizing, I wondered why a true story that sounded so amazing had—these many years—stirred so little retrospective press interest. True, along the Rodgers Road it remains a topic of pretty continual discussion.

Myself, I will do anything for a story. Plus I am truly not a snob about what's possible or not. For instance, I have written five features on area haunted-houses. I've spent whole nights in about three. Yes, I saw things. No, I can't explain them. I am in the reporting, not the explaining, business.

People laughed off my account of a seeming funeral-home resurrection. The auto-accident victim, believed dead, was mere minutes from becoming embalmed. Waking, considering himself still in his car, smelling chemicals, he imagined he'd arrived at a service station. He sat bolt-upright yelling, "Fill her with high-test!" The attending mortician nearly died of fright. That really happened. I spoke to both pertinent parties. I've kept the recordings.

In other words, I am not shy about reporting events which strain credibility. My one worry is that Richmond will be more guarded, secretive. The Fan District might prove too refined now that my taste has sensibly relaxed and possibly coarsened in Falls, NC.

One reason Larry's saga has gone unnoted for three decades: The Winsteads, if a respectable farming family on record hereabouts since the first U.S. census of 1790, have never been a rich one. Another cause for his flight's weak coverage might sound more esoteric.

—Tornadoes do not merit human names. Such storms are categorized only by their listed force then seasonal ranking. Larry's? simply called F5. —If some personally named hurricane had grabbed him, if she had been called, say, "Conchita," more attention would surely have been paid. —In 1953 hurricanes first got tagged with human names. Women's ones only—alphabetical from Abigail to Zelda. Then came 1979. Feminism intervened: Didn't lady-monikers imply that semitropical property-damage must be a periodic, tantrum-y female by-product caprice? Thereafter hurricanes alternated monikers from male to female.

Still, "Conchita Sucks Up Farm Boy, Sends Him Down Unhurt" has gale-force headline impact!

—"F5 Lands Lad Safe" made, I believe, a smaller grab at local attention.

I used the storm's approaching anniversary as my excuse to spearhead a *Herald Traveler* "Memory-Lane Special." I phoned Winstead's home but the wife answered, startling me. I should've hung up. Instead I explained that, what with this commemorative tornado-supplement, I would, of course, need a full sit-down with Larry Winstead himself. His spouse stated that the thirty-third anniversary of anything was, even for a weekly as small as ours, "one raggedy-ass date to make much of, idn't it?" Mrs. Winstead certainly had a point.

She explained that recalling the storm still pained her husband. She stated that her Larry did not intend to visit his particular F5 upon people too young to actually recall one. She said I should remember that Larry's identical twin had been killed that day.

"Understood?" She hung up on me.

No sweat. Hang-ups merely pique a good reporter's interest. Given my youth, my almost-horndog need-to-know, I endure "terminated calls" three to five times weekly. The First Amendment permits, indeed demands, that.

But I did feel coerced to reach out to my catfish man and the well-dressed bride's intelligent mother. I told them I had hit a definite wall with Larry. I asked their help in loosening him up.

I'd learned that Winstead was by now the father of young kids. I suggested—in my follow-up note—that he leave some written record of the storm's havoc, "as a legacy that might be someday treasured by your sons." I laid it on pretty thick, I guess.

Larry did not answer. Naturally I had to drive out to his farm on a non-invasive scouting mission. I observed, parked beside the two-story log-cabin, his Duke Energy company sedan. Winstead's vegetable garden, surrounded by deer-proof fencing, is indeed huge. It is so neat it looks like an illustration from some how-to manual. But, seeing me guiding my new-used red pickup back and forth past his pond, one large man summoned wife and sons indoors. He gave me a look not-unusual-hereabouts—land-proud, country-tough, definitely gun-owning.

Next I hand-wrote Winstead using official *Herald Traveler* stationery. I enclosed a copy of the original article. My own crime-scene time-line questions I jotted in its margins. No response. So I needed to attend Larry's church. I asked deacons to please single him out for me, and so they stepped right over, pointed my way and told Larry I had come into God's house "a-prying." Being a gent myself, having already been forcibly seated on the empty front-row, I actually stayed for that whole two-hour service. And Larry? During "Announcements" he slipped out the choir's side-exit.

Desperate, I now contacted all those who'd ever urged his child-flight story on me. I chose a single date for our whole group to phone Larry, urging him to finally tell it. The poor guy probably dragged home from work to find his answering machine glutted. I'd planned to call last but the tape proved full. Finally, after two more tries (never at dinnertime), I caught him by phone.

I begged for any or all of Larry's philosophy and observations. I mentioned being interested in "how the storm helped form you." I vowed wanting far more than the fireworks of yet another disaster story, however good. I craved Aftermath. I was open to lessons, confusions, the unsavory payload left behind once the adrenaline has first saved then abandoned you, etc. . . .

I admitted being ambitious and a short-timer in Falls. My eyes were already fixed upon a more glittering Richmond two hundred miles to the North. There I would work for a famous daily, not our beloved farm-village weekly. I conceded my own drive had likely lured me to imagine the heights Larry had already scaled, by age eight. There came a breathing silence. I braced myself for another hang-up. His admirers had been reassuring me: whatever the tornado'd changed in Larry might, thirty-three years along, drive this flying boy to open up at last.

His unpromising response: "How long you figure it would take?"


## ACTUAL UNASSISTED FLIGHT INTERVIEW


I BROUGHT CHIANTI and a whole-wheat baguette from our Farmers' Market. I wore understated denim but sure shined my best black church shoes. I arrived prompt: Saturday eleven-thirty a.m. His comfortable log-cabin-kit home dominates Winstead's ten-acre farm. It stands just off the Rodgers Road, one mile from the site of his destroyed childhood trailer camp. Larry's homestead is almost scarily tidy, all its painted surfaces newly coated. An anti-algae compound has turned his round pond the disturbing chem-blue of cleaning products.

On first entering the Winstead home, you see a framed advanced degree (an "M.Eng./M.Sc."; "Master of Engineering/ Master of Science"). Its placement reflects the pride of someone pretty much self-made.

He is a big man now, Larry, large and loping, not un-magnetic. He'd put on a striped tie for my visit and that made me ache for him; I myself felt disrespectful, underdressed. It was hard to connect this silvering red-haired bear of a fellow with the alert child seen blinking in school photos. Winstead offered me any of five kinds of ale on-hand. One he'd personally brewed. His burliness suggests enjoyment of this drink.

Larry has a ruddy complexion and his manner is accepting and interested, very present. When he looks at you, you feel strictly examined but accepted anyway. You sense you're in the company of an experienced survivor, getting on with things. You sense he would, if possible, defend you. (If only because you are, now, his guest.) I had plotted so long to meet him, I felt jumpy as I get when around the few film stars sent on press junkets to Raleigh. At first I found myself staring just above Larry's eyes and head.

The cabin's interior makes you know at once that Larry is a major fan of his alma mater, North Carolina State University. Its athletic teams' red-and-white school-colors so constitute his residence's décor the home appears almost a Red Cross headquarters.

Being myself a graduate of UNC, State's archrival, I chose to keep my true-blue affiliation quiet. I did risk, "How a**bout** that Wolfpack this season?" But I soon saw the topic was far too precious to be taken up so lightly, and certainly with a stranger Ohio-born.

Instead we started talking weather (which at least has storms in it!). Larry admitted he'd begun feeling fidgety about his F5's upcoming anniversary. He acted gloomy at having sort of promised to finally go on-record today. I asked if he would mind taking his tie off, to make *me* feel less on-duty? He gave me a look of pure relief. He loosened it between red clawing thumbs.

Winstead referred to the tornado as "my storm," sometimes "ours," sometimes "it." He conceded how, on its date each year, he always takes off from work, a "Personal" day. I asked how he commemorated—possibly returning to the flight-death site a mile away?

"Nope, never. Besides, the land's got all built-up. Fancy houses, paved streets. No, Mom and me, that night we just have dinner alone, just sit remembering things about Barry."

Winstead said he still gets approached by folks who miss his brother. (Larry's even set up a Facebook page joined by thirty-six Friends of the dead boy.) Larry claimed it's an odd thing about being a twin. He said you can be so much a twin that, though the other half is technically dead, you still feel full of him. "Your twin becomes almost your . . . GPS. Especially, I guess, 'identicals.' "

Showing me around, Larry reported being quizzed by certain family members. They still wonder how he really got from skinny-dipping to that hilltop grove of pine trees on a farm adjoining. "How do you *think*?" he recalled answering. "You figure maybe I rented a construction crane to lift me? —I don't really need to understand it. It's already only *happ*ened to me. They still trying to make me feel guilty for being the one that lived?"

I sensed what he meant, but hoped to explore this further. Larry now led me into his den, walls paved with autographed sports artifacts; I asked if he'd let me tape-record his answers. Larry never answered but, shrugging, did not audibly object.

*　　*　　*

I started with technicalities: Larry's young father died early, a bulldozer mishap while working in school-construction, right? I mentioned Larry's mother, her seeming a very warm diligent single-parent. I'd heard how her farmer parents offered strong support to the fatherless Winstead twins.

Larry explained that he and his brother had been only moderately good third-grade students at Delta Grammar School nearby. They spent most of their time in the woods leading down to Doane's Creek. "We had camps and caves all back up in there. Found arrowheads and even white quartz spearheads. Knew every inch of it and slept out many a non-rainy Saturday and Sunday night. No adults around for a couple miles. Those times felt safer outdoors for children. Nowadays? I won't let my boys sleep two feet from our back door in a tent without me being in it between them. Times change. Seems people tend to be way more harmful now. Maybe overpopulation brings out cruelty? Anyway, things'll grab you more now, you know?"

I nodded.

Larry Winstead's later life sounds ordinary enough. He married his high school sweetheart, one Darlene Braswell, now thirty-nine. A childhood neighbor, she had been friends with both well-liked twins, and that, Larry said, mattered to him. After high school, by working construction and rewiring older farm homes, Larry put himself through NC State. He stayed on to earn the Master's degree in Electrical Engineering. His thesis is still on-file online, "Anomalies of Conductivity in Voltaic Piles Esp. When Deployed in Wetland Setting(s)." He went to work for Duke Power. Nine years back, Larry himself became the father of twin boys. He says he is glad that twins often run in certain families.

"And I do mean **run**!" He signaled outdoors, laughing toward sons now passing a football. The carrot-topped twins wore matching black towels looped around their necks as today's superhero capes. A spiraling lawn-sprinkler claimed half their playing field. Kids scarcely noticed—enjoying getting ever-wetter.

Winstead attends Red Rock Methodist Church. He admits his more home-rolled kind of faith is locally judged unorthodox, spiritually wired "not-to-code."

As we drank ale, I searched his den's sports souvenirs for one memento of the lethal storm. Noticing, Larry finally squired me down a hallway to the blue Master Bedroom.

Framed here, all known snapshots of his often-smiling twin. Young Barry had two new prominent front teeth. The freckled face showed a sweet beaver-eagerness. It made Barry look appealingly humorous, in on whatever joke.

As we reentered the cabin's comfortable great room, Larry's own twins were still heard at side-yard scrimmage. On this farm I felt a sense of grounded practical safety. Larry pointed where I should sit. My chair matched his own puffy red leather lounger. Mine likely seemed Darlene's favorite spot.

She kept well-clear of me but could be heard making her family's lunch. I'd arrived before noon bearing bread. I admit hoping they'd ask me to stay.

Alongside Larry's easy chair Darlene now placed a Tupperware container of fresh-picked butter beans and one empty colander likely meant to hold the husks. She seemed to guess that, if he was going to tell this right, Larry's engineering hands would need gainful employment. Winstead soon made shelling beans look like so much fun, I reached over, soon tossing in my share. Unlike me, he could crack open and empty several pods at once.

Activating my excellent German-made recorder, I formally told him how his neighbors held him in real high esteem. "Well . . ." He averted eyes and leaned right. I explained: his would be my last story for the Falls *Herald Traveler*. I reiterated how the idea for this piece had come from citizens who respected him. They insisted he'd been changed by whatever his experience midair.

I said I admired the original article reported by my deceased colleague. But Larry himself had then been just a kid probably left in shock. By now, further insights must have settled? I admitted to collecting certain after-death experiences, ones that always draw extra interest in my Features Section.

By now Larry had three decades' perspective on his own balloon-like ascent (if that was accurate). Now Larry's sons were older than he and Barry had been that disorienting afternoon. No one had ever accused Larry of being a bully, before. But folks said he'd afterwards grown more thoughtful and gentle, not just a better student but a person far more serious and "real." I asked if he agreed that one unusual occurrence, however brief, might alter someone, even a kid age eight?

"Well," he answered, studying his busied hands, "some."

I sensed hesitation. So I tricked him. Maybe I cheated. I asked him . . . if he would at long-last tell me *it* . . . what I called—melodramatically, perhaps—his "secret." The big man soon grew very still. Gazing straight ahead, he even ceased shelling beans.

I had simply played my hunch. Our sticking solely to tired facts would just not lift us to the altitude I hoped he'd somehow reach.

## TEXT: TRANSCRIPT

HE TOOK ONE LONG swallow of ale. His eyes are startling in their blue honesty. Fact is, as I met his stare, I remembered being late with quarterly taxes.

I reminded him he had forgiven certain loans to pals. Others swore Larry even overlooked a couple of un-neighborly acts— irksome, even actionable. A suspiciously burned garage after his Pee Wee Football team became state champs.

Larry stayed silent. Some people find praise torture. He sat studying the red light blinking atop my recorder. He kept combing thick fingers through those beans we'd shelled. His wife, hidden from view two rooms away, soon quieted around his unease. Her overly noisy cutlery quit chopping. Darlene called, "Larry? Like I said, you don't **have** to. They never understand anyways. Especially non–North Carolinians. —No offense."

"Naw," Larry called back just loud enough. "This kid's done his homework. **He** can't help where he got born. I've kept him hunting me a whole year. Don't know **why** he wants it but he does." Larry pressed a fingertip across his lips then nodded in his wife's direction. Had she forbidden him to talk?

I truly fought to stay silent. (I am told, when on the trail of an assignment, I can become at times over-directive.) I did, however, risk pushing our microphone one inch nearer Larry. (Darlene wouldn't see.) I might've whispered, "Stories will 'out.' Got all afternoon. —Whenever'd be fine. To start."

(The machine caught my own shallow breaths. One long exhalation uncoiled from Larry's big red chair. At first his voice came halted, compressed.)

\*    \*    \*

"Sounds simple but it's not really. For a while afterwards, you do have, like, double-vision, very . . . there's this thankfulness.

"First you go back to trying and be like 'before.' But you are already 'after.' Months later, it's like you need an alternator.

"As to the storm, most of it is there in print. Nice lady, the lady reporter. Got right down on her knees to be at my eye-level. She cut her leg then, I remember. She was soon just walking around talking to people, bleeding, not knowing, more trusted for that.

"You keep going back over some details. Probably natural. The mind trying to crack a code. But just one twin got favored. After that, there's no putting it back however much you'd like. See, I am already making no sense. You will have to go in later with a hacksaw . . . straighten things out, cut you a route.

"As for so many kinds of weather turning up at once? I can say, from a science background—it was likely just some fluke of fronts meeting, wind-speeds mismatched. Freak-type thing.

"I keep trying to learn the order that everything went down in. For others along our road, see, September fifth might mean the day I flew. For me it's how my twin got killed.

"You would've enjoyed my brother. Not a clown, just one of those people's naturally funny. A talker, like you. Little things happened, he would turn them into jokes. Almost like a junior 'stand-up' even about certain birds in the woods. One time he made our hard-shell Methodist preacher laugh! Barry was the best of us two. I'm a bad copy, not a patch on what he was already growing into. Wrong one died. Storm hit without warning. Those days before 'Weather Channel'? we had about as much notice as the birds did. Less, maybe. And, living in a trailer, we were about that protected. (But, if brother and me'd been in*side* our trailer with Momma, things might have gone even way worse, all three of us crushed.) Brother loved making model planes, was always saving up to buy his next. Grown, I studied engineering, Electrical, but Barry would've gone with Aeronautic design, I'm sure. NASA, maybe even. Every plane of his, decals and all, got sucked up with me.

"I'll try and say how it felt or happened. Fewer people ask me lately. They see it makes me bashful. Feels like I'm to blame for getting to enjoy all I enjoy every day. Will you just look at this beautiful cabin? It was a kit and the model-name is 'Ponderosa.' Me, I am free to live here with these folks that put up with me. A few neighbors still want you to retell your whole tornado. But it's like being asked to sing a song in a room of people that are only talking. Even so, ever since then, I've always felt saved back *for* something.

"Maybe every healthy person has a hunch he's put here for serving some one purpose, you know? True, your purpose often stays unknown your whole durn life. Still, you wait. You know you want to help others. You try and make the most of whatever your talents are. My gifts have turned out regular enough. I am a good engineer, I think. I still work at it. Somehow Duke Energy has kept me on payroll these two decades. Was also lucky enough, right out of the gate, to meet that wonderful woman in there. (Hey, listening, Darlene?) She is my definite current-capacitor. 'We brought each other up,' I like to say. Mom was something of a loss after we buried Brother. She blamed herself to where she said, 'I should not have named Barry "Bury."' I told her those were whole different words, but she was onto that self-punishment the first year especially, taking the fall herself, you know. She'd been being the strong one, having to, with Dad out of the picture so soon. And now this. I tried and make it up to her but never really could. Not till my wife and me had our twins, those over-frisky ones you hear now refereeing each other. Mom still lives out off Cedar-cliff and she is all over those boys, has never missed not one of their games.

"If people claim anything about me, most of the time they seem to call me 'Upbeat.' I don't know. Songs tell you, you never know you were happy till your well runs dry. Maybe that flying-day jammed my gears into a single 'Stay Upbeat' setting. I wouldn't call it Happy, more just Clear. Still, I reckon you could do worse. —See? See what I just did? by saying it like that? I am someone is determined to be satisfied. (Turns out, that's rare enough!) At work we joke about the positive statements we're always e-mailing our higher-ups. Like: 'TEST RESULTS ARE PROVING EXTREMELY GRATIFYING' really means, 'We're just real surprised the stupid thing even works'!

"My habit of hoping, it's what's left over. From how I felt once our storm took me up. (Felt happier, of course, when it set me **down**!) But that very second, the same F5 was crushing then drowning Barry. It being September, Momma had already packed away our little wading pool. Still, the day turning so warm and sunny, we begged her to fill it one more time.

"She had to blow it up herself by mouth, though we all took turns. She is a lifelong smoker, Mom, so it did take a while. There was already, now I think back, this feeling so late in the season with school already open? of 'one last time . . .' at having any summer.

"Mom was sitting working in the trailer with the window open. Was sewing somebody's wedding dress beside her radio. I could hear her Singer bumping along. She made clothes for high school girls out our way, prom things, Easter dresses. Hats, she did their hats, too. My brother was then considered the cheerful twin. I was kind of a grind, I guess. I could be mean. I had done little things, experiments, on lizards, birds, one lost baby raccoon. Barry just watched, kind of concerned, but never lifted a hand to stop me. 'You **know** you are hurting it like Hell, right? You know they feel what-all we feel.' I could see he worried why I'd go on and do such s— to harmless things. People claimed I was The Worrier, having come out nine minutes before Barry, probably fretting what was taking him so long!

"That day, he chose to sit nearer the spigot hooked under our trailer's foundation. I could tell by his face he was considering lifting the hose and squirting me a good one in the snoot. Between two trailers I'd just stretched into what sun warmed our pool's outside rim. Dark clouds boiled up overhead that fast. Blackness shut over our trailer like maybe a lens closing.

"Momma's radio still played Patsy's, 'Cor-azy for feel-ing so lonely.' I could hear Mom's sewing machine treadle-rocking as the reporter's voice broke in to announce danger. I heard Ma call, 'Boys. If weather gets any—'

"It came down on us that quick. Temperature dropped forty-odd degrees. Sky went ink-black, not a bit of blue in it. But the trees, some autumn color by then, stayed bright with all the sunlight left inside them. Almost hurt your eyes. My skin . . . it squeezed, pressured. Then came six crackings, sounds I think were our oldest Whispering Pines breaking apart, sap scattering.

"One wooden shed behind the Lassiters' flew to splinters everywhichaway. The sound to all sides kept beating like some waterfall down at its bottom where the tons of most water hit. Barry's freckles and front teeth were right before my face and I said, 'Better run, Ba—' But our legs, see, were tucked up under us and, at that minute, our trailer, just to my left and behind him on the right, heaved like something living, shifted more our way. . . .

"You don't get a sec to think, 'Now I'm rising.' Some of our wading pool's water came up with me, a plug around my ankles and me still in it, then scattered what looked like ball bearings.

"There's just no choice. No chance of your giving a signal. It has already happened by just happening. And you're knowing this without a bit of control. Admiring, kind of.

"But I had adrenaline. And that *seemed* control. Keeps your mind as clear as anything. I must've used about a year's voltage concentrating those next ninety seconds.

"Of course, I was a third-grader. Man, **kids** don't know what's likely! If I was to walk outdoors now and call my boys to come pack for a trip to Mars, they'd ask how heavy a wind-breaker to bring! You know?

"I guess if I'd feared the worst I would have gotten only that. Didn't have time to worry over Barry. Didn't doubt myself. Felt like the wind had tied its biggest rope around my waist then lifted me. I was like its . . . yo-yo. It shot me up, me straight overhead. Wind across earholes. The land below me looked half-blue. I noticed our trailer where I'd just been. Back then I weighed, what, fifty-odd pounds? You'd never know it, seeing me today!

"I felt excited but, the strange part, not afraid. Later, yes. Not during. You hear about it when people see ghosts or know a head-on collision is about to get them. Instead of feeling scared, they see right **through** it. Two chess-moves ahead. 'Let's just notice how this is going to have to turn out.' Comes like that, a calming voice that is your voice but smarter, maybe older. I did move my arms. I hung forty to fifty feet in the air over our trailer camp, looking down. It seemed simple. You know the way a kid—when he's up walking along the peak of some house-roof—will just naturally throw his either arm out for balance? mine reached out, too. Not flapping like wings but just getting that bit more leverage to aim myself midair. Like swimming, really. Treading. Only you happen to be in sky not ocean.

"At least I could keep my head mostly at the top and my feet pigeon-toed off to either side so's I could see down past them. And I flew. Thanks to no effort or planning, no particular brain-wattage on *my* side, believe me. Wind had me kite-high before I could even calculate how. Sky around me was a black-green I've gladly not seen since. The wind that held me let me study whatever it was picking to do next.

"Sometimes I'd spin in space. That let me see the whole three-sixty. Soon I fell off one kind of wind and flopped ten feet. When a force of different temperature caught me in a scoop-like. Meanwhile, on land, trailer-tops were peeling open like an Advent Calendar my teacher had. Bird-high, I could peek through the roofs of trailers not yet flying off due-West.

"I saw one of Barry's plastic jets shoot past me but not, of course, flying as it should on the level, but moving straight up in my direction. Rocket. That, see, was part of the unfairness. No one in our county would have enjoyed this flying more than Brother.

"I remember staring into *our* trailer, seeing its roof curl back like a sardine tin's. Never came to me how Barry might be underneath it. I kept checking other parts of sky for him. Since I slept on *our* top-bunk, I guessed he'd just be riding air right below me and mine! I saw Momma yet bent over her machine and the wedding dress rose white around her like a bell and she looked up, her mouth this round hole. She was seeing me dozens of feet above her, jaybird-naked. Hanging there. She pointed to a chair beside her, like ordering me to come right back down and sit there this very sec, hear?

"The whole time there were like two charge-portals in me, two things running dead-opposite. The 'Head Camera,'

I thought of one, was taking in everything, real precise. But, lower, my true body was being lashed like some free little whip. It couldn't save itself. So, like boys will, there was just a joy in being as reckless as this. And the split between these two parts, AC-DC or BC-AD, the two poles, they never ever after came quite back together correct again. Like, afterwards, my hearing got way better and still is mostly. But the taste of things never went back. I used to love sweets the way kids will? but right after the storm I wanted salt. I wanted sauerkraut. Just eight and I was ready for beer, man! Desserts mean nothing to me past how nice they look. Most of what I eat now tastes metal or of strong mineral spices. But that's become my favorite kind of flavor. Look, maybe it was me *growing up* in ninety seconds? My sense of smell got good to where I could smell little exceptions inside other smells. Our trailer-park's pines broke to twigs and sap went turpentine and burned my eyes. But inside of that stink I could smell ladies' face powder or a bucket of enamel. Part of that black paint slung over my left leg.

"I knew every person living in our Park, I could watch whose place shattered next. It was interesting. Why did some get spared? I was in no hurry up there. Bright clothes were busy in the dust over the Hobgood sisters' place. People said those young gals had more clothes than God. Now God got them back! The chicken coop behind the Caspers' went to being torn screen and a million feathers with the few birds left alive flying like eagles at my level. Being yard-hens, they appeared as amazed to fly as I was. They gave me a steady look, like, 'Help!' Up there, they didn't seem as stupid like folks *say* they are, chickens. What did *I* know about flying? I had my arms out, period. I mainly used the weight of my head to guide me some. A boy my size, a third his weight's in his noggin. Blasting sand burned my legs and wrists. One of my legs was black from windblown paint. Crazy stuff was flying, school papers, truck-stop place mats, even green money.

"I did know I was moving in an arc and starting heading down now more towards the Youngs' farm now.

"Old Man Young still had an outhouse. His wife, she'd gone and bought herself some fine indoor-plumbing, but he liked the old ways and I guess he was sitting astride his one-holer when wind hit. I saw his johnny-house's roof pull off, then its side boards jerk loose and he was left squatting there, cussing to beat all, pants around his ankles and one hand covering his bald head, the other cupped between his legs. He looked like a toy built to do just that. Even flying, I laughed.

"The air around my bare back and bottom felt ice-cold. We never bothered with swimsuits. Now it seemed some harness had me gathered safe up under either arm. Felt like it pulled me in a swipe over everything being destroyed. I didn't fight it. You've maybe seen pictures of the Arch in St. Louis? Way I figure, I flew about that same shape and distance. Then wind started setting me down more toward ground and me with no shoes. I might've slammed onto my head at many miles-an-hour, or got thrown onto all that bent metal, glass.

"These days I go to Church. Served as Superintendent of Sunday School out at Red Rock three years running. But I still cannot say I am all that sure about a supervisory God, son. Friends claim I ought to be grateful for favors paid me early-on. Funny how after hurricanes, people go, 'God stopped that flood one inch shy of drowning us in our attic, Lord be praised!' But who set the danged thing into *motion*? I lost my Dad when I was four, my twin at age eight. Our mobile house got peeled, trashed. (Momma and myself were saved.) But, when it comes to there being anything smart with His Eye on the Sparrow? I'd say He's One Wall-Eyed Watchman! But you know we've got something almost better. We've got other forces so amazing, see? Papers later called me 'Miracle Boy,' but we don't need any such magic-show thinking. Don't need it, considering the pure interlocking engineering set up everywhere. We shouldn't bother with magazine words like 'Miracle.' That's just us being nervous, just us whistling-in-the-wind. It happened to be me sitting soaking on the sunnier side of a wading pool. I knew— if forces had crumpled *me* under our trailer then pressed *me* down in water—I would not be quite so high on these particular forces. But it didn't. So I am.

"Maybe every boy pictures he's the Batman or one the other of the Wright brothers. All kids imagine flying. I flew for real. No training necessary. 'Having flown unassisted,' that lady reporter wrote me up. I'd had no plans to. Just found I could. Flexed into whatever shape kept me mostly upright moving at about a forty-five-degree angle. Jerking, stopping, snapping, I kept studying how trees broke, cars rocked onto their sides like dogs rolling over on command.

"It was a ride offered for free. So I took it. I saw Youngs' farm coming. Noticed their stand of newish pines. If my body pitched into sapling limbs, those'd maybe slow me a bit at a time. So I aimed away from old oaks and more toward scrub, shifting my big head as ballast. I was set—dropping, landing at a sort of a run.

"Once down, I waited. I just knew to. In one place. The whole ground, see, was jagged with all broken things and me barefoot. Barefoot all over! Kept panting, maybe from fear or the adrenaline but not from any effort. Coming down, I did no wing-flapping. (Imagine, later, how *I* felt watching people hopping off those burning skyscrapers and trying to bat their arms like wings while falling like pianos.) No voice of God. I had no help. Nothing saved me. It'd been just bare me and Physics, and my little pecker all standing upright in the sky.

"Soon Falls' sirens sounded something terrible and a woman come trotting my way. It was Old Lady Young found me. 'How did *you* get way off over here and naked, li'l Larry?'

" 'Wind,' I said.

" 'Wind *who*?' she said.

" '*The wind*. Done toted me.' Later they figured, considering the timing, this must have been right. Nobody ever called me an out-and-out liar. But finally one the Hobgood girls ran up in her nightgown, said she'd thought I was a Christmas statue flying, pink and gold, shooting over everything.

"I stood on solid ground but felt uneasy, being bare-assed, two hands bunched over my you-know-what. The prettiest Hobgood guessed and kindly pulled a beach towel down around me. I stood without shoes and, with all the flying jagged windowpanes, had not even cut my bare feet. So they saw I could not have walked clear uphill to the safety of those pines. A cousin in his Ford drove Momma right up where I stood. When she climbed out, I saw the whole front of her dress was wet like she had been bending over a pond. Then I studied her eyes and she looked ten pounds lighter, her face gone white. 'Barry,' I said. She nodded and fell on me and all but mashed me into her.

"The second he died I felt my IQ double; I took in all Barry's talent. Like later? at college? they urged us freshmen to find a study-partner? but me, I'd enrolled with one. Could never have got a Master's from State without Brother's nightly help. And that's God's truth.

"Well, I am forty and in right good health pretty much. (I could do more sit-ups, maybe. No, I could *not* do sit-ups, but should try.) I dearly want to live to be seventy-five or eighty so's I can see my sons marry and have kids. I will lay odds that at least one their future wives bears twins, too. You would not believe how happy it makes me—imagining which of my boys hollering out yonder will have the luck to father twins. I imagine these babies being sons. But two of the other kind would be fine with me, girls. Their being born healthy is all I ask.

"I would rather not die, of course. But you know you will. I could also wish I might fly again. Even once more'd be nice.

"Of course, I feel sad not to've had my own twin with me across these years I've got to splash around in. Barry was the kind and carefree one. But I think I got his easy nature the second he died. Wham, it passed that quick clear into me. A double-strength came with the luck of my flying most of a mile unhurt."


I sat pitched forward, actively holding my breath. Winstead stopped and all our beans were shelled. I felt I'd heard some specimen of sermon. There is a school of interviewing that objects to 'Leading the Witness.' Still I longed to ask, "Any closing life-lessons, Larry?" Cheap. Such summaries don't value experience as such. Experience must mean more than whatever fortune-cookie Moral trails it. Experience outranks everything. Certain acts must be respected just for having been endured.

First Larry turned toward the bay-window, half-smiling. He was checking on his sons at the meadow's fifty-yard line. One shrill voice called, 'Said, "Hut-two-three" and that means **you**, Idiot!'

My host kept silent, smiling. He swigged, finishing his ale.

"The rest of it—marriage? work? kids and friends? I've been playing overtime innings since I was eight. Already had my death and skipped it like a grade in school. Every minute since has been pure gravy.

"As an engineer I have to rule out any type of afterlife theme-park cloud-deal. We've got a joke at work: Some folks see the glass half empty, others half full, but engineers know the glass was made twice too big to start with.

"But wherever we wind up, in whatever amount, I think we'll exit riding some force to show us out. Death is room-temperature. It has no mass but is a Fact. And nothing's out to torture us except certain other people. No hidden meanness is waiting to trap us. When I was up in the sky, all's I can tell you, son—*it knew what it was doing.*"

Our interview seemed over. Larry made that clear by standing, stretching like someone waking after trans-oceanic air travel. Next he shook my hand so hard it hurt. I felt how strong he was and is. I turned off my over-heated machine. He carried our shelled butter beans toward his wife. I knew Darlene had been listening; I'd sometimes heard her sniffling from a room away.

She made me happy asking me to stay and eat. Darlene Winstead served one exceptional home-cooked country lunch: ham, corn on the cob, buttermilk pie. Rare treat for bachelor-journalists in a Falls-sized town. Larry acted endearing around his boys. They look exactly alike but he interviewed each for me. He kept trying to prove how different were their interests. One preferred baseball to basketball.

Soaked clear through, before eating they wrapped up in big bath towels. On a clothesline outside, black capes hung drip-ping. All this made me think of those earlier twins, one about to die but both still happy in their blue rubber pool.

Not wanting to overstay, I thanked Darlene. She gestured

me into her kitchen. She pointed to the black recorder I now clutched like some prayer book.

"You got new stuff out of him," she whispered. "Unbelievable. I'd say about a tenth of that he said? *New.* To me, anyways. That about the bunk-bed, and more."

I was bound for my truck when the twins asked me to throw them a couple of long ones. I got off three, fairly passable. Larry looked pleased but seemed a bit too surprised. My aim never quite lasts. I sometimes know when to quit.

I guessed that transcribing his testimonial would take me many hours, probably all night. But despite the deadline, while driving back toward Falls, I felt scared to go much faster than thirty. Teenagers soon tried passing me. Fists were shaken, a can of foaming Budweiser slammed into the bed of my pickup. Being youngish myself, I understood kids' impatience. But I've had too many speeding tickets. Always rushing from story to meeting to bar. And now, at twenty-five, for the first time ever, I signed to them: "Please just go around me." I often feel half-sick with all the galloping-no-place testosterone (weekends especially). Now I was half proud of my Larry-like readiness to fly-or-not, live-or-die, to just to be passed. What if I failed to stay alive long enough to set down his tale? True, I had Larry's recorded voice. But my truck might burn with that and me in it.

Easing into Falls as sunlight ended, I seemed to see the town for the first time, not my last. Its green water tower. The band shell on the Commons. Everything that made it look like any other village now marked it as peculiar and mine.

Somehow my own death seemed very near just then. Hot-rodders had finally passed me, on the right. To make my surrender more their victory, boys all shot me the finger. I just laughed. —Looking back, I recognize one of those moments when you feel your life begin again!

\* \* \*

I parked behind the paper's office. This being a Saturday—with my editor at the beach—the workplace was deserted. If you're alone in a building usually crowded, you can hear sounds that seem a message meant for you alone. I drank buckets of coffee, not-great but at least provided.

I spent nine hours typing, reliving Larry's flight. Just at sunup I finally landed this piece you're reading.

I found myself still hunched at my desk when I noticed something strange in the paper's lobby. I'd already packed for Richmond. I'd bribed my cat into her traveling case and left it near the door. I would take along that old blue blazer—ripe for urban resurrection. Off Craigslist I'd found an adequate little garden-apartment. The *Richmond Times-Dispatch* is a distinguished daily, a step-up from this rural weekly. But, even before leaving Falls, I felt cramped with homesickness. Was I wrong to quit so small a town in search of a larger success? Wasn't I leaving the place just as it gave up to me certain privileged secrets? But I could always move back, right? Right? I had sworn to friends that I would grab this final breakfast at Millie's Diner down the block at seven-sharp. My hope (soon confirmed) was a surprise-going-away-pancake-party. (Love you, Millie and the gang!)

In the *Herald Traveler*'s linoleumed lobby there's always been one stainless steel hat rack. Only raw daybreak made me finally see the thing. Its strict design must've looked rocket-cool around 1950. We run a free classified "Lost and Found" column and, for years, any recovered item gets left in the lobby. This spares our overworked receptionist from filling her desk with single mittens.

By now that rack tilts under decades of unclaimed finds. It has become a hobo's tent of plaid raincoats, crocheted hats, dog-collars, kids' spelling books.

Red dawn made every random thing stacked there look specific then valuable. It somehow came to me: all these human items—never reported missing—had nonetheless been found. They've been right here, waiting in plain sight for all these years. But, only this morning, when about to leave, did I get up, walk toward these losses found, stand marveling as before the burning bush.

How many other citizens have flown unaided? I should ask around.

Goodbye, friends.
Goodbye, town.

We grant ourselves so little daily hope.
Meanwhile, barely noticing, we've already managed wonders.

# A FOOL FOR CHRISTMAS

WELL, WELCOME TO my mall, stranger. And "Merry, merry" back at you. You just come in off the highway? All this ice is scary, idn't it? They say traffic's backed up near-bout to Charlotte.

—Saving this stool? Well, aren't you nice. Me, I'm Vernon Ricketts and I manage our Fin, Fur and Fun franchise. Third-busiest pet store in eastern North Carolina, so they tell me.

Yep, finally closed, Christmas Eve. Not to brag, but my staff and me today? we "moved" more animals than ole Noah ever did. And while each of my pups and kittens goes speeding home toward sleeping kids? Mr. Manager has swung in here for a big old final drink.

Bet you're glad you're off that interstate. Lucky you found

our county's one place still open, it being a holiday after one a.m. . . . .

Kirsten runs this bar; there she is yonder. Still beautiful, 'm I right? We went through school together, her and me. Survived the same crazed Pentecostal church. Had our own big Bibles, our little tambourines. Kirsten's husband left her flat with two young boys.

Ran off with his horseback-riding teacher, a ex-Marine like him. Shocker. Oh, but Kirsten dealt with it, got a lot of spirit. And, for us mall-insiders, tonight only, she always makes personal eggnog. Family recipe, grates her own nutmeg, brings the home-blender, everything.

Yo, Kirst-en! Looking fine in that red ermine-lined mini. How those twins? We'll need a couple your famous eggnogs, me and my new pal here. (You'll see, they're super-tasty. I keep trying to "reduce" . . . but hey, man, it's Christmas Eve.)

Tonight is even more than the start of a whole day-off for Vernon here, it's secretly my anniversary. I can't help remembering, with us in the middle of a blizzard and all. Yeah, this same second be 'xactly one year ago, in my exceptional pet shop through that very security screen, I did something. Still don't know how, nor why a certain person trusted me to help with it. Got us both into newspapers, the Charlotte one *plus* Raleigh's. But, along with being exceptional store-publicity, turned out to be the best darn thing that ever grabbed me. Finest gift a woman ever give me. And right here at the holidays. Even before it happened, I was a fool for Christmas. Well, imagine me now.


I ask you, is that eggnog or is that not eggnog? Kirsten, keep 'em coming, honey. Merry merry. —First time I seen the girl that changed me so majorly, poor thing was already being hounded. We do got a "No Vagrant" policy at this shopping center. Never was enforced. Not till Vanderlip stepped in as mall manager. He was soon all over our drifters, skateboarders, even the rich old men nodding off while wives tried on every shoe in each store.

Vanderlip is one strange bird. Seems there's lots of the military-minded taking charge these days. He come up hard, like I did. Attending night-school after having two kids while working three jobs—you got to respect that-type drive in a family man. Big churchgoer, too. Big Baptist. Vanderlip witnesses for Christ, right at the urinal, feeling sure you'll stand exactly **there** at least till either you finish or **he** does. But seems-like the better Vanderlip does in life, the harder he is on those he passed during his scrappy climb clear up to mall manager.

Man ain't that old but he's always acted sixty-five, born taking names. Too proud of being in charge. Even of a mall like ours, with just three the fountains working and no Restoration Hardware.

First we thought he'd be **good** for the place. Didn't he bring in bigger palm trees? Didn't he release dozens of my shop's largest goldfish into reflecting pools? (Till the tossed pennies or the chlorine got them, one.) Was then Vanderlip caught a retired couple pocketing three-for-a-buck canned tuna at Dollar General. He marches them, sobbing, into the back room he's labeled "De-Programming."

Thirty minutes later, old guy comes out of there . . . on a stretcher. Heart attack. Thin line between "background check" and "torture." Us merchants, we'd first nicknamed Vanderlip "the Enforcer." By now? he's "Terminator."

But yes, a new girl was seen on the mall. "Terminator" Vanderlip spotted her first. Oh, she tried blending in with other pretties that age. She would settle, keeping her back to our usual standout blondes monopolizing the popular benches fountain-side. Young gals are always dabbing glitter makeup onto each other, then taking cell-phone snaps of their new navel rings, sending these to lucky farm-boys out in the county. But this recent gal wore just an old sailor's peacoat sizes too big. Had limp brown hair all down in her face. Plastic barrettes pushed bangs into being the little awning letting her hide in plain sight.

Prettier girls, bare-midriffs, migrate like birds around our Grand Concourse. All at once they'll rush like mad to avoid or attract some clump of boys just arrived.

I saw this darker new child follow that crowd, but only at a distance, just so's she'd fade in a little better. They ignored her. She acted like she didn't notice being snubbed. But at that age that's **all** you notice.

Me, I noticed. While settling Siamese kittens into our cedared bay-windows, I wondered why this one gal, of all fifteen hundred mall-visitors per-day, should catch my interest. Or my pity, maybe?

I guess she was not what you'd call real attractive, only tiny, you know. Small in a way that frog-gigs the hearts of big ole fellows like me. She kept to herself. She fell somewhere betwixt twelve and seventeen; she fell between looking not too interested and completely . . . lost.

Why **her**? Well, you know how in your smartphone's photo files, among all the snaps you took of your smiling friends and new real-leather furniture, there'll be some mess-up shots?

Maybe sky, some jet-trail and two flying birds, or even your own knee shown against the red steering wheel? What's odd, you flip right past the *good* pictures and stare longest at the ones gone somewhat wrong. It's *those* ones make you think, "Hell, I could be a pho-*tog*-rapher!"

She was like that. Off to one side, a throwaway, kind of nifty but nearbout by acci-dent.

Right off I seen she was clever. Never settling real long in one place. Avoiding Vanderlip's catching steady sight of her.

Carrying a different store's bag each day. Always chatting into her cell-phone, body turned in odd directions, hunting privacy. But Terminator was right there behind the new palm tree, talking into his wristwatch. With his nose for sin, Vanderlip guessed her story before I did.

Man walks in short steps so he always seems real busy, busy. Never without the tie; its knot big as a thermos. And since 9/11 and these mall shootings every week, two lapel pins right and left, the American flag opposite one white enameled cross. Wears them like personal ID.

Just after each Thanksgiving, Vanderlip has signs hung across our mall's four sides, "Jesus IS the Reason for the Season" and—under that—in small print, "and happy hanuka." Spelled "Hanukkah" wrong; some say on purpose. His own church-choir has been singing carols here every Tuesday-Thursday since Halloween.

My new favorite, she now fetched up only on the rainy coldest days. Seemed she was saving back our shelter for when she'd need it most. Never really stepped into *my* shop. But, like everybody, she would gather before our snow-sprayed windows full of wriggling pups all wearing red bows. I'd see her sort of grinning then. I willed her to visit Vernon's menagerie. I thought,

"Out yonder, hungry, stands somebody's daughter." I imagined her as being mine, then shuddered. I felt **more** scared for her after that.

So, was three weeks before last Christmas, I seen something I wasn't supposed to. That sweet sad mouse-girl steps into the ladies', leaves her cell phone on one fountain-side bench. Well, I figure here's Vernon's chance to be a hero, see? So I rush out to save the cell she's been chatting into constant for these three weeks, especially when Terminator's staring.

But hers? it's just a toy. For kids. From Dollar General. Black block of wood, cheap decal sticky on its front.

So lightweight I all but dropped it. I set it down real quick and run off, huffing. I figure: let her keep her secrets till she can't.

(Thanks for the fresh eggnog, Kirsten. Each glass a meal in itself, huh? —Look, do I got foam on my chin? Thanks.)

Girl ate alone in our International Food Court. I saw how sly she worked that place. She'd make a off-to-one-side meal out of dispenser ketchup, leftover croutons, hot water. She'd garnish this with lemon wedges then a li'l Parmesan from Mamma Mia's. Out of a bin, dainty, she'd lift one large soda cup, wash it good at our water fountain then drink Classic Coke all day. One time I saw her stash her cup up high on a ledge so's Vanderlip's over-busy cleanup-crew wouldn't snag it. Girl's jacket hikes up and underneath, I see: she's like ten months pregnant. White belly squared-off to where it seems she's swallowed a twelve-pound dice.

What **next**? The shopper I really like best now, the one I find I'm waiting to see daily? Pregnant, 'bout fourteen. Just Vernon's luck.

Me, see, I basically, even romance-wise, I run Animal Rescue. Even while retailing brand-new creatures, I am really running a orphanage. It's the same, even on blind dates, which my dates mostly are. I guess gals don't like it when you act real **kind** to them.

I try holding back and sounding semi-mean. But look at me. I am, on sight, a softie. And they guess. Reckon we've all got faults.

I think I do pretty good for a GED-type person. Got me the vintage Camaro, '67 SS-3838, stroke four-speed, cherry-red. My condo's half paid-off, real-leather sectionals "Merlot-Maroon." Plus, before they closed, I had seen everything at Blockbuster twice, and not just Tarantino, neither. I don't know why gals all feel there's too much of me to be much of a catch.

But, Christmas-week coming in hard, we got us a bad ice storm. Like tonight's. Driving slow to work, I think, "Good. She'll be in easy sight today." Does show up, round noon. I notice orange mud is caked knee-high on her jeans. I guess she's not used to being this dirty. You can tell from how she moves . . . her boots are soaked.

My runaway is still too used to regular home bubble-baths, see. Nobody can live anymore at ease in ditches and out in the woods. Even Pioneers, you wonder how they managed. And her "with child"! to use Bible talk. Coat-collar up, she looks all shivery, talking her grown-up secrets into a dollar toy.

So, well, I, I carry out our blondest possible cocker puppy, big plaid taffeta bow round its neck, naturally. Hold it down to where she slumps beside the Ann Taylor bag fooling absolutely nobody. Meanwhile Vanderlip stands describing her into a walkie-talkie lots more real than her phone.

I go, "Hi. I'm Vernon? in charge of that there pet-store? Would you mind picking up a little change for sitting out here holding, like, the cutest dog in the whole mall? Because I been looking somebody to demonstrate this animal for potential buyers. When folks stop and pat young Butterbean here— (meet "Butterbean")—you just refer said customers to my shop yonder. —Pretty easy money. And I think that you are just the charming gal, the very mall-regular, to put this over."

She finally whispers but right toward our pup's brown eyes, "This one's such a young one, ain't it?" Gal holds that lickin' pup so close its nose is hid under her hairdo. But from certain shoulder motions, I can tell she's crying.

Then I say, "Look. I am going to laugh 'cause Security is, like, so on to you. I'm about to pretend you're funny and we're friends already." I do that then, you know, I chuckle. People ex*pect* that from guys my jolly Santa size. But under my breath-like, I start telling her:

I know her cell-phone is a block of pine wood, know she's crying 'cause this here's a baby dog and she is toting another baby all over creation and my mall. I add as how I'd like to help if I can. Especially seeing how it's the holidays and all. I say if she *does* carry Butterbean clear from Penney's down to our Dillard's even a couple-three times, expect to meet me at Chun-King Express around two for her free demonstrator's lunch, okay? I warn her, I go, "Don't you cry, now. You get me started, there's no stopping it. Some say I'm a fool for Christmas. Some say just a fool. —But don't be feeling mopey and too bad, child. 'Cause Vernon, he knows your story now."

Well, at the Food Court, over fried dumplings and Butterbean, I ask what I usually ask my dates: who her kid's **real** father is. Holding the pup between us, this girl speaks extra-soft. I tilt nearer to hear her go, "He's Warren. Just started his third tour o' Afghanistan. He's in Bravo Company. They got him carrying his rifle through a city made out of clay like flower pots and Warren he's clearing it one apartment at a time. Says he never knows what he'll find from door to door. There's days he says he cannot catch his breath. First tour, him and his buddy had to make theirselves extra armor out of parts of things like old 'frigerators.

"But Warren swears every door he opens is one less any other American boy or girl will have to. He's lost his two best friends there. Soon as he makes a friend, says they get killed.

"Warren swears he won't be shot, says **third** tour's the charm. Says a person just knows these things. Three's always been **my** lucky number! 'Warren' doesn't sound like a name that's too exciting, but he is. Before tour three, I wondered what I could do to **help** him back here. Didn't want the boy to just get blown up like them others. I hated he would have nothing left to show for even being on earth. Figured he deserves at least a Junior.

"Oh, Warren can play three instruments, and talk about can sing! When he gets through this tour, he is going to Nashville to produce CDs that are half-rap, half-country. It's new. He'll be the biggest thing in music since the King, m' Warren. Having his son was all my idea. He don't even know about my projeck. See, I stuck one of my barrette-wires through all our protections. My Dad, he preaches part-time? and he told me if I ever got in the family way not to even bother coming home. So, I left before I showed any. Warren, he give me fifteen hundred dollars.

"Still got most of it. —This Chinese egg roll, I would say, is excellent."

I see Vanderlip about to head our way. He will ask her if she's had a complete browse-and-buy mall holiday experience, and what have been her purchases these last few weeks? Receipts, please.

So, just to talk, I start quizzing her about where she lives. Then she gets all stiff, speaks real cold into her fortune cookie, "North of here. With my aunt, why?" I thought, "Yeah, north of our parking lot, in woods with more ants than *one*, probably." So when Mr. Mall Manager does bob up, I explain she has this dog out on approval. A trusted regular.

"Merry Christmas," she smiles up to Vanderlip and he just looks her over.


With eight days till Yuletide proper, she finally steps to the back of my shop, bringing Butterbean in from their latest demonstration tour.

Before I even see the girl, there comes this hush. Now, my animals don't usually react to a customer one-way-the-other. Maybe her being so pregnant struck them? Or her quiet habit of taking not one thing for granted. Even two full-grown jumpy Maine coon cats shift forward in their cages.

My all-time smartest African gray parrot says in a Vernon-like voice that cracks up our beauticians next door, "Eww, who did that to your *hair*?" Well, hearing, she laughs like a kid then. Under bangs, I see her teeth. She shows part of one great eye, brown.

Soon I had her helping my trusted assistant-manager LaTonya do preliminary grooming. I leave the big Labs and shepherds for our sturdy after-high-school boys. One thing is,

I have a amazing staff. (Listen, you cannot sell a hundred and nine holiday pups plus fifty-two kittens without having you some able helpers, are you kidding?)

I liked seeing our new girl use the blow-dryer on a apricot toy poodle. She looked totally into it, finally *training* for something, you know.

During one of her many bathroom trips, LaTonya and I found the wallet in her peacoat, us scouting for some family phone number. But she'd smartly marked the contact-info off of everything—that determined to do all this alone. I noticed she was down to ninety-nine dollars, mostly ones and fives. Like me, LaTonya had already offered her a place to stay but our little girl she was too proud. Kept talking about her being a guest of that fancy aunt of hers. Well, to judge from muddy boots, that aunt must've lived in a cave.

Was three days before Christmas we had downpours, sleet, high winds, and she goes missing. Naturally I'm worried sick. Already I am picturing this pale gal, dead in a ditch beside her new baby. Used to, I'd go crazy waiting for my mom and grandma to get home from the box factory. Now I had LaTonya checking three times daily all women's rooms mall-wide.

So that night right after work, I aim my Camaro out toward our lot's far north corner. Leave my brights on, whip out my cell phone's flashlight app, go squishing through puddles.

I aim toward huge walk-in concrete pipes, all lined up to be part of that new Target going in next door. They been dropped in among our last few sassafras and sweet-gum trees, all that's left of old American woods herebouts.

The sky, from low clouds and strip-mall signs, shows oxblood-red this time the night. My breath clouds. Musak carols drift clear out here, words and everything.

*How still we see thee lie, above thy dark and dreamless streets,*
*the silent stars go by . . .*

But, funny, my mall, from this back-dumpster angle, tonight
looks almost ugly. That's from my missing her, from my worry,
I reckon.

Then, before one big pipe, I see flooring made of scrap plywood, laid just so. Bricks circle a cold campfire. Inside that four-
foot pipe, my flashlight finds garbage bags stuffed with leaves
for bedding. Two empty cans of Old Milwaukee. And, hooked
to one wall, a little round hand-mirror.

Hanging on to it, I see an old Smurf doll with all of one
girl's pink barrettes clipped into that toy's orange hair. Well,
that tore me up.

I don't know.

People are so **brave**, you know?

I hear another body's shoes slushing the dark nearby, and
Vernon jumps like from a horror movie but calling to her, cry-
ing almost, "That you, babe? Say you're safe." And here stands
Vanderlip.

Strange to find him in his suit, snooping out this far, Sunset
flashes his lapel pins red, with all the rest of him left dark. He's
like, "So, Vernon, come out here after work, do ye? Get a little
steam off? Girl that low, living back out here like some rat in a
hole, and you standing in front of her pipe. That's it, idn't it?"

Old as I am, being forty, you forget you can still feel shocked.
But I have been living so far past such filthy thoughts as his,
first I-I-I didn't even understand him. Defending her, I knew I
was going to say what I'd never dared speak before to any hall-
monitor like him.

"Might could surprise you, Mr. Vanderlip, with your pray-
ing into our loudspeaker every morning for sales, with your

church-choir handing out Sin leaflets noon and night, but there's still some good folks left on earth. You feel s'fine about yourself you expect everything **but** good from others. There's way more sin in your mind than you'll find out here at the edge, where most people just try and live. She's one the good ones, sir. She's your daughter Tammy's age and no worse.

"You invent an enemy a day. That's your caffeine that wakes you up. The others ain't enemies at first. But they **start** being, once you treat them like 'at. Her boyfriend's off serving in Afghanistan, sir. I ain't ever been out here before tonight. It's that she's missing. How'd you even know about her camp?"

"Security reconnaissance. She's been building off-site fires, code violation. Why? What'd you do with her body, Vernon? You're just the type. I know you've been slipping her the odd tenner. I have my sources. Funny, when I started here as manager? you struck me as a real retail-leader, Vern. You knew how to mix up the big and little breeds of pups, Great Danes beside Chihuahuas all wearing Easter Bunny ears in one Old English window. And you got **points** with me for that. Did. You could always stop thirty customers dead in their tracks out front of your shop. Sure, you need to drop about a hundred and fifty pounds. But, once that's done, you might could find a future even higher up in management. Instead? you've got half the high school working for you where one qualified adult'd do. You overpay them out of your own pocket. And now you put that little skank on payroll right at Christmas?

"God knows what other bag boys she's been kneeling in a pipe and doin' back here for pocket-change. Wise up, Vernon. She's carrying somebody's else's load."

I felt tempted to tell him about his daughter Tammy's reputation. I was about to sound off about what lessons Baby Jesus's stable taught, but I just let it go. There is too much to explain to any man this sure he's the Baptist angel-grade of "good."

So finally, after her going missing three full days, come Christmas Eve closing time, I see the Terminator's Security boys surround a small person at our Grand Concourse fountain.

LaTonya alerts me, "Vern, it her, okay. She back, but she looking *real* shook." I rush out, tell them she's my niece and I'll handle our own family mess. Good thing Vanderlip was off chasing Dillard's formal-wear shoplifters into Day at the Beach Tanning Parlor. As I bend down to help, poor child says, "I hitched halfway home, but they're too churchy to take in no bad girl like me. This old lady outside Ahoskie picked me up, carried me to *her* house, but she kept trying and get in the bathtub with me. Vernon, it got to where it was almost kind of weird. But right along, I kept thinking I've just got to get back to Vern and them pups. —But, am *hurt*in' some."

She stares right up at me, her face dead-white, emergency. Then I see as how her jeans are soaked clear through; her waters had done broke. If I knew little, she knew less. At least I had the delivery of eight hundred pups and kittens under my belt. In the valley of the blind . . .

LaTonya, knowing my tendency with strays, tried to warn me. She stands behind the gal, shaking her head no. And I understand LaTonya's right. So I tell the child, "We need us a hospital, girl. This one's beyond even me, glad as I am you're home." Then that child sandwiches both her little paws around one slab of mine. Gal says louder than ever she has spoke before, "Got no *in*-surance. My folks is probably already told the police I'm missing. Be a world of trouble if I step into a ER. I don't want to get you into no bad fix on my 'count. Us not being kin, doctors'd send you off anyways. But I couldn't stand for this to happen among strangers, Vern. Please. See? with Warren away, I done come clear back to **you** for this. Please— I'm strong."

Well, when somebody's chosen you, however much you might want 911? you are, well, you're . . . chose.

So while Vanderlip is scaring naked folks in tanning beds, LaTonya and me get her back into our storeroom. A trail of water on linoleum.

Hiding from Security, LaTonya, a big CSI fan, mops up evidence. The DNA, whathaveyou, it all tells a story.

Right off, I run to my beloved Internet. Vernon Googles keywords "baby" "human," "delivery of." Kept the printout folded in my back-pocket all that busy day.

Things stayed pretty hectic sales-wise, it being Christmas Eve and ever'thing. We do 39.3 percent of our business after Thanksgiving. Yes, Vanderlip goes rushing everywhere, grilling everybody about where she's **got** to.

Man never knew we'd lock her safe back here with us, behind stacked bags of every Hartz Mountain Canary product.

So. —So, yeah, it was right at a year ago tonight, about this exact same minute, see? First I send LaTonya home to her four kids. Then I move my Camaro clear down to the Hardee's lot toward Old Raleigh Road and hike back, huffing. If Vanderlip had seen my '67 cherry-red nearby, he'd of barged into my shop with cops, social services and his own crazed finger-wagging preacher, probably.

For once, I lock my store from inside. Turned out all the lights except aquariums'. Now, I tell you, the sounds of a pet shop is easier to notice in the dark. Fish tanks' bubbling becomes like ticking clocks, a sweet background—calming. Lights off, you can even hear our reptiles move their own sand. Around one a.m., her and me perked up and felt a bit afraid when the mall's great outside metal doors slammed shut then echoed everywhere like inside a whole castle.

My girl kept trying not to scream. By then her jeans were off and I had our store's every space-heater putting pink light to all the sides of her. I tell her, "Just us chickens. Don't hold back none now." Well, then she flat lets rip.

Shrieks echo across a sleeping mall, bouncing off each glassy storefront. This place will feel forever more alive for that, for me.

She screams in waves and rows, and I called down into the heat from her breath and body, a little stove. I found a way to coach her, "We're getting there! You can! You can! You are, girl!" I see now—every creature must be valuable if each birth takes this much work.


It was not no holiday night-off. But I guess I might call this the most testing, flattering thing that's ever once been asked of ole Vernon here. To be so trusted, and on Christmas Eve and hid with her among our animals!

Then it got so sudden, and even the top of the head looked like a human head, because it was, it *was* one. Somehow it got out whole, we got it out. Amazing that she'd hung around my mall and drew me a bit forward, found me. I cut the cord with my highest-end dog nail-clippers (but brand-new, plus sterilized). Amazing that, when the time was right, she had hitched clear back to be with me here, and that I *could* get down there and pull and coax and catch it—then hold its ankles up like it was some lizardy pet but slapping into it the air that made it go human.

I had saved back one tartan-plaid Burberry cashmere dog jacket, softest thing in the store beside birds, and our most expensive. I wrapped her child in that and laid it in the mother's arms.

By the end, she says, small, but meaning it—"This here's the first **real** thing I ever done, and you was with me ever' step, sweet Vern."

I goes just, "Thanks."

Well, it was a male one—I mean, it was a boy.

Oh, he was a pretty little thing. Black hair spread out like damp feathers. But of course I **would** call him pretty. I would, as his—whatever—as her substitute, as at least a fairly good pet store manager. Then I did something foolish, but it felt great. I let out all the puppies and kittens, ones that had not been sold in time? And it did not take them long to drift back here and find where all this new mewing was coming from. My best African gray flew over to perch on a pegboard partition and look down at her and the babe and asked, "Eww, what did they do to your **hair**!" Well, she cracked up.

Yeah, was just last Christmas Eve, lit by saltwater tanks, behind the staff lounge in my dark belov-ed pet store, in a mall with just us three, and other animals surrounding us, locked up tight from the outside-in, together.

The baby dogs and cats could smell her built-up milk, hoping it would fountain out soon, first real mother's milk. And the excitement of her scent and the blood and this slick new little life, it made them crazy with the kind of joy and jumpiness I'd never seen, not in all my years of retail here.

Of course, I couldn't keep her and him hiding in my storeroom forever. Even *I* knew that. And she didn't think it right, her staying long at my place without us being married or nothing. Oh, I understood. But she'd have forever been safer-than-safe living life with Vernon here. Whatever she wanted, I'd of dealt with it, really. Even being an ample person, what with eleven-hundred-square-feet, I had plenty of room for little folks like them.

Finally, I did get the parents' phone number out of her. Called them. Told them she'd had a son, named both for Warren and for her father, which would make that boy the fourth. And there came a stillness and the mother finally said, "How *are* they?"

I drove them both to the Raleigh airport in my Camaro, waxed perfect. I got as near the gate as the person without a ticket *can* go nowdays. And, just before the X-ray machine, she turns back, tells me she will make "Vernon" an extra middle name of his, which was . . . quite the Christmas gift.

Sometimes her mom still sends me pictures of this ideal baby. I sure save every attachment.

Just did what anybody would have, really. Still, I've taken his best baby picture and—well, he's my screen-saver now.

Oh man. Sorry. Blubbering here. Can be such a pushover. And a big ol' boy like me, too.

But hey, this time the year, could be—getting a little sentimental's legal, right? You been s' nice to talk to, really. Yeah, well that was *last* December twenty-fourth. And, I guess I'd have to say it was—of all Vernon's Christmases—his most . . . per-sonal.

You got to get on the road, I see that in your face. . . . Kirsten, precious, can I settle up the tab for me and my newest friend here? You kept us real well-supplied.

What? No, Kirsten. Not this many, not for free! Naw, Vernon cannot "accept." You give others way too much, girl. —Well, but . . . well, just looks like I'm going to have to sneak you and your twins something extra up ahead. Their birthday's March eleventh, I believe?

Guess I'd best be speeding home, too. Snooze me fourteen hours straight. Holiday emotions this big, they wear out even a plus-sized person. Hey, good luck on that highway, getting where your folks're all expecting you tomorrow.

Imagine Kirsten not letting me pay for any of our many eggnogs! Old family recipe, made with hand-grated nutmeg in her own home-blender.

Oh, I know folks say I tend to be a fool for Christmas. But, I swear, once a year, maybe we should all just go ahead and admit it:

Ain't people wonderful!

# FETCH

SOMETHING IS THROWN. *We retrieve it, without quite knowing why.*

If you'd been on that blue-pebbled beach (and today, of course, you *are*) you would've seen which drenched creature survived it, and by how much.

This spit of rock juts into the Atlantic. Currents fight separate battles along its either side. April in Maine is really January anywhere else. The waves, jade-black, still look sludged with cold. Thirty floating gulls—born into this—appear miserable anyway.

Last night's nor'easter left this quay littered with the worst of what's man-made. Against stone-gray, torn plastics show all the colors found on flags. Yellow nautical roping binds a splintered ping-pong table, its net still taut. Most of one young oak has been blown here roots-intact. A car pulls right onto the beach. Swimming seabirds shift. Whatever drama's coming matters as their latest chance at food.

Lost on gulls: this being a Swedish station wagon, bone-white—so new its back-window shows a scratched-at dealer's sticker. Under radials, pebbles grind like molars testing molars.

The driver clambers out, lanky, scanning. He seems at ease with this bleak spot, half glad for violent wind. Sandy hair, parted like a schoolboy's, gets flung back to front then front to back till, laughing, he rakes it free of his eyes. Handsomeness has outlived early freckles. Stepping to the passenger's side, he pockets a massive key ring. Its weight hints at boats, other cars, two homes, maybe three.

Despite superior care—he's nonetheless gone forty-five. His shape is as yet straight up and down. There's something gallant if tested in how he aids the woman standing. She rises, stretches, as attractive as he, if darker. Full mouth, long nose, her movements imply a dancer's history. Her beaten-gold choker, its matching cuff-bracelet, demand appraisal. But the neck and wrist look somehow whittled, thinner now than even fashion might require.

His right arm supporting her left, the man half-pulls her across slicker rocks toward surf. His pale hair whipping, he helps steady this old woman somehow his same age. She moves like a person needing sleep. He stage-manages her climb uphill toward a spot they seem to recognize and like.

In motion, you catch his recent habit of subtly offering just enough energy to always catch her. Without seeming to cling. Facing horizon, the pair arranges itself, cornering the pivot of each luff. They rest now, staring out.

\*    \*    \*

She keeps balanced on her left leg, while rubbing, favoring the right. Wind pushes her hair straight back, makes the cheekbones, so recently chic, look dire. But she just nods. Her eyes, as if blind, shut over half-a-smile.

Terns and gulls, in search of snacks, now flap ashore.

Strobes of sun start then fail, return, lose interest. Having squired her to this highest spot, he points toward a jet-dark eddy last night's undertow carved. The few swimming gulls avoid this clouded channel. One tern's orange beak scissors up a glint of sea-colored minnow.

The man is glancing toward their car, seeming worried as for some child left there; she holds on to him a minute longer. Their clothes, the most careful of careless natural fabrics, press back snapping along limbs. Her short dress shows legs now so thin the knees look swollen.

A gale arrives direct from the Canaries. This pair lean forward, almost welcoming such strain. It seems they've come here for a test more visible—if less treacherous—than recent inland ones. Clutching each other tighter, in the din of surf crashing against rock, they say nothing. Maybe they're too showily prosperous to have let the rites and woes of childbirth impede their style. Even out here, they seem used to being stared at. But, now alone together, mussed, they each act opulently off-duty.

Till lately, they must've looked younger than their years. Now they move at a pace more understated, somehow resigned.

He leaves her, goes padding toward the car, wary over stones. Boyish white wrists V-out beside him, balancing. She waits uphill, arms wrapped around herself. One palm smooths her throat, resting on its collar of beaten gold. Is this item ancient-Greek or by some designer we will hear from soon? The thing's simplicity makes a claim about its beauty and, till recently, hers.

The way both people have just opened to this elemental place, the way they've grinned at its sewage scents and steady battering, makes you feel they know and somehow claim the spot. Maybe they've been coming here for years.

He unlatches the back of their station wagon while studying her. Feeling observed uphill she twists his way, lifts a hand to reassure. The bracelet wobbles. Even in repose at half-speed this woman inhabits a daunting force. For all the beauty left her, she might be someone with more imitator-admirers than close friends.

From the wagon's rear, he pulls forth something alive. Given the wind's factory-whistle howl, considering the surf flume and sucking sounds, hearing human speech will be impossible today. This might help explain the pair's relief.

With something more of eagerness than he has shown in leading her, he coaxes forth a heavy squirming thing. After hoisting it, the man detaches onto stones what is surely too big to be a baby, too heavy for the old frail lady it resembles.

Wrapped within a collector's Indian blanket, shaking itself awake, one ancient and quite fat black Labrador dog sniffs around itself. The creature has a podgy instant grandeur like the aged widow Queen Victoria. All black silhouette, its comic plumpness seems to comment on the couple's thinness. The man settles his animal—from the look of it, a neutered male— careful of its footing among loose stones. The dog appears so glad of his whereabouts, he tries, chin-up, eyes squinted, to entirely circle himself. The tail is fat and bent and jocular in sudden whipping. Before the creature fully finds his legs, such motions lurch toward a dance that nearly topples him. His red collar is, along with that startled oak-leaf green, the plastic trash, her distant gold, the rare brightness on this gray beach.

One black tail flopping side to side seems the single witty thing out here. The man smiles down his pleasure. Above the dog's silver muzzle, eyes narrow, accepting customary praise. Amber eyes are set somewhat too close together. This gives the beast a look of scholastical absentmindedness. His roly-poly bounding is unrestrained. Overt with pure response, he seems everything his smart and loving owners cannot, would never, be.

*If they've just begun suspecting they are no longer young, they might love the dog for not yet knowing he is old.*

From the stone perch, she bows, then pats one thigh, summoning her animal. The man steadies a barrel-bodied creature her way. He lifts its collar, helping maneuver the Lab around these first few boulders. Soon the old dog finds his natural trot. Still, stones prove unsettled. The beast half falls while going mainly forward. As he fixes on her, the dog's whole head and neck make involuntary swivels. At last he trudges huffing smack into her right palm held open for his nose and tongue.

The pet is soon inhaling dead fish and the iron smell of Greenland; he blinks as if offering the horizon his own rubber-faced tourist greeting. As usual, his jester's timing makes her laugh.

Stacked in the station wagon downhill, overnight-luggage, good French bags of optimistically small denominations. The kind you'd take to a hospital only for some procedure "exploratory."

Today and in everything that follows, in this couple's farewell to a well-known hook of land, in their relation to the dog and one another—something new and weighted is revealed. Usual motions slow now. You sense—in this last rite of driving onto the rock peninsula—some tacit farewell. It seems they are about to deposit their dog with his favorite grad-student-sitter before speeding straight to Freeport, some small plane bound toward Mass. General. To the best—certainly the best—oncologist on earth. No one—but the gulls, two terns and you—will see them strolling-limping here today.

Strong winds cause each to twist aside while keeping necks locked, heads raised. United, the three scuff toward the sickled point. Smells alternate: rock salt, spoiled celery, tonic water, dead birds. They've come here *for* something. Their walking proves challenged by wind but goes easier along the elevated center of this mineral path into the ocean. Clouds throw moving blue-gold scallops that go noon-to-evening with odd suddenness. Daylight itself seems the likeliest retraction. This spot looks either desolate or beautiful. It assumes whatever mood you bring here with you.

Though the three are regularly beaten side-to-side by northeast wind, the Lab lowers his weight and simply drags forward. The couple lock arms. Approaching any incline, the man, automatic, grabs their dog's bright collar, steadying. As this group proceeds, the woman's limp reveals itself. Being here, maybe she's given up pretending to look well. Maintaining inland appearances must sometimes seem, especially for a person this naturally visible, half-taxing as disease itself.

The old dog, released, bounders ahead. Purposeful, porpoise-like in forward lunging, he goes at-sniff half-tottering across each slicked stone. A born clown, he seems to love his role, judging from how he keeps glancing back at them. Every twelve feet or so, he'll pause, check. He's waiting approval of his bumbling route while keeping tabs on theirs. He is, as in his younger days, still guarding them, though time has changed the terms without his noticing.

Smiling, the two separately study him. Each seems to savor his sense of avid always-forward life. This morning the Lab's springy front-legs, some extra glitter in his eyes, recall his better days. Does he sense how ill she is? Is he playing his game extra-hard today for love of them? Or might their present exhaustion make him appear—by contrast—even more the pup they were unexpectedly given, then came to adore and now sort of worship?

This group seems so at peace here on this blasted quay. They might be wandering the chrome solarium of what you guess is a good-sized cliffside home not far up the coast. At last, they've trekked at their agreed-on pace to one high spot two hundred yards beyond the car. The man idly lifts a found blue bottle. The dog's front half immediately starts bouncing. This is the old-age version of his famous ground-clearing puppy leaps while playing Fetch. But—with ocean moiling on either side—that game will not do here. The man, catching a motherly head-shake from his partner, sets the bottle down, and slow.

The people move arms-around-waists. In their very word-

lessness, they achieve a hobbled working concord. Their dog
twenty feet ahead keeps always turning back then going on,
turning back. Even for the healthiest, these rocks—all round
and each one scummed unevenly—make for ankle-twisting
hazards. Gulls follow the party. Birds flop down just ahead
of these intruders, shifting in irritable ten-foot flights. Birds
appear expecting benefits from any guests crazed enough to
come here after last night's storm.

The woman's slight hunching now gives way to opening her
mouth then leaning forward. Sick, she waves her companions
on ahead to show she simply needs privacy. Her mate follows
orders. Her grouchy gesture seems in no way irked at **him**.
None of this seems personal. She is already that sick. She simply bends forward. Gulls—sensible—surround her.

And, while the man and dog go on ahead, she does cough
up a little breakfast. The Labrador keeps looking back at her,
taking six or eight more steps, checking around again but, head
lowered, with an air of philosophy or fellow suffering. She has
hardly wiped her mouth with the back of one braceleted hand
when birds mass across her ankles, fighting for that spot of yellow. Cursing, she kicks through leathern wings, manages to
keep moving.

The Lab, attuned to her discomfort, barks at gulls. He
turns to greet her in awkward circles, yapping out to sea while
slobbering some. His timing theatrical—he goes straight to
playing the fool. Even in her smiling struggle for breath, you
see her shake her head with mock-exasperation. This has
become the woman's most frequent sign of approval for both
her males: half-wince, part-grin. Even so, as intended, the old
creature has just fetched for her one moment's distraction.

The dog makes sport of yapping up at flying gulls. One

tern dive-bombs him, scolding him with hard yellow eyes. The woman, hand to sternum, still shakes her head, peeved with her upset-stomach, a social lapse. The blond man, hoping to amuse her if stupidly (half-copying their dog), hurls himself down a rocky incline, achieves the surf. Waving both arms, leaping like some chieftain, he tamps one palm across his yodeling mouth to give off war-whoops. He intends such foolishness as a diversion. But he seems surprised by the very joy he's faking. He, after all, is still healthy and not un-young. How many months now has he slowed his gait to honor gravity's sudden tax on hers? Even before the diagnosis, didn't his body sense a darkling visitor in hers? But today, out here, he dances, briefly freed. This guilty vigor surges and he feels himself again. Before whatever is waiting, he wants to bound around once more.

The animal stoops, defecating, behind one nine-foot boulder. And from a second uprooted oak, the man rips a forked stick then shakes it overhead. Then as some last proof of his vitality, he chucks this limb end-over-end into surf. Foam pushes it, experimenting, only to suck it nine feet out with one smooth inhale. Such undertow. And he acts pleased. Till noting her eyes cut left, till seeing how she seems to curse. Her hand whips toward horizon. Their dog, from behind his shielding boulder, has somehow seen a stick tossed. Any stick is his. He has just belly-flopped into one very cold Atlantic. Their prized pet is swimming out to fetch a prize these two do not want. She clambers nearer water, shaking her head as if not believing. First she points to the man's watch. Then, one palm pressed to her throat, she hollers accusations. Her partner goes very still. She screams out toward a dog impervious.

She is left simply shaking her bone fist at the ocean.

## II.

ONE LABRADOR RETRIEVER has found his daily chance: to retrieve. Fetch is the single game this beast will play forever. Night can fall. Favorite foods will go uneaten. He must love the joy of fetch for its being perfectly mutual, a standing appointment.

The man, face stricken, now turns toward her. An airplane, on its runway, is being fueled. Doctors are likely reviewing her charts, scanning MRIs. Now this pair's Lab, fourteen years old, dog-paddles off into a frigid Atlantic as if bound for Ireland. The creature is fixed solely on a green V-shape in this zone of rolling mercury. And all because of one dumb moment's pure exuberance. She appears furious with him.

Neck muscles vexed to cords, she finds the nearest good-sized stone. He expects she will now spastically hurl it toward their dog. Instead she heaves it right at him as hard as she can. It strikes his shoulder with force enough to knock him two steps backward. Then, shocked by such savagery, her features imitate his sudden grimace. Her face goes ashen as she reaches out. But, even as his hand presses the worst hurt, he shrugs, admitting he's just done something idiotic. He has already turned, is running toward water.

Given this sea's Greenland temperature, considering their afternoon's likely schedule, the man trots as close to jagged foam as he can in his Italian loafers blond as he is.

The tide's been shifting. Last night's storm has added a whole new pitch of whistling roar. This makes any talk inaudible. What, anyway, to *say*, especially now? Flying gulls resettle on water, again at-swim to see whatever action must befall these guests. Birds shriek news of fresh currents, dangers only their ruddering feet perceive. (They now rotate forty degrees to face the dog's own poorly chosen route.) Water surging past this point goes coursing south. But waves keep slamming east to west. Undertow results. Till now, this day has been the gray of the beach's million dry rocks; now it turns the color of those wet ones varnished seal-black.

Two people, together standing separately—one near the surf, another higher on stone bluff—each stare toward a floating branch, pursued. They judge the likely energy of their pet now paddling oblivious toward it.

The couple's upper bodies lock, studying a darkening whorl curving not thirty feet beyond the dog. This new channel feeds a greater suction turning off the point. Already the sprig of greenery goes spinning toward it, some compass-needle crazed.

The woman, farther uphill, folds at center, points then hollers toward the man or dog or simply hollers. The man signals, showing he's already seen the risk. He has accepted her stoning, but is now urging her (via downward sweeps of both his open palms) to at least not panic their dog, please. All this might yet turn out fine. Well, *couldn't* it?

Since breakfast, something extra's shown in their Lab's stolid bounce. Some up-curl at the inner seam of his black lip. Old as he is, this has been one of his better recent mornings. Even his chasing a stick not intended for him proves how young the ocean's made him feel. His foolish splash of energy seems meant to re-engender theirs.

The Lab is so intent upon his game. Such sport has become his favorite way to lift their sour latest moods. In the station wagon he rode here with familiar dreaded luggage; these people are world travelers; the dog knows the signs; he has been left before. So, even as he paddles toward that branch, he seems to take his time in chill water, eager for activity, relief, glad to hold them amused on his beach.

You sense how truly smart they find him, at least how charming and present. As both these people straighten with suppressed alarm, you guess he's always been their reckless enjoyer. They get to marvel and to worry, over-think for him. But their designated explorer has today overshot his skill, forgot his age. Surely that stick should not have left this beach. One backward shrug from the man near shore to the woman uphill again concedes this. After slamming one palm to his forehead, he hoists both hands then, despairing, lets them flop. Meanwhile, hopping side to side, he keeps screaming a two-syllable cry, probably the dog's name, all while knowing—till that stick is fetched, nothing will deter the dog—nothing can save him.


Still favoring the right leg, she fights her way down a graveled bank toward surf. She forgets herself and falls in her struggle to somehow help. She scrapes her knee, barely notices, scrambles upright. What can either of them **do**? The water temperature would stun, then, take them under. Even the dog, in weighing less, is—slowly—being pulled now from behind. The stick seems all that matters as he bashes through successive waves. Each hides undertow. Riptide's force is visible mostly in its smoothing the tops of all the breakers that it implicates. The old dog, feeling only safe in his companions' gaze, just goes with it. He heads toward the green. He imagines that his own male energy creates the tumbling drift that already has him.

\* \* \*

They hear the point's down-turning slough, gone louder now. Everything is pulled toward and into it. She, reaching water's edge, eager to consult her man, totters up to him, touches his back. He—deafened by wind's shrilling, unaware of her approach—jumps as if shot, lifts one arm to actually defend himself. He at once shows he regrets this. And pulls her waist hard against his own right hip. They both turn and—joined— are screaming at their dog. They wave free arms. They separate to run like mad-people up and down the beach. Anything to distract their pet from his goal, anything to bring him in while he yet has strength and body heat.

Once his usual game of Fetch begins, there is no devaluing the contested object, ever. As with love, substitutions don't apply. Even so, they whistle, hooting favorite nicknames, acting utter fools. This eager to become his saving amusement, they imitate then gladly *become* him. (She, by drawing near the ground, coaxing him at child-height. He, via kinetic spins, by playing superb ghost-Frisbee.) This show begins to seem their farewell-thanks. Maybe they can mime him toward recalling his own confidence? He will need that. To pull himself free of a vortex waiting—roaring—at the point's far end. They should never have fed him from the table; every ounce of extra weight today becomes a peril. Already the current has tugged him forty feet past shore, toward some claiming horizon.

He somehow snags the stick. They literally applaud. He does a crude proud U-turn. He paddles toward shore. Now he faces them, how small his head looks bobbing out there. Black dot, smiling. Full stop. Then they see the gulls flying-shifting into better positions out beyond-behind him. Floating birds all shift his way. Ready for spectacle. They know more about the harsh shared currents than do any humans ashore. What are the gulls hoping for? Do gulls hope? Does any living thing for long? What are the odds against us?

What of the dog? As yet unaware, even while locked in combat with undertow, instead he shakes the stick! (Tough-guy, probably growling out there to prove his moxie.) But currents already test his haunches. Smart as he is, the creature fixes on the expressions his companions offer. Likely two white masks of tragedy. And only now, in his reading these, do you see the creature's sideways jerk of consciousness. Awareness flattens the animal's black face. His head is visible, now not, visible, not now—behind repeated jagged waves.

His paddling redoubles. But now the dog advances not at all.


The second they see their Lab release his stick—no longer remembering why he even **liked** it—his companions start to cry. Herky-jerking arms far wilder, dancing ever-crazier, one weepy man goes into manic pirouetting jumping jacks. She does a faltering remembered ballerina-turn, a pas de chat, then settles for simply hopping frog-like side-to-side. Odd, now instead of favoring her bad leg, she seems to pound its whole corrupted foot against rocks. Sickened, she gives over to the un-discipline of outflung arms, then whistling with two-fingered tomboy force.

The dog half-notices. And you soon hear in their torn scraps of sound how they no longer simply tease or coax the animal ashore; theirs have become cries and screams ascending to the pitch of non-believers' prayers. Are these two yelling orders for him to save himself? Are they crying for themselves? Is any separation possible? With winds risen to twenty-five knots, it's harder to hear the pitch of creature yelps. Undertow, as in some prank, now turns the dog one full rotation, so fast. And he, dizzied, simply starts paddling out to sea. Such screaming they do. Over his haunches, he notices, reorients. Slowing.

The man, using the butt of his right fist, clears his nose while trying to hide signs of crying. She curls down on the rocks then, forcing herself, jumps into the ocean, wades a full yard out. Simple contact makes her start. Outstretched hands both fisting. Two minutes' swim in this will stiffen her to wood. One shamed look tells him—she knows so now. But when she trudges out, dress darkened-lowered with sea-weight, she looks far more hobbled. She keeps signaling toward the animal. His rear-legs persist, then stop; two kicks more, he is going into some uneven stymied drift. Though he's floated too far to read her gesture plain, she keeps holding out one hand, down low, as if offering whatever treat he'd most like finding there. . . .

The dog is being pulled against his will—aside—then out. Along the shore they follow him. They're scarcely aware till they look back: that first oak is now three-hundred-yards away, their white car has somehow shrunk to matchbox-size. Off to the right, at the point of the peninsula, they hear a boiling suction. The stick the Lab just forfeited—in being weightless—shows his own likely route. Far faster than he would go, it is spun by six tricky currents till it reaches the point's funneling vacuum, tilts, disappears.

The two onshore begin to stare toward the great black surging channel.


Treading water, the animal is visibly starting to know. If only he'd been stupider these last fourteen years, his end might now, for all of them, prove easier. He's brighter than most first-graders and understands. If not the science of his fix, then its likely outcome.

Though his front legs continue making their usual spastic imitations of real swimming, you sense he's losing use of rear limbs. These are becoming just more ballast the undertow can use against him. The dog bares his teeth with strain. Amber light in his comic eyes goes leaden as the waves. What has left his features is simply all the native wit. You see he is now gauging only the couple's distorted expressions. His face gives them back their own despair, their lack of plan, their sinking-in middle years. Finally, out of choices, the dog even risks staring straight-overhead at the gunmetal sky, seeking help there. As thanks, he takes in water, goes thrashing under for a bit. He's out there seizing up, for one reason: he is obeying fear. Fear learned from the features he so daily and expertly reads. And, only after seeing him imitate their own recent half-deadness, do they somehow snap—fully parental—into action.

Now they move like same-sex twins, natural and unanimous in joint emergency. Along the beach, they heave themselves, casting about for props. These people have so often taken charge. They've certainly stormed—with their thinness, good luggage and independent funds—many a fine hotel worldwide. Now they try distracting him at least from his own panic at seeing theirs.

Running to a wedge of sodden plywood, she throws herself onto it, grabs one corner, tears it free. Rising, she now chucks this out toward the dog's central fan of vision. He notices, continues frontward struggling, only to recede. For one second, glancing even at this pointless target, he seems to hold a moment longer in his place.

She nods herself encouragement, finds six smaller rocks,

ones safe enough to hurl into the black current before him. She intends describing the single path that might get him to a flat stone half-submerged thirty feet offshore. She's trying to prevent his looking overhead again and taking in more water. Her tossed rocks sink at once but do leave cusps of foam. The dog is now watching each plash. He's mapping each and this helps keep him fixed on her. On anything except the drift that has him, that seems just toying with him now.

Soon she and the man have stripped the second oak tree to its trunk, tossing into salt water its last limbs, mere twigs.

First the flailing dog ignores these but as the man onshore screams, doing further calisthenics to make a taller visual target, the old dog's head fights to stare toward whatever useless bits are thrown his way. *Fetch?* You see him fight to regain something essential for all drifters—a scheme, however arbitrary. The man chucks one stone close to where the last plopped. He more or less replaces one target with another at intervals that show, if not a Major League arm, then great adrenalized concentration. Fear has given him a material control till now seen only in one Swiss tennis champ. Awed by his own aim, he envies it. Knowing this can't last.

The more the dog fixes on any target, the better does he struggle, resisting sideways drift. But there's little left to throw. His eyes are blinking, longer. He's freezing, cramping up out there. Hands bracketing her mouth, she screams more warnings, promises.

Having tossed at him everything available, now seeing him lose fixity while being shoved due east, she pulls off her gold bracelet. It is one whose "good" weight and simplicity has marked it as a feature of her arm for years. Without a thought except of him, she heaves it with good sisterly aim. And, though he's gargling in sea-foam, its plop, its familiar glint, does snag at least a fragment of the drowning dog's attention. Then pitiless she shucks her necklace, sends that into waves. This buys him another two seconds of interest.

Next, each by each, her shoes go in. They describe an arc that hints toward a half-sunken shoreline rock that might give the creature foothold. Each of her offerings at least snags some new part of his retinal range. Retrievers' being bred for such collecting helps him now. Each distraction she offers helps him plot a momentary wish. He is engaged because remembering, expecting. His next cobbled kick seems pure reward.

Now the man flips off his loafers, lobs each in turn along the only crooked route ashore. He tries to find any beach rock not so large that, if tossed, might brain his struggling pet. First the man whips his belt free and knots it, heaves. Finally he peels off his silver diver's watch and, after dangling this to make it appear tempting as some tinned food, underhands it within sixteen feet of the dog's frothing snout.

Last thing, the man pulls out his wallet. He sprinkles cards on stones then shot-puts his whole billfold into the Atlantic. Massed keys, pulled from a pocket, he lifts, weighs, pauses, keeps.

At last, the man, with nothing left to throw, notices a wooden shipping crate wound in a tangle of yellow nylon line. He yanks that up, pebbles flying, judging its strength between two hands. Some spots prove rotten. But three lengths hold firm as he knots these fast. He tosses a free-end toward her and, at once understanding, she trusses line around her narrow hips. The woman lanyards it under both arms then leans back. Half sitting, she is getting steadied on the largest angled rock near shore.

He loops roping under either armpit, cinches it about his

chest, leaving ten feet free as he dives. When the man finally bobs up, mouth gaping, hair flat, he immediately turns, despite himself, looks back at her. Gasping, he seems to take one last glance at her. For strength? And to inform her how goddam cold it is. She already knows.

She hunkers back, braced against the rock. She keeps the frayed line out before her bare extended legs, one bleeding at the ankle. Yellow roping, being light enough to float, stays visible within the surface of most heaving swells. Somehow that line—a plan to fix upon—allows the dog one stray kick, now two, alternating either numbed rear-leg. Front-paws return to their cartoony paddle-wheeling nowhere.

The man, now roped to her, heads out as far and fast as possible. A strong swimmer, he speeds at first, knowing that the time he might survive such cold is rationed. While he can, he gives it everything. His downstroking right hand grips the line's unbraiding end. It's not that he expects the Lab to bite this rope then clamp there like some show dog. It's more how the sight of it, something almost the color of a rawhide chew-toy, might let the creature jolt free of his frozen sidelong drift. The nearby floating terns and gulls, not uninvolved, give off limp cries—the interest of anything alive observing anything else alive in far worse trouble.

Three minutes more, the man has finally made it to the dog. The creature tries at once to climb onboard him. The man laughs with the joy of contact while fighting not to take in water. He catches the beast around his neck to keep him submerged if with his head free. The trick now seems to be getting this line through that red collar sogged black.

Inland, backward she tilts. Then, hand-over-hand with all

the might left her, she pulls toward herself what rope she's able to attach; the rest she doubles under arms, binds around her chest. Sometimes she'll release a foot or more but, stern and motherly in motion, she tightens it at once. Line playing through her clawed right hand first chafes then burns toward bleeding till the yellow rope's discolored.

It is ugly, these two fighting a trussed dog ashore. The dog's tongue hangs loose, looks huge, beef-colored out there. Ugly how current keeps pulling man and dog aside then back. Just to suck in air enough, each gives a sound like barking. The man scissor-kicks, amateur, frantic, but never still. He presses his face, for warmth, maybe courage, against the dog's loose neck. He must be screaming at it baby-talk as they come so slowly forward.

On her back against rocks, she herself might be dead. She has square-knotted scratchy rope around her waist. Now she reverses the field, leans back to make one fierce spinal pivot for support. Reeling her males in, hand-over-wrist, letting out line then yanking it tighter, she, laid flat, must splay aside her own bare feet. Only that way can she even see them. Just their feeling her line's intermittent tautening concentrates them. Why this faith? Because of one filament? Somehow the color yellow has a sort of magic.

At first the dog battles both salt water and his rescuer. But simply being touched again works on him like a drug. The beast's heaviness, even as his front-half tries to help, makes joint-floating so much harder. The man must finally slide behind and simply push, shouldering the old form forward while himself choking and cajoling, cursing encouragement in odd coughs and lavish spittings.

Times she loses track of them. Flattened, staring up, she must fight to prepare herself for one great swell when all their weight slides off her line. What *then*? As for her pulling, his pushing—their eventually getting the dog even close to one flat rock angled under four feet of ocean and finally ashore—how could it happen? Except by will, three animal wills. It would seem unaccountable, though we are all somehow watching it occur. How long has this taken? How many months of their lives have they just used in helping save a pet already ancient with dog-years? Will a beast so old, this savagely tested, even *live* much longer? Does that matter? The Lab has snapped out of his own terror. He has left his own permission to surrender. Fear has been granting all of them a list of perfect reasons to give way. She struggles now to stand, finds she is so tired that, half-laughing, she must use as ballast her own twelve-pound head; so crisscrossed is she with rope, so hostaged to this rock and rescue. Saving is the only thing. Headfirst she rises onto knees at least and, from here, can rein in the last of their rope, the final hardest eight feet.

In the end there's no explaining how the three of them became one single homely unit. Look, it is now panting, cleaving to this outermost rock. Soon as the Lab—now appearing more a varnished black catfish than anything big-boned with legs—soon as he is pulled up panting onto rocks, the dog vomits his morning's bribing meal. Gulls gather, wings among and atop these three. This time no survivor swats at birds. Let them.

The old creature wheezing on his side—looks half perished—but, tended to from either end, shows one wet tail now thrashing stones. Helpless, faith! One tail, beating, leaves black marks printed score-like on a few dry pebbles. The laughing man and woman salute this independent appendage. His wagging somehow makes these people heave themselves once more against their beast for warmth. The people are barefoot, with nails gone blue, their beautiful clothes darkened by salt and clotted with grit and sea-kelp and their own inglorious snot. You see a single creature-mound. It could have washed onto any beach. It appears one bulbed, joined, gulping thing. It occasionally raises one hand to pat some far fond part of itself. Once, a thin arm, purple with rope-burn and a banded ivory-white to show where gold has been, pulls aside a man's shirt. One finger traces the long open gash from shoulder to neck. All from a rock once shied at him long-ago. Then everything fuses. Clutching at dog collar, at whatever bits of cloth they can grab up from each other, faces averted, propped partly upright, these people neither cry nor smile. They simply rest here with one dog—consoling-consoled—between them.

If a chartered plane still waits, if some squad of white-coated Harvard doctors expects to gather soon, all that must keep for another day, or week, or month.


It took the couple more than fifty minutes to get sitting then finally standing. First the man, pinching up plastic cards like clamshells from the shore, made it barefoot all the way to their car. He went stepping with goat-like tenacity, cutting his soles but not daring study damage till all of it was done.

He brought back some of her packed clothes to use as towels and bandages. He brought the good old Indian blanket. He and the woman both ministered to their dog, rubbing, reviving, warming him in ways first medical then comical then both.

The man pointed, one mile into the Atlantic: the sunlight now fastened onto thirty square feet of green swells, sunlight shot full of gold, seemed about to make this spot the most beautiful on earth then opted against. Cloud-cover once more. As the sun faltered then revived, waves roared louder as if complaining as at the loss of them. This close, they saw the dog all wrapped, a fat papoose in its bright Indian blanket, just his two shiny brown eyes showing, blinking . . . on purpose. Clowning again and therefore alive.

The man carried the retriever first. Then he came back for her. Their car had somehow independently become a quarter mile up-beach. You could see how tired she was. She hobbled in a weaving almost-drunken way. He had to help drag her worst leg over larger rocks. Finally, though he feared breaking something already-jeopardized inside her, the man just lifted his friend. Tired as he was, he advanced like some stilted seabird, short enervated rushes forward, long wavery halts.

The wind had gotten colder. The surf itself was black now. Day had run its course. The yellow rope, uncoiled, had drifted tangled half-a-mile-out. Rope seemed some stand-in checkmark, unwinding offshore, already half-lost knot-by-knot into riptide

Soon as their car-engine started, he switched on headlights, flicked these up to brights. It'd be hours till official sunset. But who could blame his overcompensation, his superstition, maybe his faith?

Then, blessed with the same four-wheel drive that brought them way out here, they left these rocks far faster.

No trace of their struggle remains. No sign of their lifesaving, their tossing things into the sea, their clearing these cold stones of nor'easter's storm-trash. Such blood or vomit as just fell from them? already gull-eaten, salt-neutered, immediately wind-gnawed to nothing. The terns and gulls have gone back to swimming as usual, just this side of undertow. Birds are feasting now on many small silver fish jumping to avoid black suction there.

*Something is thrown. We retrieve it, without knowing quite what's been offered. The harder that proves to reach, the more we feel we need it. Out after it we go.*

You've endured this blue-pebbled beach. You have just witnessed which drenched creature survived it, by how much. You were promised that. Now you have it. Can you feel this ending? Can you feel how eventually we will? Even you? Oh well . . .

Wonder what happened to that couple and their dog.
   We never even learned their names.
   Never really heard them speak.
   Did she get to live?
   None of that is known.
   This is not that kind of story.
   It's the kind that has a happy ending you know is not the fullest happy ending but must pass for one.

The end.
   High tide has come.
   Their beach is underwater.

# THE DELUXE $19.95 WALKING TOUR OF HISTORIC FALLS (NC) —LIGHT LUNCH INCLUSIVE

I DEARLY DESPISE BEING late and yet here I am, three minutes behind my time. Uncharacteristic and one mighty poor example for you youngsters. Your patience is much appreciated, and aren't you a lovely, varied crowd? Big group, too, for my first day back!

As you likely know, you've turned up in historic downtown Falls, North Carolina. Our trek will soon involve some strolling. No worry. If a lady of my "vintage" can hike it in heels, even the biggest of you will do fine. I won't gallop. There's simply too much to see and say on this my return to history and the world.

Some call ours a town that time's forgotten. But *I* have not.

I am a volunteer docent, meaning every cent of your ticket goes to preservation. And doesn't our Courthouse Square look handsome in this morning light? See those cannons? the city finally varnished them. I had to nag our mayor. Children, to prove my tours are real educational: the plural of "cannon" *is* "cannon." Gather closer, please. And disarm all cell phones. These next few minutes *I* want to be your favorite form of modern communication. "Founded in 1824, the . . ."

Right off, we've a teeny problem: These little barefoot girls up front are visibly texting. Yes, **you**. (Thank you for looking **up**.) You're walky-talky-ing each other, right? Doubtless chatting about old me and Falls, even older. —Girls, how do you think that makes us *feel*?

Might any adult present be willing to take responsibility for these two? Well, could you at least stand between them or help them to hang up? Others have come on purpose—my first day back from the edge—come to hear some actual *Hist*'ry. Not those clicking speedy little thumbs. —Fine. Nothing personal, all right? Everybody feel ready to move? —It's **this** way, actually.

My name, as some may know, is Mrs. Evelyn du Pre Wells. Born and bred two blocks from here, on Summit. I've always claimed first dibs on you, our Full-Deluxe $19.95 visitors. You're a finer class of listener than those who only pay for our $4.95. *As* we walk, we'll encounter Falls' dead and living, politicians and sculptors from centuries past, persons white and black. And you know what all these achievers have in common? They would've shelled out the $19.95. —Humor, you see.

Founded in 1824, Falls—known for the purity of its tobacco and its curative River Lithium—still plays host to sixteen churches. Our township produced one minor sculptor, a major general and several beauties of national note. Could be we're more famous for those who perished here than ones we mid-wifed into being. The Civil War's oldest surviving soldier expired, not three homes from my family's, be 1940. When that war ended, the boy was still a private. But, thanks to inherited property, his pushy little wife, and the man's own narrative imagination promoted by time, he died with the rank of "captain." And here, solely as footnote . . . may I mention how today's stroll through history feels important to my own?

After the slightest recent medical setback, I'm fit as a fiddle and raring to go. After my Edmund's funeral, Falls noted I'd become housebound, unusually silent. Town offered me this small late-life career. Since then, thanks to my research and a certain grit, I've become Falls' most-asked-for guide. How? you ask. Oh, it's not just the social preeminence. —Though, there *is* that.

No, this work takes a certain kind of brain. Narrative imagination. I don't simply recite history. I interpret. Or "interrupt," as my middle-aged daughter jokes. "Mother is a licensed 'historic interrupter,'" my girl told her best book group. They all laughed. So I had to. But do you see so much as a clipboard in my hand? I know my stuff. Born here to the town's best, I *am* the stuff. Local doubters have hinted how—with me so lately under the weather—I am still not "ready." But we'll show them, won't we?

—Maybe form a loose line? and here our more directed walking starts. No, I repeat, dears, more *this* way. Yes, Falls is tiny but, as Blake hinted, the universe exists in a grain of sand. Your immersion in all that our village implies will be followed by some lovely chicken salad. It's served at our best (actually only) bistro, Sally's on the Square. Sally she's a cousin. You won't soon forget her chicken's surprise seasoning. Trade-secret. I naturally keep Cousin's recipe safe up here, on trust. Please don't ask. (Oh, I've had cash offers.)

I see *you* two are certainly dressed for comfort—if you find navigating cobblestones in flip-flops relaxing! To be honest, during the $4.95 hikes, especially on overcast days, if their group acts glum or sounds too much from New Jersey? I let their walk "go short." I call my ten-minute tour the Revised Standard Version. It naturally lacks the grandeur I intend for us today. My comeback is blessed with all this splendid June weather. Youall're entitled to my whole King James seven-block sweep.

Today will be personal. Mrs. Evelyn has far more than dates to share. You see, this is the first walking tour since my resurrection. Got your attention? I did have a slight episode. And I've come out the tunnel's far end a whole new person. I'm back, but somewhat flipped-over, more sunny-side up. More . . . available, maybe more easily surprised. Today, everything old looks freshly varnished. Everything new's gone antique-valuable. And vice-versa.

Most persons believe History only means "Back Then." Maybe that's why it's s'popular? Folks feel that—aside from hearing it—they can change nothing back there. But with me post-bed-rest, I see: History's "Right Now." Why, children, things can change in a second! Like, if I say "RIGHT NOW" again, see? Well, now we're in a whole new *place*. A new and deeper time. I'm just making this part up but it still feels solid. Maybe what we call the Past is just back-issues of "RIGHT NOW"? But today, everything's quickened. Our town's colors look pure as a Benjamin Moore sample-chart.

I feel s'healthy. I want the whip-crack of history's Now to

live and burn for you, too, especially these dear youngsters. Pretty, **that** one. (The "Founded in 1824" script? Written by a sixth-grade teacher, charming girl, my late husband's niece. But she herself sometime seems an enthused sixth-grader. No names. "Either names or tales. Never both," Mother warned. Being a name myself, I always choose tales.)

Falls doctors' wives have been filling in for me during the prescribed two months' recovering. Don't think me ungrateful. But I am told certain ones constantly flee the Big topics— oh, race, litigation, embarrassments. Mrs. Evelyn says: History **is** embarrassments. What else, in toto, was our attractive if deluded Confederacy? Children, here's an easy math problem. In 1860 there were fifty-six million Yankees, but just seventeen million Rebels (and five million of **those** were non-combatant slaves). Young'uns, guess which side was bound to win? Right you are! They should have asked **you**! Ooh, don't get me started. Well, yes, my dear bright child, you already **have**.

With my returning to the history game, expect some surprises. I know **I** do. When my truth's too bluntly presented, I've encountered resistance. But, considering the size and importance of Belmont, my home on Summit Avenue, even if I grow overly candid, what are they going to **do** to me? My recent dustup with the mortal left my appetite for answers boiled far nearer the surface.

Soon you'll all be back on U.S. 301, bound south for Miami. Once there you can scatter Falls' news to the four winds. But I? I remain. I am so old I can't name a number vast enough to describe my great leaf-pile of years. You'll never guess my age.

No takers?

Evelyn's first day back and she draws a bunch of diplomats? So much for our next hour's fun! But I do love having you young ones along. **I** once skipped like that little girl on the end. Oh, the joy of using double-energy to get not one step farther. Why, if I tried that today, I'd best first have medical help handy! Still, Little Evelyn remembers.

You two darlings, now that you've stopped messaging, you are *so* much more attractive. I think people squinting at little screens . . . makes 'em s'ugly. Why, there's a whole immediate world waiting all-up-out here! Look, two cardinals and one blue jay. Bird-colors are so good they flirt with being "cheap."

Moving along nicely. No stragglers, please. Incorporated in 1824, almost immediately made the county seat, Falls still boasts five thousand local souls. We're down from our peak seven-thousand during the commercial boom of '98, 18-98. See that arched bridge? Some say that yonder River Lithium accounts for both our citizens' soothed temperaments and for how hard we find leaving home. Few local students, matriculating up north, last long there.

On the cheap tour, I lead Yankees straight to Town Hall right past secret sites of major vigilante mishaps. Mind you, I withhold nothing out of laziness. I simply foresee which group is historically minded—like youall are. Everybody cannot handle events that once complicated these torchlit streets. Especially certain midnights in the name of hurry-up justice.

Plus, the $4.95-ers get not one dollop of the secretly spiced chicken salad. For them I might point out to Carnegie Library yonder. Might call it, "McKim, Mead & White–*like*." Little joke. Most Garden Staters don't "get" it, ne'ery a smile. Sad, public education. In New Jersey. Why, Princeton was Granddaddy's school.


I feel opened today, and isn't June simply the best? Falls was founded then, right now, June eleventh, 1824. Can't help feel that today's our start-over chance, an anniversary and birth date both. Since the aforementioned surprise medical turn, certain of my personality filters have grown more, I'd say . . . porous. Nerves tuned ever-alert. Times, sunshine almost cuts. What made me three whole minutes late? As I was walking over to greet you, I saw a mangy yellow alleycat trying to carry one of her blind kittens across Main. Just some common collarless housecat without a house. No pedigreed Siamese, mind you. Still, I stopped suddenly. And, as never before, *felt* for that feral thing. In the mother's mouth her young one hung by its neck's loose skin. Both animals faced terrible recent traffic we're getting off the interstate. Mrs. Mother Cat stood waiting for the green light at a human crosswalk. Hesitating, she looked hard left then right, her kitten swaying as, fearful, her head turning, she made sure, sure. Something . . . about . . . her . . . attempts. . . . the endurance required.

—Incorporated in 1824, ever-eager to further erode the church-state divide, Falls has given U.S. history one lieutenant governor and three U.S. cabinet-level politicians no more corrupt than forty-nine *other* states' greedy boys.

I say, "Welcome to Falls," but *would* it welcome all of us, of you? Small-town life is made possible by rarely stating one's true opinions. It's the bargain we strike to keep getting invited places. But my brief illness just showed me: Mrs. Evelyn here— a good sport far too long—has kept so many ghastly secrets rammed safe down her throat. For nigh on to a century. Secrets must, like bad molars, eventually come out, if you're to survive. Oh, imagine finally feeling sunbaked clean. Still, with inherited gifts go responsibilities. And, socially, I do think you have to *be* at a certain level in order to *see* at a certain level.

As for my naming names as we tour, if Falls' historic figures died during the nineteenth century, I consider them fair game, clear up to 1960. Our Tourist Board threatened to stick me back in the booth with the brochures. But I can talk there, too. Before my near-death experience, I defined myself as "conservative," believe it or not. Then I woke up being this whole other person, the person I'd been becoming behind my own back.

And History is the only way they'll let me talk about it!


You, you no-longer-texting pretty youngster skipping on the end? That was a yellow *park* rose, not *your* yellow rose. Well, don't throw it down *now*; you're just doubling your crime. Stay closer by. I see that you brightest children need stimulation, stories. You know bears were once so plentiful 'round here people would eat them like you'd go out and kill a hog? I yet own a family recipe, 1689, for "Bear Pie." Can you guess one thing that lets me so confidently lead you? Leadership genes.

My many-greats-back first American granddad, our founder, is still called "Grand Number One." Big handsome man. He became a Carolinian after getting voted out of the Jamestown settlement for his sanitation ideas.

Yes, throughout my family's seventeenth, eighteenth, nineteenth, and twentieth centuries, we've timbered then farmed till, alas, subdividing (into tasteful five-acre lots) this rich red soil on which we landed, 1607. History for people like us always means our next "Right Now." I won't be kept in my four-poster bed another two months. Whatever the young doctor says, I shall not be held back from my twice-daily appointments with history and you, our honored guests. There is a need to fill in Falls. And my people have always filled those. Bargain for you, and lucky for all involved. Never felt better in my life and do hope you find me making sense? Fine then. So I thought.

\*    \*    \*

Well-preserved, you say? Well, aren't you precious. Care to know my beauty secret? The Twenty-Third Psalm. Keeps coming to Mrs. Evelyn's rescue. On a summer day this warm so early, I have but to quote, **He maketh me lie down in green pastures. He leadeth me beside the still waters.** Best offer I've had in months. Say it and **your** temperature'll plunge, I swear.

On your left, my right actually, please note our handsome Gothic Revival courthouse. See its columns topped with carved cornstalks and tobacco leaves? Done by a local boy who headed north to study at the Pennsylvania Academy under respected sculptor Stirling Calder. (Man was father of the more famous Alexander, twentieth century inventor of "the mobile." Stirling's own daddy forged that huge William Penn atop one tall Philadelphia building.) Our lad from Falls flourished, shot to the head of his class but, first semester, had a breakdown involving the undraped models he was daily subjected to. Of course, to do nude park statues, you need a real stripped thing to look at.

One of his teachers, in a class open to both male **and** female pupils, saw fit to undrape a man, whole-hog—all while making some point about the finer points of the male . . . anatomy. —Is this too much?

Children? Raise your young hands if Mrs. Evelyn either upsets or confuses you. Blame history. See, it's all dead-true. That's what I'm **talk**ing about. American facts cannot be beat. I don't make anything up. In a town this small, fiction's **unnecessary.**

Why, if I told a quarter of what I know, the mayor'd disavow me; probably nationalize my lovely home on Summit. One good thing to put in chicken salad? White pepper, not black, is all I'll say. And if this detail gets mentioned at Sal's bistro later, Mrs. Evelyn is going with deniability, hear? Yes, dear, you may **keep** carrying your yellow rose since you went ahead and **picked** it.

But that art teacher proceeded to yank the cloth off the handiest example of it, I reckon, of the male anatomy. Our delicate Falls boy, whose mother had protected him, even from the minimal coarseness surging along tree-lined Summit Avenue, which you will shortly tread and, as its name implies, is the pinnacle of refined art-loving book-oriented civilized filtration, he saw, for the first time, another . . . portion of another full-grown male's full-throttle . . . anatomy.

From whatever he expected, it must've looked . . . different. The breakdown ensued almost at once. Our boy, later grown ancient, explained (to me as a wee girl) there'd been something about how that brusque teacher whipped off the posing cloth or pouch or whatever. In front of ladies! It was seeing the male model's own shocked expression. As if a man posing nude for his living had no idea as how all that extruded gear had been waiting shaded **un**der there.

In short, in wintry Yankeeland, the most gifted of our village boys fell pure apart. The lad—found wearing four pairs of winter pants, unable to leave his Walnut Street apartment—was shipped straight home to Falls. He was just one of ours to personally Appomattox, to stage a strenuous public washout up North. Me (except my college years), I stayed, and therefore stayed untested. That was your Mrs. Evelyn's fate till—after bearing a child then burying a husband—I somehow ascended, half-despite my upbringing and grim good taste, into being Falls' number one guide. —Well, it gets me out.

\*     \*     \*

Philadelphia's loss proved our gain, as you see in the courthouse capitals up yonder. Truth is, I always think his depicted corn-cobs look a little like hand-grenades. *See* that, youngsters? But the peerless veining along his tobacco leaves makes for plants you can all but smell. O how fragrant it was on market days in our Falls before the U.S. surgeon general, issuing warnings funded by your tax dollars, jinxed Daddy's business, one highly profitable crop. Yes, madam? Good, a question. Say what? The name? Of whom, dear? The sculptor . . . of those agricultural products . . . that . . . predominated . . . hereabouts   for . . . he, oh, I won't lie to you. I just forgot. But only his *name*. Not him. Is that awful? I know it is. Not to answer my dear tourists' first historical question, all while having by heart our artist's entire genealogy.

When I started telling you about that model being stripped naked? I *feared* its drama would take up those very brain-cells soon needed for entry-level information. I knew the boy's mother as clearly as I see you here—with your digital cameras and some sunscreen blobbed beside the nose of that pretty little girl with the Afro on the end, there, that *is* better— names are the first things you lose, children. He never got real famous, anyway!

I admit I am up onto the very Everest of my time. Air thins. Even ladies' hair thins. Tree-line soon teeters far below. My doctor told me to go back to whole milk after years of slenderizing skimmed. For bones. But *you* try this, twice daily. To go, Moses-like, leading tours each weekday at ten then four, without the three-ring-binders that certain First Baptist tour-ladies in their early-fifties must read aloud, read *badly*. The doctor at Duke told me I'd had "many strokes" till my daughter explained he meant "mini strokes." As in "miniskirts." Well, that certainly spelled relief!

One thing, I can still **walk**. You need to, leading pedestrian tours. Even my $4.95ers respect that. Yes, quite the hiker, my vigorous Scot tradition, kilts, knotted calves. Can still do five miles before my first cup of coffee but his name . . . Clarence! Clarence Royce Whitted! Born summer 1888, died not twenty-nine years back just two blocks north, 211 Summit.

I **will** point out his house, if one of you youngsters reminds me. Volunteers? Excellent. This pretty little colored girl right here in front. I choose **you**, darlin. Cute as a button and bright, I can always tell. Our most famous sculptor got collected: Why, his statue of Chief Geronimo (1829–1909) stands in our governor's mansion. Dear Clarence, like a much much older brother, befriended me while I was just a questioning if not-unpretty child. So, yes, folks, these crop capitals would prove his masterpiece post-Philadelphia-breakdown. —How'm I doing? Be honest. Facts console people. Folks just gulp dates down. They think they can permanently **know** a thing.

My only child blames me for "hooking" her on history, like some drug. This daughter, "Meade," family name, she's sixty already. (Time, I **swear**!) This morning Meade begged me to stay in bed or, if I was determined to risk this, at least to stick with just facts till I ease back in. "Beside the stilled waters, preparest a table for me in the presence of mine enemy, **Forgetfulness**!"

Now, feeling better and certainly hope you all are. Good. Confidence is the thing.

What say we just keep moving southward, whatever befalls our li'l scouting party? Pioneer spirit. Fact is, while still a girl, on Sunday afternoons, my parents and my friends and theirs, we promenaded right around the Square here, still wearing white church-clothes. Crinolines made their very private sound, whispery, crackling, even. A brass band's always playing Victor Herbert or your top hymns. My, but full sun is warming. Mind these cobblestones, now. Tricky even for my two-inch heels.

Do these stones feel historically accurate? Should. These are the *originals*, children. Certain ones are said to have come over as ballast on English ships. "Pavers" can snag even a low heel and break a hip. Certain local ladies my age or younger get so worried about falling, they want to spread tar clear over stones' own history. Why, if every generation did that, what'd be left to walk my tours *through*?

Good college friend of mine she just attended the burial at Arlington Cemetery, for the last sailor found in wreckage of a Civil War iron-side. Government had held his body since the seventies, the 19-70s. Finally DNA science grew sophisticated to where it could trace which crew member he was. Then they actually contacted that poor sailor-boy's living kin. This would likely be the last-ever Civil War burial. Big ceremony: Secretary of the Navy spoke, Marine band played, horse-drawn cortege waited out front, news photographers, a nation-mourns-type-thing. They saved that chapel's whole front pew for the dead seaman's modern offspring. And his kin they turned up, all right. Wearing shorts. One, I am told, in a huge yellow Tweetie Bird T-shirt. Here came grieving men and women slouching to Arlington in flip-flops!

—No, not criticizing *you*, dear. Why, that was a state funeral, and we're in summer with an outdoor group seeking more Mrs. Evelyn information. Apples, oranges. —Even so, I say a nation with no rules, no formality—with only an obese off-duty sapping casualness—it just makes China's takeover that much easier!

Let's keep ours at least a high-end $19.95 nation, right?! Humor again, see. But, in light of some of your footwear, we trailblazers had best stick to historical Falls' sidewalks, agreed? Lunch ahead, remember. You've got a secret treat in store. And the hungrier you get, the more you'll want to know her cold chicken's spices. Don't even *think* of begging me. Sally is a first cousin with a private formula and Mrs. Evelyn's lips are sealed.


We'll soon turn onto tree-lined Summit Avenue. It's been the scene of major coming-out parties, seven murders, more suicides than have ever been called that. One good thing modern is medicine. Thank you, madame, for passing me your brochure to use as my personal hand fan. S'thoughtful. Are you a schoolteacher? I thought so. It's getting toasty out, despite the spring left in my step. Guess how old? Still un-willing? Maybe that *is* personal. Oh, I hail from a long line of walkers, and I do not mean the rolling aluminum kind! Another modern advance is how the race-subject can be addressed front-and-center, at least among thinking persons like us. And especially, my lucky first time back, to draw, like ours today, a "mixed" tour.

Meade, my one child, eats and breathes history but has a willful streak I find mysterious. My daughter just idolizes Jefferson. It's beyond "having a crush." At sixty, she still calls him "Master Tom" or, after 'bout three martinis, "Massah Tom."

Meade's backyard has an eighteenth century "knot-garden" and nothing in hers was *not* first in his. The man ghostwrote our Declaration at age thirty-five and who can deny his unbelievable genius? Of course, *I* bought her all those worshipful children's biographies, before we understood the full extent of his interest in animal husbandry, if you grown-ups see my meaning. —Never a beauty, Meade. Took after my husband's mother, poor dear thing. (But is beauty that important now? I notice, out at the mall, how the utter lack of looks doesn't stop those countless frog-like couples from rubbing all over against each other.)

My daughter belongs to various local book groups. One still reads books. They bused to Monticello last month, with old me tagging along. Dear Meade keeps a copy of Houdon's life-sized bust of him in her dining room. She has propped a man's fedora on his head, cocked at an angle. I asked her, only once, why that hat was there. Meade, now sixty, answered, *"Cute* on him. —Other questions, Historical Interrupter?" She often mentions Jefferson's weight and height, red hair. My daughter likes to concede how shy he was. Except, I guess, around his personal staff.

We'd just arrived in Monticello's great foyer. As you know it's lined with Lewis and Clark's stuffed animal specimens. Our tour guide that day proved a lovely undergraduate girl, studying history at the University of Virginia. And before we were properly *in* the house, she brightly mentioned our third President's live-in slave mistress. Well, Meade emitted one sound between a hiccup, a gasp and, I guess, growling. I sensed trouble ahead. We visit Monticello so often Meade has one of their out-of town family memberships. And, during earlier tours, back in the early times when "slaves" were still called "servants," Jefferson's form of sexual exactions went cleanly unmentioned. But today's pretty tour-girl waded straight to Ms. Sally Hemings's becoming mother to Jefferson's, what? six-or-eight bright dusky sideline children.

Well, my daughter's face it duskied up. Even *I* know that things have changed and sex is more freely discussed now. Good thing, too. (Say *what*? You want more of the tour's walking part? Soon as your Mrs. Evelyn gets herself cooled off a little. But what I am guiding here aloud is *itself* quite a procession. If you'll bother to listen. History cannot be sidestepped, whatever your footwear.)

Getting back to Monticello, for the few of you still interested? Well, thank you. Meade was about to embarrass all of us. Miss Docent, dignified, trained, she stopped, pointed: "Question? *This* lady—"

"I mean," Meade began. "What could a man of his refinement and some semi-literate girl-servant possibly find to discuss all those years?"

Well, everybody looked at their feet. I just wish I'd taught my daughter more directly about birds and bees and men's willingness to do or pay anything for it. Maybe my cowardice about sex-talk stunted our Meade, you think? I've finally become a liberal but could-be too late! Oh, my daughter is intelligent, forever forcing excellent books on me. Meade is the admired executive vice president of our local college. But I should not have withheld her childhood sex-information. She's never had one boyfriend. I'd be glad with her finding a nice woman roommate, maybe a trust-funded potter out of Sarah Lawrence or somewhere. But it's just always only Meade off alone being Meade. If sex is embarrassing, virginity's worse.

But here, at Monticello, my daughter grew so belligerent toward that girl docent, staring absolute daggers. I confess to stepping slightly away from my own flesh and blood. Our tour-guide had lovely skin and you could see she was of good family. Funny, her name was Martha, same as his dead wife, Jefferson's. Confronted by Meade, she did not back off answering the question. "In common, miss? Sally Hemings was the beautiful younger half-sister of his recently dead wife. Jefferson had made said wife a deathbed promise never to remarry. So, what had they in common? Living in sight of each other here, way out here, on their 'little mountain,' day in, day out? Sex. No charts are necessary, right? We all know he was certainly high-energy and project-oriented. —Now, moving on to something more germane about the genius we've come to celebrate, ahead on your left, please note . . ."

Well, my daughter's breathing had grown so labored, she had to cross her arms to keep standing. Meade's expectations of Jefferson are, I fear, just not realistic!

She will tell you any day: her two muses are the scientific Jefferson and her dog, a pug she calls Wallis in honor of the Duchess of Windsor, one of the most selfish people ever to draw breath. All pugs, lacking actual noses, snuffle like a TB ward. To top that, *her* Wallis, he has asthma. And here my Meade is, right *in* Monticello, grabbing this attractive UVA girl by one arm to spin her around and tell her to please go wash her mouth out with lye soap, period-appropriate! She said "*lye* soap"! Implying a mistruth, I suppose.

Then Meade announces that this short tour has, for her anyway, near about "contaminated a founder"! Well, right there I told Meade this girl's welcome had not been free-form. *She'd* not written that foyer speech. (Not the way that I—being always over-prepared—sometimes allow mine to evolve, if I get, like youall, an especially receptive group.) No, Martha's had been scripted by the very historians you see on PBS. And I explained to everyone: this young coed had not *herself* climbed up on any helpless slave girl. So why be mad at *her*, Meade? But truth-telling is essential and, though embarrassed for my daughter, I basically found it tonic.

\*    \*    \*

Say what, young lady? Local hangings? Oh, my dear. Yes, a few. But, child, it is scarcely past ten in the a.m. What put you in-mind of **those**? Psychic little girl you are, Voodoo. The bistro has probably not yet deboned sufficient white meat to become our chicken salad and here we've already hit the historic racial punishment question! I prefer tucking that closer to my tour's end, once I get you all back nearer your cars. My $4.95ers don't even get to **hear** the pivotal American word "slavery."

But, you did pay nearly twenty-dollars adults, children's—five, I believe. So Mrs. Evelyn, as local hostess to history's embarrass-ing present-tense, should not deny you. Of course, I'd be going up against the Chamber of Commerce boys again. There are three main censors, uniformly Young Republicans, all named "Skeeter," each one's mind a forty-watt bulb. They'll once more likely threaten me with silence. But . . . only if one amongst you should return to the Visitors Center and gripe afterwards. Well, but you promise?

If I do tell the "whole truth and nothing but," you'll defend your Mrs. Evelyn? Show of hands. Well, I declare. I am a wee bit flattered. My first day back and maybe our nation's still a Democracy, after all!

But, should anybody care to **skip** this part, go wait over in that shady old bandstand. I'll send my teacher's pet here to retrieve you the second my topic gets easier.

Well, now that Miss Flip-Flop's gone, the answer's "yes." Some. Some hangings **did** occur. This has never before been a tour-stop. I am possibly overstepping. But, see this giant sycamore right here, silent? It did not go uninvolved. —And, m' young ones: the proper verb here is a person's being "hanged." Not "hung." That is something else.

"Vigilantism" I'd call mighty unfortunate. See, poor white workers resented freed slaves taking their jobs for even lower wages. Much of the South's trouble came down to our poor whites and how very little my **own** people, the more fortunate badminton Summit Avenue crowd, did to control Caucasian riffraff hereabouts. Gentry looked the other way. Generations living in a . . . cloud and I don't know what silly mists! Bourbon, certain ones. Sad comment—especially from a town once called "the Athens of This Far into Eastern North Carolina."

But we will always have the poor, certain uneducated bog-Irish lurking about, inebriated, intermarrying and making Saturday mischief. The facts about lynching, all over the U.S. and not merely in the South, appall any thinking person.

(But, wait. Owing to this child's question, aren't I suddenly telling you Falls completely out of order? Seems I was just getting our pretty town founded in that butter-colored 1824. To offer you a newer reference point, that yellow mother cat trying and get her poor blind baby across four lanes of traffic? they occurred right here today. Does that give you a sense of the epic pageantry involved? But this question, see, reorganizes me just when I can likely least afford it.)

I am told that, between the 1880s and the early 1960s when it went completely out of fashion, thank **God**, at least five thousand persons were done away with in this savage manner. And zero prosecutions, since the men who do it too often wear pillowcase hoods or pull their hat brims down or **are** your actual sheriff. So this very sycamore, grown up to shade a courthouse so McKim, Mead & White–**like**. Thank you for that knowing smile. I just **knew** you were a schoolteacher. Yes, African American schoolteachers warm my heart. I am proud of those who look after their **own** community. You folks and your little girl who just asked this question, I **assume** she is yours, do seem so bright, which just makes **my** work that much easier. Why, if this tree could talk, we'd pay it not to.

Two of our worst hangings depended on participation from this selfsame sycamore. But, no, Professional Educator, you hear that passive construction I just indulged? It was weak of me and is shaming. That was the **old** me talking, the pre-ministroke Evelyn, a lifelong default-setting Daughter of the American Revolution. Fact is, this tree had little to do with it. Plain human meanness inspires such acts.

Most of the hanged men, all ours were men, proved innocent. But only afterwards, see. The white girl recanted but she'd always been homely and had lied from day-one about having random boyfriends. And that stolen silver punch bowl—very valuable, made by Gorham, an early prototype of the "Viking Bowl" shown at 1893's Columbian Exposition— was later found under a dining-room table. It had been placed there the day before by one cautious housepainter, not wanting to drip enamel on that grade of sterling. The owner who reported it stolen? **she** did not know this costly wedding gift's whereabouts. Oh, and that lady she was very hard on herself afterwards. Later railed against herself for having accused a boy named Sammy, someone she'd known, liked, and hired his entire short life. It was terrible for **everybody**, really. Shocking when country men dragged that hollering child my age from a jail cell where police had stuck him just as a one-night lesson.

Poppa said I could absolutely **not** go downtown, what with this mess roaring everywhere. But you know me. In my nightclothes and slippers I simply monkey-climbed my bedroom's wisteria arbor, just came running these two blocks here to Courthouse Square, hoping to save our funny quiet Sammy. Running, I planned a speech! I feared grown-ups might reprimand *me* for being on the public street in a nightgown; but what with torches and the screaming, everybody was looking up at what was, not supposed to be, but hung twenty feet right in this tree. Poor boy. Skin ashy-gray already. And hadn't done not one thing wrong, Sammy. Oh my my. This is . . . *extra*. Must not tell, you must not tell, I ever told that.

So . . . but. I know how long she suffered, the woman that accused our Sammy wrongly, because, well, she was no stranger to me, but closely related by blood. Let it not be said I do not implicate my own family, given its central role in our town's and nation's founding.

After round-one of my TIA mini-strokes, they said I'd only keep "losing function." But I have also gained things. Have taken onboard a whole new admiration for the visible world, plus certain old secrets I am saddened to finally know. But human life and history, it's not all subtraction, children, no. We're added on to, too. Or so I . . .

Is it not a bit humid out today? Surely we heirs of these very Carolinas' founders should be used to heat by now. Northern European stock was just not meant for this Africanized tropical climate. Imagine what-all noon might bring. Should have worn a big garden hat. But it seemed, in my hall mirror, too "intentional," overtly picturesque. Even for you, the more educated Deluxe crowd. I was not thinking practically, nor of myself. So many little concessions to others. Well, what say we tarry a moment in this tree's generous shade. See how many uses a sycamore can serve? Note its handsome mottled bark, unique . . . botanically.

You don't usually *find* an Altar Guild churchwoman willing to meet with strangers on public streets, much less go near the subject of race. But me, I am stronger than that. Mother brought us up different. She made her own mistakes but the woman learned. We'll soon stroll off onto Summit Avenue, runs parallel. I'll point out Belmont, 1824, my own home but we can't go in, as it is her day for downstairs vacuuming and she'd kill me. —But some iced tea would be excellent about now. Is it increasingly hot out here or is this some . . . residue from my recent unpleasantness?

You were kind to earlier point out my springy step. That's due to titanium. This hip is made from the material that forges jet rocket airplanes. I am secretly so modern, what holds me up is what keeps airplanes in the sky! Now, watch out ahead for these huge tree roots coming. See how they've buckled the sidewalk? I've been after our mayor for years to . . . Children, said, "care-ful."

My! No.
    Ohsh! EEEee.
    Dear me, Lord. But see how fast I caught myself? Family tradition. Basically fine. Only let me, gather myself . . . somewhere. Please let me sit. Sorry. Better. Give me one wee minute. Why, thank you, child. Your yellow rose all for me? Can't people be wonderful? You are so sweet. Now that this flower is **both** of ours, I love it more for being stolen. Wish I'd broken more laws while I could still reach 'em.
    Feeling better'n better. Mustn't worry. Most of my days are spent losing then finding things and almost falling but, knock

wood, not. Just shook me's all. Here I was, trying to clear **your** paths! Typical. My nearly falling hurts way less than having it so **seen**.

Let's all test these park benches, what say? Think it's too early for our slipping into Sally's place? Could one of you ladies steal over, just tap on her door, ask if I and my today's stellar group might come in, just sit a spell under their electric fans while they ready our lunch? Thank you, ma'am, for going. I would near-about kill right now for a simple glass of tea.

Upsetting . . . Jefferson. And a grown daughter who disbelieves in DNA while living jealous of one poor trapped slave girl. My late Edmund was a whiz at earning money but not enjoying it. I had to seem to enjoy for all of us and it . . .

These spells come over me now. And, should this episode persist and expand, you will not be charged, even given how far I have already got . . . Here, more nice Victorian reproduction benches in the shade of a real sycamore. **The** sycamore. Sweet Sammy's tree.

Poor Meade. I did encourage her love of history. But historical monogamy is impossible. Lately she's joined a charismatic sect (if still Episcopal). My daughter acts so hidebound, old-fashioned. I feel "newer" than she. No, what's the concept? Yes, "younger" than she. Whenever I visit Meade she keeps trying to give me tours of her tiny town house. Lead **me**! Why, there's not one good thing in there I didn't **give** her! Seems history keeps crushing us with what we're proudest of.

Times, I just don't **know** m' precious Meade. Is she and that poor wheezing dog all I'll really leave behind? Have I made even one small stride? Doesn't our white-folks' tribe just keep falling back, ever weaker, in the pursuit of . . . pursuit? And since I nearly tripped, here I am perspiring, too. "Glowing," we were taught to say as girls. Field-hands "sweated." Now so am I.

Certainly wish that teacher would get back from Sally's. Not wholly myself today. Might some man run check where that other one wandered off to, after I trusted her? See? The restaurant's directly yonder. Their plaque is still turned with "Closed" facing outward. But there is another side. You can fall at any minute. No help then. But the main sign can so soon reverse . . . can suddenly say "Open." To us all. **As the sheep of his pasture, enter into his gates and under his palm fans.** There will be a first seating but next there will be a raising up and then the last leveling. I only hope that those, however flawed, who battled for enlightened views, those whose families treated theirs as close-knit members of . . . I only hope, in this town, which is all I know of home but which can actually be a festering little bandstand pagoda made of solid shit, if you youngsters will excuse my sudden potty-mouth.

Your children disappoint. The Bible tells us that. Do you mind? I feel I need this entire bench to stretch out on. Could that prettiest child come fan me, please? Others go stand nearer the tree, now. All of you. But someone spry do run for Cousin Sally, say, "Mrs. Evelyn is poorly and down in the Square." Hardly anyone anywhere knows now. Who my people were. When to wear real, shined, self-respecting shoes. I feel . . . where **was** I? Let us take me from the top.

"Foundered in 1824, it . . ." No. Bad. Am reversing again. They told me I might and to come quick, so if. "If so." Not good, see? Quick, send your strongest child fleet-of-foot to young Doc Worth. He got us through the dreadful Spanish flu, my whooping cough. He'll know. I **said**: Run fetch Doc. Yes, you. Said stop fanning me. Run, you pretty little nigra-girl I been spoiling. Do as I tell you, I say . . . Why stare? Have you never seen a lady? Have you never seen an actual **lad**-y, you?

Deliver me . . . someone even phone m' Meade. Text, girls,

text *now*! Meade's organized, knows everybody. Scolded me this morning I was not ready. This concludes any walking tour's possible walking . . . Full refund. How much can one con*vey* in an hour?

And now that I look closer at you people, I find you're all unknown to me! Not one family resemblance present. Why, you've swarmed into Courthouse Square uninvited, empty-handed, wearing shower shoes. Pretenders. All you've ever brought us off that godless highway is carpetbags, Dutch elm disease and fire ants. You're squashing local cats and being absolutely no help to your elders.

Eager to be *told* history by those who're mainly made of its embarrassments. And you expect to hear that for under twenty-dollars per riffraff-head? Oh, Mrs. Evelyn thinks not. And I've already spared you half the worst! Lady school-principals caught working as actual Raleigh whores. Mayors stealing us blind for thirty years and then forgiven. Preachers corrupting little boys . . . I mean, of diaper age! I've never given one tour worth even $4.95. Why? 'Cause, if I took you up to the full-twenty-dollar truth-level? your ears'd bleed. Admit you're here to suck culture from us, the way black snakes put fangs into Momma's white hens' eggs.

God gives so little guidance to His faithful guides. He must've taken early retirement. Left no practical instructions. Where *are* still waters to lead you people off beside? Presence of mine enemies, oh, I know you now. Such cold stares from false familiars. Have I just lost *all* my last looks? You the country posse come for me?

And, as for you, ma'am. Why should you of all people wear short-shorts? To show us those huge white tree legs? Sequoias of foam-rubber! Is such germ warfare your Jersey way? Nasty.

Please cover those. History's hard enough without your needing to display all that! No shame? No home-mirror? You think
Jefferson would've been caught dead looking like you anyplace?
even in his house? even while doing Sally anywhere? even after
candles-out? Where's the least bit of **dig**nity?

Here, you people, at least come help me to stand. That's all
I need. Will breathe easier. Well, do as I *say*. Here, you and you
and *that* on the legs, come help me rise. Try leaning me up
solid, back against Sammy's tree.

All right, you Federal spies. Hard bargain you drive. Those
your final terms? You were always going to win. It is: use seed-
less green grapes, white pepper, lots of mace, toast those damn
almonds. And now you've got our secret? go home up North.
Back off away from me.

Believe I hear help coming.

Falls' ambulances will know me.

Mustn't be *found* like this, fallen among barefoot strangers,
down, and in a public park.


But, wait, attention, group.

Last thing. And I'm meaning this.

Look! Why . . . there . . . so suddenly . . .

Directly to your left.

It's . . . it's . . . —**Green pastures!**

# FOURTEEN FEET OF WATER
# IN MY HOUSE

COME MIDNIGHT I was the sixty-five-year-old owner of a river-view Colonial, asleep on his second story. By three a.m., the river was my first floor and wanted my second.

I kept an aluminum flatboat in the backyard. Hadn't thought of the thing since last bass season. And yet it waked me like some good pet. Its prow kept beating gentle against my upstairs bedroom wall. Spooked, I set my bare white feet . . . into six inches of cold gritty water. I soon went headfirst out my highest window into a waiting boat. It was all so weird it felt natural.

An aged outboard motor, untouched for months, somehow sputtered to life. Starting off I felt fearless as a boy. No streetlamp worked. Just a crescent moon refolding over currents as I chugged between treetops.

Prediction, as usual, failed us. "This is real," I told my Evinrude's racket. "Dad's house is ruined. —Boat seems fine, though. People probably stranded. . . ."

Our neighborhood is called "Riverside." No lie! Three-acre lots, four-car garages, one dock per home. This happened September 15, 1999, a North Carolina hurricane named Floyd. Winds, threatened all afternoon, proved nothing much—the unexpected sneaks in after dark.

Tonight what first seemed silence became a million suckings, bubblings, gurgles. Instead of rain driving down, it was black wetness canceling us from underneath. Wind spares *some* things. Water, climbing, testing, claims them all.

At least in mid-September it wasn't too cold. I sound like my late wife: Jean was always finding the glass half-full. Now everything was.

I motored our Alumacraft from house to major house. I made all my usual walker's shortcuts but now at roof level.

The Hutchesons, half-dressed, on their third-floor turret, stood behind two barbecue grills set ablaze as signal pyres. I tied up to their Flemish-bond chimney, calling, "Ride, folks?"

"Well, well, our favorite insurance agent. We covered for 'acts of God'?" Hutch, wearing only polka-dot boxers, sounded amused. "Because just yesterday I paid a man twenty-six thousand for finally painting this doggone barn!" Hutch kept gesturing toward water, hinting with his arms that it should split like the Red Sea. Hutch laughed till he coughed. His wife gave me a look. Their teenage daughter said, "Even tonight, Dad, you talk only about money, Dad. You're sadder even than *this*,"

and she nodded toward our former neighborhood. We all eased
Hutch into my boat. He kept laughing.


Familiar streets seemed the canals of Venice, and we always
had right-of-way. Humidity sogged your clothes then shoes.
The darkness smelled of transmission fluid and ginger lilies.
We heard roarings from the distance.

In a friend's sunken carport, his new Lexus acted mighty
shorted-out: under five feet of green sludge, it ran every possible
lighting combination, brights to dim flashers, oddly beautiful,
a dead loss. —Which neighbors were home, which drowned?

We tacked by all three Alston boys paddling boogie boards,
wearing just Hawaiian swim trunks. They told us the mall was
still above water, rescue trucks gathering there.

These kids had surfed since age six and now, splashing off
no place, called back to me, "Is this not *awesome*?" —For once,
the word fit.

I might've shouted: "It's not some mountain stream you're
swimming in. Our neighborhood's gone septic tank, kids." But
they would all three learn this later. I just let it go. You can't
monitor everything.


On top of a gazebo, Charlie Hague, four-time winner of our
Top All-Round Golfer Cup, kneeling in pj's, stared out of an
avocado facial. Tonight Charlie showed how he'd maintained
his Hollywood handsomeness. Face caked green, the guy
looked like some cannibal headhunter. The Hutchesons helped
Charlie and his tough-talking third wife down into our sixteen-
footer. The wife rose behind him, pressing one finger across her
lips. For her, a flood seemed almost worth letting all of River-

side see how her ex-Marine CEO primped for usual beauty rest. —Turns out Charlie, as my late wife called it, "moisturized."

*Moisturize!* Our mall lot, overlit by twelve generators, gave the only brightness for square miles. Approached by boat, it looked like the shores of Heaven, I swear. I started dropping off my neighbors. Nine drowned bodies were already stretched beyond the dumpsters. Seven had been non-swimmers from the projects.

People said not to worry, refrigerated trucks were on the way.

## II.

I JUST KEPT BOATING back for more. Excellent—staying busy. Since Jean died, aside from my golf-and-coffee pals, it'd been mostly me and the leading sports channels. One genius secretary pretty much ran my office. I had perfected Sitting on My Dock with Bourbon-and-Water, had brought that sport to new heights.

Now? I'd been shanghaied back to action. Odd, but losing everything made me feel decades younger. That couldn't last. (Adrenaline, always a good idea, seemed the opposite of prediction!) The other side of pick-up is pure letdown.

My neighborhood stood two stories deep in . . . well, in shit. Wasn't this some early practice-form of dying? And yet, at first at least, I felt alive because again a little useful.

Didn't know quite how this mess had happened. But, some way, I knew exactly what to do.

\*  \*  \*

Bart Tarlton waved a flashlight, signing I should boat on past, just leave them atop their carport roof. "Others will be by, and she's not . . . ready." He shone the beam on Caitlin, squatted, arranging soggy child-photographs across their roof's white gravel.

"Cait's got lots of Saran Wrap up here." Bart sounded sad. "She's busy sealing all of Carolyn's baby pictures. Keeps saying, 'First things first.' —Thanks for stopping, pal, but we've got to get through this part. Hell, where *else* are we going?" He shook his head. "Oh, and Mitch?" he hollered as we passed. "Sure glad your dad didn't live to see this. I know he thought the world of your house."

It amazed me that while his own wife sat playing paper dolls with baby photos, Bart would be imagining my father.

True, this would have re-killed Dad. In 1950 he overpaid for our stone manse, guaranteeing my boyhood social standing. On a street known for its two brain surgeons and one college president, my dad managed Milady's FootFair. To make the fierce down payment on our 1939 Colonial, he gladly knelt half-a-century before Falls' best and worst female feet.

Dad's wish? That I run wild with our Episcopal rector's delinquent (if platinum-blond) sons. We did shoot hoops; we raced our boats; we made bourbon both a daily staple and a science experiment. Still, neighbors never called Dad anything but "Shoe" Connelly. "Proves I know my stock," the sweet guy smiled.

He titled our house "Shadowlawn"; put a sign in the yard; painted its front door a shiny tomato-red. Pals forgave me. Being scrawny and funny, I knew to never claim that much. Always sent these buddies home when Dad, back late from work, three vodkas in, started, "Best in town? I'd say young Diana de Pres has the toes of Greek goddess. —Joy to see, touch, and serve."

Dawn came pink and gold but with many a wet and sorry sight. We puttered by drowned long-horned cattle—washed into town from where? They'd stacked up under a bridge like something from the Wild West. And on top of a pile of such carcasses near the underpass? two live deer, a mother and baby, just stood grooming each other.

I heard, "Mister? Boat! Mister Boat!?" Soon I wrestled onboard two skinny water-treading black kids. They'd Australian-crawled clear from the projects. The weakest swimmer was looped within an inner tube he kept blowing up while kicking it forward. Grateful, each tried shaking hands, even while—with my bad back—I fought to pull them in. Water beaded like mercury across their hair. Kids were about fifteen and looked scared to death. We didn't talk much. I had a boat. They were in it now.

With them settled, I figured I'd go rescue a gal my age I've always liked. She'd probably be alone tonight: her dashing husband was two-timing her with his freckled college-boy "executive assistant." Every local knew except maybe my friend.

I motored toward her now: our generation's all-time Riverside glamour-puss. The face that launched . . . at least one bass boat. Diana's were certainly the feet that kicked off my dad's highest praise. "White marble," he'd announce, as Mom and I gave each other steady sickened stares. But Shoe Connelly was right, Diana looked ideal. Unfair advantage in a town this small.

I hated loving the very one my Dad would want for me, for us. I lacked the looks, height, trust fund. Only had such access as Shoe'd overpaid for. (Dad would love seeing me tonight, boat at the ready, with an oar and a tarp. I'd become a beloved entitled ole coot, so naturalized he's colorless.)

And yet, even now, with me sogged and sixty-five, I still pictured my ninth-grade crush. She'd be stranded on her second-story balcony, wearing satin like her "Juliet" in our school play. Figured I'd go muscular up a vine, then bring her to my waiting gondola below, her satin frock pressed damp within these brawny arms, etc., whatever. Pathetic. Still, I aimed her way. —I am a widower now.


Churches, as sunken as private homes, somehow looked sadder, having once claimed more. At least their steeples gave every boater bearings. As I motored past First Baptist's chromium upright, it showed steel rivets, a fuselage of copper flashing, so much rusting armor now. But, poking above our waterline, each denomination still insisted on itself.

In our Williamsburgy town, even the synagogue sports a Georgian portico.. Churches are often set face-to-face on corners opposite, paired like fighting cocks. A minaret might not be long in coming. —Ours is a God-fearing community. Afraid of what? Plagues? Floods?

Looking clear downtown, I saw just trees and steeples bristling into the distance. And over all this, without form, and void, news-channel helicopters getting great shots of poor people clawing up their chimneys, waving bedsheets.


You didn't need to be a structural engineer to know that most of Falls' old homes were done for. You let a house, however well-made, stand in twenty feet of wastewater for one week, that's curtains. The mold alone will kill you ever afterward.

I sputtered past the Epsteins' pink-stucco Spanish Colonial, the Murchesons' replica of Andrew Jackson's home, the Hermitage. In its basement rec room I'd first felt a girl's breast, the left one only, but enough aplenty to interest me for life. Now I banked behind my dead wife's girlhood home. The breast in question had not, I'm afraid, been Jean's. But, here among the camellias of her mother's formal garden, Jean and I were married. Now around our altar-pergola's Corinthian columns, sewage bobbled.

I chose not to Alumacraft past *my* house. I recalled overhearing a local dowager say, "Those shanty Irish *would* shoehorn themselves into the biggest home right on the river." Photo albums were most of what I wanted, and my bronzed baby-bootie that Dad made much of. Those, stowed in the attic, might still be safe. But for now I had *people* to collect . . .


My boy passengers sat discussing friends: "You think Lottie still be on they roof? Wouldn't leave the little ones. Somebody bound to find them. Could be, this city man, once he finish gettin' his own folks out, might could go on back, fetch Lottie and them . . ."

So my passengers saw me as a town employee! Paid to rescue them. Hmmm. That was okay, I guess, but strange. (Son of a "Shoe," after all.) What had I expected, a Lifesaving Merit Badge? Did it really change anything—being assumed? Till now hadn't that been pretty much my family's life's goal hereabouts?


Unlike the boys' friends, most of mine had been rescued by first light. Other Riverside boaters, using personal canoes, Sailfishes, and paddle wheels, had hoisted neighbors off their butlers' quarters, SUV roofs, pin oaks, and from the head of at least one life-sized bronze Saint Francis. My bass boat had fetched maybe thirty to the mall when we finally sloshed into the yard of the woman I have loved since age thirteen. (In fact, her left breast was my first breast, ever. I can admit that since she wouldn't remember it.)

Her Wright-style low-slung home seemed missing in action, but I saw she'd breaststroked toward the only sturdy vertical around. I found our town beauty treed like a wet raccoon.


Prediction so regularly fails me: For fifty years I've believed she was maybe meant as mine. Dad encouraged such faith. He thought our owning in Riverside outranked lace-curtain Irishness, made us Lord Proprietors. Man never really guessed that "Shoe" is a servant's name. (I fought to keep it from him. Of that at least, I'm proud.)

She'd been born rich with red hair and green eyes so you didn't know if you were coming or going. Seeing how I and six other boys from our cul-de-sac all loved her, she had already found a substitute for me. Diana promoted her plainer sidekick for my romantic attention. She offered me the girl who let Diana copy algebra homework, who held her coat and laughed at her usual jokes. She was Diana's gal Friday who personally delivered her sarcastic notebook-paper come-ons to us sad hopeful males. One such note, hand-brought, explained: *Jean here is smarter than I and looks-wise grows on people. She has scads more tobacco money than I'll get (even when Dad finally goes). And trust me, honey, she loves you WAY more. Choose Jean, Mitch.*

I stared into the fine if simple face of this love-note delivery girl. She could not know how its contents had just shifted her future and mine. "Return answer?" she, innocent, asked. —I smiled at her.

I kept that note for twenty years. A town beauty always makes such matches for her handmaids. And I somehow had done as told. Was Jean also following orders? Dad, even knowing Jean's exact net worth, still always treated her with fond pity.

And yet our marriage proved fairly lively, forty years. Maybe not a love match at first, but . . . practical. We were really just best friends. I guessed my own face's sketchy net worth. I'd really wanted to head north to college, where my brightness— or goodness, whatever—might get me noticed as more than the by-product of flat-footed others.

My Jean had proved a wit, a "man's woman" regularly out snagging bass with me from this same boat. I had chosen well, at least, in picking the one who picked Jean *for* me.

The treed survivor's hair, this wet, had all but disappeared. Not since our thirteenth year had I ever caught her without benefit of makeup. Now, aside from orange-nylon panties, poor thing was damp and bare as God made her. Coiled around a rough-barked pine tree, her white marble looked curdled all over.

"Uh-oh. That old lady she butt-naked," one kid observed.

"It's okay," I said. "I **know** her."

"Gosh, it's Mitch. And me hoping to be rescued by some handsome Yankee new to town. —But, hell, no secrets 'twixt old friends, hunh?"

"Diana." I nodded as if greeting her at the club.

Her lips were blue (the nipples also, truth be told). I had the tarp in my boat and soon saw her wrap herself as if in sable. This old lady left up the tree should've founded Flirters Anonymous. There have been years when I worried I still loved her more than I did my wry, quiet wife.

## III.

WHAT I REMEMBER best is how the flood confused or dignified our animals. Some neighbor kids I ferried would hold their
tetchy Siamese cats or keep their shivery Yorkie terriers wound
in doll blankets. I saw how it comforted even three-year-olds
to take care of something still smaller than themselves. Two
swimming water moccasins tried crawling in the boat with us
and had to be discouraged. But I couldn't bring myself to hurt
one with the oar. You'd just redirect them and hope they'd find
some log somewhere.

A few birds were very noisy, as if sounding the alarm for all
us other creatures. But crows, being real intelligent and often
loud, kept oddly silent. They lined up along lower tree limbs,
looking out and down like disappointed tourists.

The oddest things floated. A yellow high heel. One oil-
painted photo, some bride and groom shown smearing cake
across each other's mouths. Its wooden frame, like a life pre-
server, bobbled them along.

I felt more shocked by each dead drifting dog (a boxer, one
beautiful collie). Here came swollen pigs and cows. We'd pass
clever living deer swimming here and there in a strange mild-
looking panic.


At eight-thirty a.m., having found the two boys and then Diana,
I figured I had my boatful. Could reverse direction.

I did a last hairpin curve over the former Shady Circle Drive
twelve feet under. The kids stayed quiet if with teeth chatter-
ing. Though teenage boys, they kept their arms around each
other for sheer warmth. Diana sat hidden within tarp, silent

as royalty, looking out at the water hiding her holy stomping ground. She seemed undisturbed, staring in a clear and noiseless way that made me remember why I loved her.

The mall would have its bonfires, media, hot tomato soup. First I'd just swing back by, check if Cait Tarlton and her photo show had been saved.

Odd, by then it seemed that I, full of tidal surge myself, would **always** run this bass-boat-shuttle out of our disaster. I liked the work, this leg-up shoe-clerk service. I felt relaxed in ways that might have been hysteria or gratitude or both. Water seeks its own level.

Without one real possession past my clothes, this motorboat, a wedding ring, I felt lightened, simpler. But also babyish. The damp fetus somehow gone sixty-five and out on good behavior. A nineteen-room house? Dad's idea. Marrying Jean? Some great notion of Diana's then Jean's then all the Riversiders who adored us two sweet runts. "Good idea. Who else will they get? I think they're **cute** together."

Surely I could finally move on.

We heard a terrible yodeling. It sounded pitiful but violent. I glanced back at my passengers. I could tell they dreaded whatever sight such sounds would bring us.

I chugged across Hutcheson property, over Greta's beautiful knot garden spoilt beneath brown water. At the corner of Carter and Shady Circle, in what was the front yard of some new doctor from Nash General, we came on two young golden retrievers.

Flailing, by now they were barely afloat. Dogs kept paddling in gulping circles, reduced to saving themselves by climbing up onto each other's backs. Nails and teeth of each had slashed the other bloody.

Seeing help, they howled and, spastic, flapping, angled to

face us. But what most struck us in the boat: Though water here easily went down fourteen feet, despite higher ground's being visible close by, these yellow dogs still made themselves swim—whimpering circles—right over their owner's yard. No wall, no street was visible, only drifting deck chairs and dark free currents coursing everywhere. And yet both animals stayed put, treading the very water they were bloodying. As if assigned one jail cell, pets spasmed back and forth, floundering in that one brackish narrow.

We called to them and, treading half-under, they gladly turned and watched us. But each kept whining in place, wanting help yet scared to come for it. One kid behind me asked, "Why they hanging *there*, mister?"

I only knew while answering, "It's their 'Invisible Fence.' They think the power's still on. So scared of one little shock, they're drowning right over their yard."

We slapped water: "Here, boys!" No go. The dogs' collars were fitted with electrical stunners meant to keep them in the yard where a triggering line lay buried. Electricity citywide had been shut off since three a.m. Their owners were not home to help. I saw one dog had actually shed its collar. Still the poor creatures stayed. They must have scrambled up the house's sides as water rose, then onto its roof, and finally out to the property's front edge. And here they swam in bloody goldfish circles hours later.

I tried explaining their security system to the kids. But, dazed, boys didn't quite register the setup. It would've seemed overelaborate, wasteful in their neighborhood. Seemed that way here, too.

Diana kept silent. I was now so glad for these youngsters' strength. As I watched drowning dogs going under, snarling at each other's necks, I started feeling sick. I went half faint myself—from motor fumes? Maybe stress.

Since waking to find my first and second floors sodden—I'd had a surge superhuman, pure attention mainly for others. Heck, I'd been in the boat for, what? six hours straight. Need be, just peeing off the side. But now I understood I hadn't eaten since the night before, and then only a bowl of warmed-over oyster stew.

Could I somehow be a skinny old guy suddenly at retirement age? Oh, definitely. And, considering another rescue—of dogs so crazed and young and heavy—I felt myself go weak as water. Such gratitude now as four able brown hands (ivory palms) hooked the one poor creature's collar then got another's foreleg while heaving both with damp loud **thwunks** into the bottom of our rocking boat.

Soon as the gasping dogs were with us and safe on their sides, their tails, almost mechanical, beat three times very hard against aluminum. For a split second they looked over at each other. Just that once, but with such great joint effort. Then both fell dead asleep. This, of all things, shook me.

Of every triggering sight today, this seemed so sad and wonderful, their being saved if bloody, their staring at each other to acknowledge that, then **out**. I could see now: one was male, one female. So, a marriage.

The way they'd checked on each other before agreeing to lose consciousness, that was a true killer. I cannot describe it well enough. But when I looked at the kids astern, I felt glad they'd gone wet-eyed, too. Pals sat hugging. Diana barely noticed anybody, gazing at all our water as if it were just some mis-delivered Amazon order. Then, oh, but I wished my best friend were here. People always praised Jean's jokes and smile as "dry"—a holy word today. Shouldn't I have felt more grateful, forty years spent riding alongside someone so forgiving? I'd been the worst sort of snob—mine, a store-clerk's snobbery. Now, finally qualified, I wanted my wife back. Now I was **earning** her.

One of the boys saw me shaken. Polite, he waited a few minutes before calling, "When you done with this load? If you still on the clock? Figure you could maybe take us back to where some **our** folks need help?"

"You bet you."

With final prizes—three people and two live dogs, after all— I could head to higher ground. Our neighborhood smelled of raw pine sap so strong it burned your eyes like Lysol. You got a snootful of hog waste and this strange new scent, almost sweet. It was the smell of so damn much water left all to itself and allowed to rush anywhere, everywhere.

Dust had powdered each twig with a pinkish talcum (dust flying in odd puffs as if scared of becoming mud). But far under our boat, braiding currents pushed blackness over former golf courses and car lots. We squinted in the smell of what's **wild**. Freedom, chaos, everything let loose at once.

It was something not even my great-grandparents got to sniff: it was the smell of wilderness, doing all it wanted before any of us ever got here.

—Doing all it will do once it has finally shed **us**.

IV.

FIVE YEARS LATER and I just turned seventy. "Mitch's Boat People," they call themselves? they threw me a surprise party.

Antoine and Sam and Lottie and her grandkids all turned up. Plus Diana, again looking forty-eight if a day. And the Hutchesons and Charlie Hague (with his skin like a girl's).

Before floodwater dropped quite four feet, I'd already retired from insurance. If you think that *pay*ing it is hard, imagine the torture of quadruplicate recordkeeping. Went out of that office like I'd bailed from my second story. (Insurance had been Dad's idea: "Take advantage of our *con*tacts," Shoe winked.)

The flood made me a thinker, made me mad, or smarter. Not sure which. Was it a breakdown afterward or some gush of overdue insight? Maybe all the above. A flood, after all.

That night in September, we'd been on our own. And somehow we briefly managed for each other. There truly *was* no government. No electricity, no property lines, no valid houses! There was whoever, in swimming distance, needed your little boat.

One thing I know now: It's a privilege to at least *try* saving each other. It's also a full-time job.


Riverside had been our one blue-chip sure thing, the citadel everybody in this eastern part of our state aspired to. Now? it's a huge contaminated park, river view, not one 1939 "Colonial" still standing. So much for American history (a series of revivals anyways, I guess).

Five years after our night of high water, the number of people in Falls still seeing shrinks you would not believe.

Me, I actually have a new lady friend. Great bridge player, a widowed former school principal, Grace. Total charmer, too. Must be doing a little something right. I was spared owning even one salvageable stick of furniture. Blessing in disguise. And Dad's "ancestral home," very well-insured? So much harum-scarum flagstone way downstream.

These days I occupy a year-old maintenance-free condo, three miles from any river, thanks.

I like it here. White interiors, no floral wallpaper. One table, one bed, one real good couch. I guess I live like a 1950s shoe clerk staying strictly within his means. I live like a renter.

Retired, I scan three morning papers online. From the *Times* to the localest, I read them religiously. Aside from sports, I had let the world drift to hell in a handbasket. It sure got worse without my monitoring! Prediction and leadership keep failing us. Is it as bad as it seems or does this just mean I've entered my seventies?

Corrupt as it is today, Washington, D.C., must now smell like Falls did after the flood.

These days, maybe only the old and semi-brave should even bother keeping up with current events?

Only those with boats!


Now I sit quiet and dryly puzzle out my whole career: the choosing insurance, the marrying Jean, the not waiting for Diana, my old choices. Probably unadventurous to have stayed put in my hometown, in that Founding Father palace Dad bought for me, one high heel at a time.

"Never let Shadowlawn pass out of family hands," he begged at the end. —Poor old Shoe. He died believing in American permanence. He'd never noticed others crowding behind us in line. He never guessed how fast we'd squander our country's foolproof inheritance.

Finally, post-flood, I could live anyplace on earth. Some locals my age moved en masse to bone-dry Phoenix. But so many folks I know are still here, still getting over that one night. All my life I'd been waiting for something. —Was that it?

We've become good company for each other, way better than before. There are new kinds of people in my circle. I now know an artist that paints several "abstracts" a week. Keeps her busy. And I've come to like two gay guys that live together, and one of them, I swear, is the best golfer Falls ever produced. These days, between us, post-flood, so much can go unsaid. Since that night, I've given lots of Jean's family money away. It never really felt mine.

Now that I can really begin again, I seem to have chosen to be here. It's no longer my father's neighborhood, not Jean's or Diana's. And, that's what makes my staying put a choice. Pretty late in life, you can come to know your place.

But these five years afterwards, swimming animals still agitate my dreams: *I'll walk into a mall, our mall, and it has been sealed then flooded as if to make a skating rink but it's overfilled with floating scared wild animals, smelling not terrible but more like wet-wool overcoats. These creatures make no sounds except the slaps of paws, the kicks of their hard hooves knocking against mall glass, mall stanchions, mall Sheetrock.* I wake, sitting, terrified.

I am Mitch, now high and dry, and somehow seventy.

Before our flood, my drink of choice was Jack Daniel's and water.

These days, I take it straight.

# MY HEART IS A SNAKE FARM

I HAD A SNAKE FARM in Florida. Well, Buck really owned it, but I believe I'm still Board Chairlady. Almost overnight, he hand-sculpted a one-stop two-hundred-reptile exhibit right across the road from me here. At first it was very clean. It drew lively crowds from the day it opened: December 24, 1959.

Then President Kennedy went and excited our nation about putting a man on the moon. That sicced the Future on any act just roadside and zoological. Tourists soon shot through our state, bound only for Cape Canaveral. Our Seminoles? Our bathing beauties? Passé at eighty mph.

I myself had just retired from life as a grammar-school librarian. I was an unmarried woman of a certain age, imaginative as one could be on a fixed income. I'd felt a growing hatred of Ohio's ice, of shoveling the brick walk I knew would break my hip if I stayed another year. I was and am a virgin, my never-braced teeth too healthy. Toledo's secret nickname for me even as a little girl: Threshing Machine.

My worst vice? Letting others see me gauge their foolishness. So claimed my lifelong housemate, Mother. Even so, fellow-librarians did make me a national officer, thanks to my way with a joke, my memory for names, my basic good sense. And because, at our dressy conventions, everyone looked better than I and they all knew I knew.

An old college friend urged Florida on me. "But, Esther? Be careful where you first settle. Danger is, once you're sprung from those fierce Toledo winters, the first place you find in the Sunshine State you will—like some windblown seed—take fast tropic-type root." She was a prophet. I drove past Tallahassee and, eager to make good time, got only as far as a crumbling pink U.S. 301 motel called Los Parnassus Palms. "That's almost *literary*," I said, hitting the brakes of my blue Dodge. Been here ever since. Rented a room by the night, week, then year, and wound up buying the whole place for less than my Toledo town house cost. I still keep the towels fresh in all twelve suites.

A previous owner had named (then plaqued) each luxury efficiency: "The Monterey," "The Bellagio," etc. True, I never knew what such titles meant. But I accepted them as part of History's welcome by-product, Romance. Some suites I lined with library shelves, others served recreation needs. E.g., 206-B, "The Segovia": Periodicals, Ping-Pong, Reference.

I didn't care to chat up strangers nor wash the sheets of hairy men. So I eventually switched off my place's wraparound neon. But a motel cliff-hangs its highway as waterfront property has lake. Salesmen kept honking, believing that dead signage (plus one cute wink) might mean a discount.

Now, to me, Virginity and Refrigeration have both always

seemed blue. Ditto one small steady "NO" under the pink and blinking "VACANCY." So, months into ownership, royally sick of explaining myself, I flipped on that blue "NO" full-time. Redundant, you say? With my age sixty-seven or -eight? Well, let's get this part over.

As to sex, I had one chance once with a beautiful boy but I chose not to. Actually, it was the father of a friend but it seemed wrong in their sedan in the countryside, and I thought there would be other takers. There were not. You can wind up with nothing; but, if you claim that and don't apologize and forever tell it straight, it can become, in time, something. It's not for everybody to marry and have kids, or even to be, well, homosexual. Or even to be sexual. But you can still retire and move to the semitropics and wind up on the board of a Serpentarium. You never know—that's the thing. And I say, thank God.


Except for two middling hurricanes, my first year in Florida proved ever quieter. I'd always said I liked my own company; well, now I had twelve cubic suites' worth. In identical bathroom mirrors, I found one tusky similarity saying, "Esther, you again?" True, the most intellectual Baptist ladies hereabouts invited me to join a "Serious Issues" book club; yes, I re-linoleumed my whole second story; by then it was almost 1960.

The previous October, Mother'd finally ceased ringing her favorite little bedside bell. I had put it there for emergencies, but soon a moth in the room, any passing car, warranted much brass chiming. By the end, I asked the morticians if they would settle Mother's service bell right in the coffin with her. These large, kind men remembered me lording it benign over their grammar-school library. They now said, "How sentimental. So your momma, in case she wants something, can ring for someone else in the next world?" I lowered my eyes. "Exactly," I said, but thought, "And ring, and ring!" I let gents believe whatever version of me they found easiest to take.

Now that I'd retired to wearing flats, finally becoming my own silent hobby, imagine my alarm when the two acres right across my highway here blossomed into Carnival overnight. Someone had leased the swampy inlet and its entire adjoining beachfront. He'd claimed my sole view of the ocean. One morning, two black Cadillacs, sharky with finnage, rolled up, pulling silver-bullet Airstream trailers. A pile driver soon pounded what looked like sawed-off telephone poles right into sand dunes.

The man in charge, I saw from my perch, was a big tanned white-haired fellow, all shoulders and department-store safari gear. He supervised via barks and back slaps, using his beer bottle as a pointer. I always resist such show-off males. (They never notice.) I'd served under three similar swaggering principals, mere boys. Any Ohio man willing to be called "third-grade teacher" got promoted above capable senior women. Now I watched this particular bull, six-two, fifty-eight if a day. Dentures probably.

Across the poles, he hand-stretched huge canvas placards pulled tight as fitted sheets. Each showed a different Wild Animal of the creeping, crawling, biting variety. The ocean? Already upstaged. (First a showman hides something, then he describes it so you'll shell out the admission.) Braggart images looked wet with all the drippage colors of tattoos. Crocodiles were shown, big as floating shacks. Black snakes glistened in figure-eight oil spills that lashed up the legs of screaming white girls scarcely dressed. The more pictures this hatchet-faced lion-tamer rigged aloft, the slower flowed traffic on old U.S. 301. Beasts scaly, beasts spiny, swarthy, twisted, fanged. "Come one, come all." Not wholly uninteresting.

Meantime, I dragged a cushioned bamboo lounger out of "The Santa Anna." Arms crossed, jaw set, I settled in, daring him to get one centimeter tackier.

The salt-white dunes soon swarmed with antlike workers. Into sand, using driftwood, the head honcho drew a large scallop shell, outhouse-sized. He pointed where he wanted it built. Mexican-American bricklayers scratched their heads then shrugged but, laughing, nodded. Many cinder blocks got unloaded. Within hours, the men had formed three steps, each mitered round as a fish gill in *Fantasia*. Atop these stairs arose one little Aztec ruin dropped beside the sea—a ticket booth, glass-fronted, scallop-crowned.

As masons mosaicked, Jungle Jim praised his artistes, fed them grilled sandwiches, wielded a trowel while squinting past his cigarette. His big piñata head moved side to side, judging, as he framed all this beauty between his thumbs. He once backed too near traffic.

Three attractive young women, using hand fans, kept their folding chairs aimed wherever he largely stood. By six o'clock, his cinder-block fortress, shaped like some goldfish bowl's hollow castle, had been painted an odd pistachio-meets-swimming-pool green.

All day, knuckles on hips, making a jolly silhouette, the man laughed and threw his head back sort of thing. He seemed as entertained as I by how his fantasy could rise in hours from sketch to housing. Come ruddy sunset, these circus folks threw tapering shadows that spanned traffic, just hooking their heads and shoulders into my parking lot. The showman (roughly my age, I now decided, though some men carry it better) mixed two clear pitchers of possible martinis. He and his dark workers toasted their structure and everyone watched the sun sink ruby-colored behind it. Then the boss—with a bullfighter's slash—

tossed his whole martini up the stairs, cocktail glass shattering into sand. His women, stirred, saluted him by knocking back their drinks in single gulps. Thus ended their first day here.

If such a white-trash eyesore had sprung up across the street from my Toledo mews town house, I would've stormed City Hall with two hundred other irate owner-career girls. But here, even with my oceanfront eclipsing fast, I stared from my green-house (formerly 202-A) while pretending to read fiction, doubting that things could grow more gypsy-ish.

The level of construction across four lanes of traffic soon became almost too complex for even me to track. Then two huge snakes arrived UPS. How, you ask, could I know the bundle's contents from this distance even while using Mother's surprisingly helpful mother-of-pearl opera glasses? Hints: serpent-package length, two added suitcase handles, triangular orange Caution stickers, air-holes thickly screened, and how the delivery boy, wearing shorts, held these out like barbells, far, far from his plump legs.

The carnival's first six days here, I played hard to get. I deprived management of my company. I did not even wave. They seemed to be coping all too well.

Nothing like this had ever so directly threatened my privacy tropique, my sense of self. Of course, the previous year, our retired librarians' newsletter, *Ex LIBRIS*, had announced, "Guess which colorful national officer just retired to and purchased her own 'compleat' Florida motel? (As yet unlisted, she is 813-555-0152.) Yes, our Esther!" Librarians fetched up here so thick I thought of it as filing. I stuck the Altoona crowd in 104-A, "The Sangria." The louder Texans I sent on purpose to the leaking 307-B, "The Santa Anna," an Alamo pun only I got.

Eventually, I hung sheets over my office doors and windows. And, slowly, even those big-time lending librarians greediest to borrow a free sunny room got the hint. Circulations dwindled.

Alone I was again. Mother's bell had been muted by six feet of Ohio loam frozen solid. My studying the ocean? Worth maybe three full minutes daily. Now what?

The ringmaster across my highway finished digging a whole lake using his yellow rental bulldozer. From floor two and then from my flat roof, I caught chance peeks at his radical new land use behind the screening placards. Finally, one afternoon as I sat reading, all at once, in the bull's-eye center of the lake he'd scooped, up spouted a wild central jet. It went off like Moby-Dick sighing straight aloft. This secret fountain caught me utterly off guard. I felt surprised, then half scared by such a tacky surge, felt something possibly akin to sheer dumb joy. A column of white foam shot forty feet, then fell heavily aside to make a plash half violent, half joke. My every suite seemed cooled some eight to ten degrees.

I rose. I saw that I had been a snob. These tanned, pretty circus folk were new here and living so en masse—and God knows I was none of the above.

I finally understood it'd been Mother, that old eighty-five-pound Denver boot, still holding me back—her scoldings about manners and the standards required of a family fine as ours. She'd never let me play with my favorites, twins, "coarse, grocers' daughters." Having risen, I now slammed shut Pearl S. Buck's *The Good Earth*. It was my third time through. Why be trapped in a book as some Chinese peasant girl when I had Maturity's sloppy, festive here-and-now?

Darting downstairs to my office-kitchen, I pulled forth a fresh-baked piping coffee cake, carried it bold across the highway (as soon as the steady stream of Key-bound tourists allowed a gap for a running gal my age). That's how I first met Buck and his wives.

"Well, aren't you the perfect welcome wagon," he himself spoke, deep. "We noticed you seemed to be in every window. Sure you ain't triplets? Does your coming over mean you forgive a guy's road show for complicating your property value? But aren't you scared my prize Burmese python will wind up in your"—he studied unlit neon—"Parnassus Palms dresser drawers?"

"That a threat or a promise?"

Well, this cracked him up. "You're a right good sport."

"Looking like this, do I have a choice?"

The ladies laughed, he didn't. I am such a patented virgin I can say things only some ancient cross-eyed nun might risk.

"Everybody has a choice," Buck met me head-on. "That's what we mean by 'sport.'"

Soon, over a berry-pink daiquiri in his teak-lined trailer, I asked Mr. Buck how many snakes he owned—did he hire them from some animal-theater agent or catch them by hand? The man's voice had gathered accents from pretty much everywhere. These were basted in a unifying baritone the hue of Myers's dark rum.

"Some, lady, I personally snagged in Brazil. Gators just seem to find me. Mowgli, why, she swam up a service-station drainage ditch in Kissimmee. I rescued Stump after he fell into the pool of some bad motel, no offense. My alligators start, like seeds, you know, small, but you feed them into becoming attractions. Funny, but they're loyal in their way. The fancier snakes I have been known to order by phone but will probably say I caught bare-handed. I did, by dialing Princeton, New Jersey, same outfit that pervides mice to your finer cancer labs.

Yep, always have been fascinated by the cold-blooded. As a kid, I tanned muskrat and otter pelts, kept corn snakes on-hand, pretty, non-poisonous. Been on my own since I was nine. Lost Mom to diphtheria, Dad to a traveling lady preacher. So be it. A longish adventure. —But enough 'bout me. What's your setup, Esther? You didn't start in Florida. Naw, you're like me. On the lam from another buncha lives squandered elsewhere, eh?"

I lowered my eyes, unwilling to seem simple as the word "unopened." But then Buck did something unheard-of. Awaiting my response, he looked unashamed, a tamer of beasts, right at me. I peeked back up. I stood here and he stood there, with his ladies slouched to all sides, and he did not avert his eyes or flinch, not even men's usual once. "Ouch at first sight," I call it. My teeth are independent; each has its own unique sense of direction. And my hair, despite backcombing, had grown somewhat thin on top. All my life, even when I was six, males have treated me like the Maiden Aunt. A self-fulfilling trend. But this Buck, he stared straight at (not through) me. Seemed only he was strong enough to take it.

Buck soon bounded clear across north- and southbound lanes, inviting me to his show, for free. He'd asked everybody door-to-door for miles. He included massage parlors and churches, all the same to him. By now his toy-like bulldozer had piled real hills around Buck's spitting lake. He'd imported full-grown royal palms. He'd made the white gravel paths look almost natural, going nowhere, if fast and in four-leaf clovers.

Pastors, bleach-blond masseuses, two education-minded Cuban couples, and a bunch of glum little boys gathered, plus me. "Everybody 'bout ready? Come one, come all. Price is right, if today only." Then he performed his entire test spiel. Buck's first jokes did seem stale, even for 1959. ("Welcome to Florida, Land of Palms . . . all open!") But it was like a starter try for us all. If he tended to ramble, en route Buck charmed. He mapped out Amazonian rainy seasons, warned of visa requirements, described his sleeping-sickness onsets. He showed early claw damage to one forearm. Facing certain snakes, he recounted their especially nasty captures. As he grew loud, his creatures got stiller and even beadier-eyed, as if out of guilt. He draped any creature not gator-weighty around his neck. They looked like leis that flexed; they seemed to enjoy it.

When Buck laughed, he gave off a smell like flint, ham, and 3-in-One motor oil. Active as he was, one of his fingernails was always black-blue, coming and going. He lived in his great-white-hunter gear, jagged khaki collar, epaulets. Pall Malls got buttoned into a customized slot, the Zippo lighter slid snug into its own next door. This man had a brown face like a very good Italian valise left out in a forest during World War Two and just refound. Weathered, but you could still see how fine its starter material had been.

Buck owned alligators, about forty, and three were the stars—huge, I mean as big as ever I saw in Mother's precious back numbers of the *Geographic*. As with cows, they each had whole sides to them. They loved their new lake; most showered in its hourly fountain. Large amounts of lettuce got eaten. (Buck had already payolaed the produce clerks from Piggly Wiggly and Winn-Dixie to bring their cast-offs here instead of leaving them lonely in trash vats back of stores. He also fed his reptiles frozen chickens—claimed the birds' iciness made a crunch the beasts considered their own achievement.)

I soon noticed grocery trucks over there at all hours, as much for curiosity as delivery. TV stations covered his Grand Opening. By now, the show was charging (except for me) full admission and Buck let each visiting child feed one gator apiece. Only the bravest dared. The kid would inch out on a diving board wearing rubber gloves to keep from getting lettuce drool on his paws. Parents took snapshots. I feared a lethal topple. I briefly wondered about the Reptile Farm's insurance picture; then, suspecting no coverage whatever, thought of something else. Smelling chow, gators hissed like gas leaks. Large white mouths opened. Seemed it was always time to feed the gators. Anything could be tasty. Loose luncheon meats, crates of limes, you name it—they ate each thing before deciding.

Till Buck and his wives appeared, my afternoons had been somewhat less eventful; the local library (open three to five Tuesday afternoons) featured only past-due bestsellers stinking of Coppertone. Come one p.m., I had been mostly monogamous with my favorite soap, One Life to Live. Sure, Fridays I might go wild, pop popcorn. But, finally, in the Parnassus Convent vs. Reptile Coliseum battle for my interest? No contest. By then Buck had made me a charter member of the Snake Farm Family Board, meaning I always got in free.

His one request: "How's about you arrive five minutes prior to showtime wearing a flowered hat and carrying a purse, Esther? Just to keep up our sense of how my place is classy, scientific, er, whatever. Pretending to listen like you do gives my talks real tone, your being the retired educator. Eyeglasses would be good, even your reading specs. Hell, hon, with old school smarts like yours on view, I can charge a dollar more per customer."

Oh, he was sly, that Buck. He wore a cap pistol rammed into his holster, had on thigh-high treated boots, double-thick to keep rattlers from snagging clear through. He would be wad-

ing into their humid glass booth, where thirty snakes curled
clicking like seedpods on a binge.

Nobody hates snakes more than snakes do. That's part of
why we fear them. We recognize our own self-loathing, but
slung even lower, it's armless-legless with self-pity. And yet,
even during a heat wave, snakes piled one atop the other like
trying to form some sloppy basket. I did not get why. Myself
being a single person, myself with typing margins set Maxi-
mum Wide, with me needing 13,500 square feet just to feel suf-
ficiently dressed, simply watching such constant summer skin
contact made me feel half-ill.

Sometimes if I saw a crowd of especially nice cars—
Lincolns, Caddies or Imperials—I might wander over. First I
limited myself to Mondays and Wednesdays—plus, of course,
weekends. (Mother had always rationed my attending other
children's birthday parties: "You come home a sticky blue from
their cheap store-bought sheet cakes. You forgive their whispering jokes about your . . . features. Listen to you, still wheezing
from having run around screaming till you sound asthmatic,
Esther. —No, we're alike. Too sensitive for groups. You are one
overstimulated young lady. So let's just sit here a few hours and
collect ourselves, shall we, Little Miss?")

Buck's wives swore that if I stayed away too long certain
snakes sulked. How could the ladies tell? You mostly recognized
different reptiles by their size and how much of that the others
had chewed off. I got to know on sight Buck's largest rattlers:
Mingo, Kong, and Lothar. Stumpy was the hungriest gator and
often got in the way of others' frozen chickens. Stumps never
learned. And he paid dearly with his limbs, his tail mass, and,
finally, his life. God bless his stubborn appetite.

After-hours, hanging out with wives in the Reptile Post-
card Shop & Snack Canteen, Buck claimed he had once bought

Hemingway a rum drink in Key West and got invited home to "Papa's" hacienda for an all-night poker game. I usually asked him what Hemingway was *really* like. Buck would shake his head sideways: "Good talker, sore loser."

During tours, I don't think Buck's grasp of species names' Latin was all it might have been. More than once I heard some pushy customer loiter before a ragged cage, jab his camera toward Exhibit A, and demand, "Hey, what kind of snake is this un' hiding here?" "That one? That's a big mean red one is what that is. Sooner bite you than look at you. Now, ahead on our left . . ." People would laugh, not knowing if he was joking or muleheaded. But, with this level of poison around, considering his German Luger and hooked stick, no one ever asked Buck for refunds or repetitions.

After one show, I quizzed him: "I guess it's that people love to be scared?"

"No, dear Esther. It's: people love to be scared by something new."

I looked at him. I sipped straight bourbon.

In time I'd learn that Buck had been married four times, and three-quarters of his troubles were still with him. "Buck's harem," locals soon called them. Each gal kept her sleek identical trailer parked behind the backmost palms. I heard tell Buck visited a different lady every night. I'd never stayed up late enough to see. Some part of me did wish he would at least come nap in any of Parnassus's comfy settings. I kept the central fans of all twelve suites going, just in case. He plainly had no sleeping place not already warmed by a previous nesting wife. "Feeding them's cheaper 'n alimony," one local boy claimed Buck said. But that sounds like any of the hundred rumors that made his stint here on our highway so lively during those glory years of latest Ike-Mamie, earliest Jack-Jackie.

Buck's wives seemed another sort of specimen collection. They wore stage makeup, as if competing with each other during those long hot afternoons spent waiting for Buck's last show to end. Of all ages, his wives were either very young now or had been even better-looking pretty recently. Each still appeared sun-baked with strong ceramic traces of her starter glamour.

Working the concession trailer, they were supposed to sell the tourists food and souvenirs. They mostly smoked, drank Cokes and ate the merchandise. They'd say funny things about our paying customers. "With those ears, we should stick ole Clem there out in the monkey cage," or "Some of our exhibits eat their young, ma'am, and if you can't quiet those bawling twins of yours we have the livestock that will." "Now, ladies." Buck came in laughing. He liked them spirited. Of my outfits, he preferred me in the lilac-covered hat and the white patent-leather shoes with matching bag. He wanted his wives to lounge out front—like auditioning—in halters, waving at the cars, bringing in considerable business. (Me, I'd drag a kitchen chair into shade off to one side.) Truth is, the girls looked a little better from sixty-five mph. But don't we all?

Come drink-time, the former wives changed into beautifully ironed off-the-shoulder gypsy blouses. They sported pounds of Navajo silver and turquoise squash-blossom necklaces that would bring a fortune today. They were always painting their fingernails and toenails or working on each other's. You felt their tensions crest only at the sound of the final blanks Buck fired to end his show. When at last he stalked in, there'd be this pinball ricochet of love-starved looking: him gaping at the nut-brown breasts of one while another studied Buck's flat backside, as the other kept glowering at his front. Nervous, I once blurted, "Can I grab anybody a cold Coke?" and got one hot unified glare. They all seemed to *like* this body tension. Would just not be distracted.

His exes were intelligent girls who had not enjoyed my state-school advantages. They'd once felt too attractive to ever need much additional information. Doing crosswords out loud between shows, they'd squeal at how often I helped. "Flanders Fields!" I found myself yelling as my mother told me I should not at parties. The girls soon treated me like Einstein's sister, and I admit I humored them.

Christmas and Easter, I had the whole crew over to Los Parnassus Palms for my turkey, dressing, pies. The wives arrived in drop earrings, evening gowns. Slinky and powdered, they unfolded from matching Caddies. Buck would wear a crumpled tux that looked like Errol Flynn at the end.

Beloved fellow snake farmers seemed most impressed by my owning countless solid-silver napkin rings from Mother. (Funds she might've spent on her only child's teeth braces.) "Good weight," Buck said, testing, as all his holiday ladies nodded, giving him hooded looks. His wives had each been in or near the Show business. Buck's first, Dixie, once worked as a juggler's assistant in Reno; Peggy, numero dos, claimed to have been a buyer (estate jewelry) for Neiman Marcus; Tanya was runner-up to be a studio player at Metro pictures in the class that included Janet Leigh. Over wine, they revealed more of Hollywood's sad secrets. Hearing the crazy vices of the stars, I cried, "No, not him, too. What leading man'll be left for Esther!" The wine flowed.

(Later, some local yahoo tried telling me Buck had never

married those three girls, said that they were just part of his roadside attraction, that their separate trailers made nightly cash admissions possible. I don't believe it for an instant and I think some people along this road have very dirty minds. They adored him. That was all.)

Not long into Kennedy's administration, the wives sped off to buy new outfits in Bradenton where the circus folks retire. I saw their fin-tailed Cadillacs scratch off around three, and at four I notice Buck, waving a big white hanky to make cars stop, looking sick as he come staggering across four lanes of traffic toward my Parnassus Palms. I can't say I hadn't pictured this house call before. But not in crisis, not owing to illness. When I opened my screen door, he frowned, head wedged against one shoulder, and his face was all but black. He handed me a razor blade. "Esther? Some timber rattler, either Kong or Lothar, snagged me a good one in the back. Here, cut an X. Then pour ammonia on it. Go in an inch at least. I can't see to reach it and my focus . . . It's already all over, focus sliding, Esther."

He whipped off his shirt. Front down, he fell across my rattan lounger. I now stood behind him. Two fang marks weren't hard to find because of all the purple swelling. "Okay," I said. I dashed to get a towel and some ammonia. I splashed a dollop of cold water in my own face. Buck's upper back was seizing something terrible. And yet its shape was very strong, copper-brown, tapered like a swimmer's. I cut far deeper than I wanted, then blotted at least two pints into a large white beach towel. "Now," Buck said, "I'm going to have to ask you, Esther. And for a friend like you I'd do it in a heartbeat. Feels I . . . feels I'm going into shock here. I'd never ask for any reason shy of Life and Death. —But, honey, would you suck it?"

I might sound funny if I tell you my thin legs nearly buckled. I fought then not to faint. Blame my seeing his dark blood, or my viewing his entire back. More than once I had pictured him across the road being worked on by his full swarm of wives. I'd imagined how Buck might look shirtless, and he looked better, even with the blood, which made this more a movie. With Buck in the lounger, I could not bend forward far enough to help. "Here." I lifted him and led him to my davenport. He was only half conscious and the weight of him was wonderful and tested my full sudden Esther strength. I helped him stretch out there, facedown. God, how he trusted me!

I settled on the floor beside his ribs. Finally, breathing for two, I rose up on my knees. My teeth are bucked, as you'll have noticed. My own low-cost form of fixing them has always been to make the joke about them first. "Need a human bottle opener?" I once heard a handsome young man quip to pals (and me only seven, trailing embarrassed pretty girlfriends). But now, knowing I might finally be useful to someone, I managed to say nothing. No Esther jokes today, Esther!

I tottered on my knees then pulled the hair back off my forehead. My eyes wet, I drew closer to his snake holes. They were like twin tears in cloth. At last I pressed my lips down onto those warm slots black with blood, then, slow, I pulled the poison out of Buck. Into myself. You might think I'm exaggerating when I say that I could taste what was poison, what was blood. The poison was bitter with a foamy peroxide kick to it. But blood seemed only salty and, by contrast to the venom, almost sweet.

"Spit it out, Esther, spit it on the towel. Get all that out of you. I cannot have you harmed, not for a sec. You're so fine, dear. Bless your soul for this." I did as he said. I spewed it out then, just as he told me. I was stooped here over him, him flexed out below me, star-shaped, Buck. I fought wanting to cry like some little girl would then. Crying not from horror, not even from gratitude, but more from simply knowing: **This is my life I am living.**

"Esther, now please hit me with ammonia. Takes acid to counteract snake acid. There. Yeeks, burns so good. Now I'm going to need some shut-eye, pet. You sure did it, though. You got it all or most, and I can tell, dear. But let me sleep, oh, twenty minutes tops. Then I'll be fine. No more than that or I'll get dopey. I will need to do something when I come to. Need to have you walk me around. This has happened maybe ten other times, so I know. But when I do feel stronger and can roll over, I am going to thank you, Esther. Living across from us these couple years, you've made our being here just so much more livelier. More civil. And now this. You be thinking if there is anything whatever I can do for you, girl."

Then, at once, he passed out or slept. I eased onto my breezeway. Had myself a cigarette. I'd only ever smoked two before. But somebody had left half a pack in "The Segovia" and I did enjoy that one slow Lucky, pulling smoke way in, letting it find its own eventual way out. Laissez-faire. Then I realized: here, the only time a man had ever told me in advance I could expect something memorable and I was making my big mouth smell like an ashtray. I had to laugh at myself as I dodged into "The Bellagio" and swigged down half a bottle of Lavoris. By doing this, I saw I'd made most of a decision.

I only woke him because I felt scared that being out too long might give Buck brain damage. I stooped beside my davenport again. "Time," I said. Facing downward, he just yawned then aimed his elbows out, as if nothing much had happened. So . . . male.

My couch had a new hibiscus print on it, maroon. Whatever blood he'd shed, it would blend in. But I wished that some might stay there, permanent. So sure, he turned over with a sleepy grin and growled up, "Hiya, lifesaver." First Buck kissed me full on the mouth then more *in* the mouth. It did not prove so repulsive as it always looked when you suspected two movie actors were sneaking doing it.

Then he told me he'd forever been crazy about me after his fashion right from the start. Said how his liking me so, it had nothing to do with my first aid just now. Not simple tit for tat. "So to speak," I said.

He told me to go pull the blinds shut, and I did. He got himself to sitting, woozy still. Then he patted the cushion right beside him. I, dutiful, feeling frail as if I had been snakebitten, settled just where he showed me.

"You won't forever after blame me or be jealous of the others if we do this once, to celebrate my coming back to life with your great help, right?" I shook my head no. He said, "Nothing to panic anybody. No breakage, Esther. Just one thing I want to do. I am too weak for offering up everything right now. I would black out. But this I know I want." And he slid down off the couch and, first, Buck warmed his right hand between my knees. In recent years I've been given to wear half-stockings and he soon rolled those fully down with all the care of the earth's best young doctor. Next, he hooked his hands around my drawers' elastic and pulled the pants out from under me, showing me how to lift up so he could do it easier.

He knew I could not have borne to let him see me all undressed. It was just too late for that much. Too late to do everything. But as I kept my hand on his one shoulder not swollen, Buck's white hair, bristly as a pony's, disappeared under my housedress. There was no false start, none of the snaky seeking

I had feared. His tongue was there all at once, its own blood-hound locator system, and it could have been a hundred and sixty degrees hot. I had no idea. It, his tongue, soon seemed to be a teacher of infinite patience, then like a sizzling skillet, a little pen flashlight, now featherweight, now flapjack, then just a single birthday candle that—in time, strengthened by doing lap after lap—becoming the forest fire. I had no notion I would ever respond like this, way beyond where Language ever gets to start. In brief, certain sounds were made. Snake-farmish sounds, only it was me . . . I. The "I" that soon had her leg crooked around his shoulder, pushing him away, but he leaned into that so it felt like I was playing him in and out of me at exactly my own speed. He was regular as a clock and I was always knowing where he would have been as I allowed myself and just went off again and again and off again, my calves St. Vitus, my feet dancing spasms. The first time was sort of a sea-green, the second time more a bronzy blue—there came a red moment but it ended all steamed in hard-baked stone-washed sunflower-yellow.

It ended only because I was too proud to let it go on as long as it wanted to. Which would've been as long as both his life and mine. Finally, I said, "There, oh my . . ." and started to make one of my jokes, but some sudden dignity stopped me. Funny, I didn't feel ashamed. I felt dignified. I never understood that this was possible. Having another person here, it was less shaming. It was more a way of knowing we are all alike in this. It was beautiful. It was once but it was beautiful.


"Bacon and scrambled eggs and coffee cake," I chanted, gathering myself to stand. I knew I wouldn't risk the ugly comedy of pulling up my half stockings or regaining my step-ins. Instead

I would eat a meal with a man who had just taken my knickers off and he would know that, while we ate. I'd placed new oil-cloth on my little table here in the Main Office of Los Parnassus and I felt glad the room looked nice. He stayed right on till 7:35. I asked if he wanted my help to get him back across the high-way. "Hell, no, girl." Buck smiled. "Let me picture you right here as you are. Know what? You're a saint from heaven and one wonderful, wonderful woman. You're so strong. I love that in you, Esther."

"Well, thank you," I said, not doing anything funny, not daring to ruin this. I helped refasten Buck into his blood-soaked safari top. We had eaten as he sat there in the half-light glow with his white hair tangled on his chest and the swell-ing already going down. He was that healthy, it was cause and effect, once I had Hoovered most of the bad stuff out. Fact is, I could still taste him or the poison or probably the mix in my mouth. A blend: walnut, allspice, penny metal, black licorice, lamb medium-well. I watched him go.

The traffic parted, like for Moses.

"Come one, come all," I whispered through my screen door.

It was Buck's fourth wife that took him to the cleaner's. She was not in residence. On Independence Day, we heard she'd sud-denly demanded half of everything; and here he was already sharing with his first three. Her lawsuit tipped him into bank-ruptcy. I hate that kind of selfishness in women. In anybody. He gave so much. Then she had to claim his cars and wallet. The sheriff served a summons mid-show. Flashing lights, sirens, horrible for Buck.

What else shut him down? Not the Health Department, though they could have. Grilled-cheese sandwiches were served to customers off a greasy G.E. appliance meant for home use only. Buck's vats, where the gators did their shows (if you could call gators' being gators *shows*), those might've used a weekly hosing-down with ammonia, Clorox. I had not volunteered to rush over and help. But *you* try and Ajax around thirty moody rattlers. All I knew, just when our neighborhood's social life had grown so routed through the Reptile Canteen, just as I'd got, first, the taste of poison, then a taste of what other people's physical-type lives must be like and, I guess, daily—here came the state to close him down.

There was a huge new sign:

*Selling Truly Giant Snakes/Gators.*
*Under Chapter Eleven, Everything Must Move.*

Buck soon sold the rattlers to researchers who believed their venom might someday cure cancer. A nature park outside Orlando sent a huge yellow Allied Van Line truck for the gators. All thirty-nine (Stumps, deceased, excepted) left here with silver duct tape wrapped clear around their heads, stacked like wriggling cordwood in the back of that dark truck. Oh, it was a black day along this overly bright stretch of U.S. 301, I can tell you. I stood there in Florida's latex glare as the van pulled off with every creature blinkered and discounted.

In honor of the reptiles' exit, I had worn my lilac hat and all my white patent leather and every Bakelite bangle I could find. We held on to each other, Buck, Dixie, Peggy, Tanya and me. Plus some young gents and the teenage boys the girls had flirted with just to keep them buying Cokes. Buck didn't shed a tear. He was the only one. Said, "Well, I've gotten out of tight corners before, girls. But this is the End of the Age of the Snake Farm, probably. Hell, I'm a realist. All their rocket talk and hating the Russians has nixed many a laugh. Eisenhower and Mamie might've been customers here. But, you know, those European-type Kennedys? No roadside attractions for people that French-speaking and stuck-up. Type that changes clothes three times a day without noticing. Thing is, it's not personal, way I see it. And that's the problem. The Future is here and it gets hosed off way too often. And don't you girls suspect it's all based on Bad Science? I think nobody gives good value now, much less put on a decent doggone show. And where the fuck is the energy and fun in any of it? Excuse me, ladies."

"No sweat," said I.

Next morning, hired guys rolled up all Buck's signs. Those now proved no more substantial than window shades, and yet, for almost three years, they'd got to feeling pretty monumental. During windstorms, their canvas snapped like the sails of the *Mayflower*. That sound and the surf's slamming had made this seem the New World after all.

Suddenly, signs gone, the Atlantic's raw horizon showed again. But it'd lost its charm; looked like one lethal paper-cut. Buck's home-dug lake, gatorless, appeared about as exotic as some miniature-golf water trap. Gravel paths bound nowhere now.

I'd planned a major farewell breakfast in honor of my friends. But they left overnight in the middle of the dark. I later saw that as a kindness, really. The very next noon, a Haitian crew—carrying radios blaring French tunes—arrived to dig up all Buck's store-bought palms. Root balls were still wrapped in burlap from their last sale. Seeing those trees go off lonely and akimbo on one flatbed truck? was like witnessing a slave auction of friends. Unnoticed, I waved. From the second-story breezeway, I was physically sick. Well, guess who felt bleak to the point of suicide, of moving back to Toledo mid-February?

Weeks after, you would see a Piggly Wiggly truck pull up, not having heard or believed, and with enough slimy salad in back to feed all terrariums on earth.

I never doubted Buck's tale about beating Hemingway at poker and what a whiner Papa was over losing sixty bucks. I believed my friend about Papa's being overnight with my favorite moving picture star, Ava Gardner. Buck would say no more than that, except, below his dancing eyes, he kissed all his right hand's fingertips. He admitted just, "Ava? Ava was a gentleman." And since Buck had once told me I was also somewhat one, that helped.

Buck had been exactly Ava's type: the best gristle-sample of manhood ever to spring up on the wrong side of the tracks. And a man still male enough at sixty-five or -nine to keep three exes fighting for some stray lettuce-head of his tossed attention. He never bragged, except maybe to tourists he'd never see again. You might think Buck had too little to boast of; but there was, in the high times at the Reptile Canteen, in our sole evening of sucking the poison out of one another, a kind of grandeur I can only hint at. After his wives, too loyal and numerous— having heard his final pistol—powdered their noses and freshened their Cleopatra eyeliner, all of us knowing our last show was ending, once that day's clump of tourists spent a few last wadded dollars on plastic shark-tooth key chains, Buck would come chesting in. He'd give us all a cobra smile, teeth white as my patent leather shoes and, including me, he'd say, "Que pasa, girls?"

Oh, he had it.

That is all I can say.

Buck definitely had it.

\*     \*     \*

Once the Farm closed, if you dared walk over there to consider the sandy blankness and those holes where rental palms had stood, you realized most of the cages had been nothing more than double-thick chicken wire. Made you wonder why the snakes had stayed. Maybe for the reason his ex-wives (and I) did. Because this really had been a working farm. Because everybody did their chores. Even the snakes, who struck against glass, aiming for the sunburned leg of some plump passing tourist-boy, just to make him scream and force his mother, once she found no fang marks, to laugh. "It didn't mean it, Willie. That's just nature being nature, is all. That's what snake farms teach us, son."

Even now, one snaggled fact still stands there. Greenish and flaking, it is chipped like a Greek temple salt-preserved in Sicily; yes, the ticket booth's rounded cinder-block steps arranged in a shape as close as possible to a scallop shell. And up on top there's the little cement platform, five feet above the sand, where people stood to buy admission for their families. Two hurricanes chipped the booth away in two huge molar chunks. But those steps yet survive.

I told myself not to expect to hear from any of the wives or him once they'd slid out of sight. That proved righter than I'd hoped. Still, wherever they washed up next, you wished them well.

(After all, when these show folk found me here in '59, my lady library officer's drink of choice—learned at conventions—had been a sticky cherry cordial. And by the time my snake charmers left in the middle of the night in '63, I'd worked my way straight up to straight Jack Daniel's. Who says there is no human progress?)

Those greened steps now stand framed against only browning palmetto scrub. But here's the funny part. On a cool afternoon, if you park down a ways then tiptoe back, if you take a peek at the little stage that platform makes, you'll often catch three to seven dozing there. Real snakes sound asleep, wild ones. They must love the heat a day of sun leaves banked in those old blocks. Maybe snakes enjoy being dry and up out of their usual mud. But, cottonmouths, water moccasins and, once, a red-and-yellow coral snake, they all seem to be waiting. It's as if local reptiles can yet remember Buck's whole vivid show. Like they long, as I once did, to simply hear how he'd describe them!

Soon as the government closed Buck down, things grew silent fast around Los Parnassus Palms. I could not have simply left here with them when my friends drove off. I owned property. Besides, they never asked.

Still, I knew that, if he ever thought of me, Buck would want his good-sport Esther to be getting on with this, her latest life among the others she'd spent elsewheres on the lam. My heart had lately grown so . . . unsystematic.

When first I bought Parnassus, I turned off its signage indicating rooms available. But bargain-hunting oversexed salesmen kept making me explain myself. So I'd lit just those two low-watt neon letters. My "NO" warned cars away. Through monsoons and dry spells, one blue skull and crossbones—my spinster coat of arms—blazed day and night against stucco.

Five months after the Reptile Canteen closed, as I lounged around the Main Office—alone, naturally—I noticed, there beside the table where we'd eaten our aftermath bacon and eggs and his favorite coffee cake, two light switches. Decades back, these'd been marked in some stranger's tidy pencil script the welcoming "V" and, near it, the canceling "N." I now reached over and, inhaling, with the flair of some magician's assistant, flipped off the "N." Then, taking in two lungfuls of sea air, instead I just hit availability's "V."

I let it burn, out in plain and common view. I cannot say it didn't partly shame me. Pink and raw and overly visible, so all by itself (in its upright fifth-grade cursive). I retreated to our crucial maroon davenport. I settled here, now facing our highway's every southbound headlight.

I crossed my arms and felt surprised to find myself this ready: I would wait again. For what? Something. Anything, though not quite anyone. Heck, I'd already had the best. Oh, I might need to make a few concessions next time; I knew that.

Buck used to flatter me: "Cozy how my big Show attraction stands right up across the road from your nice Shelter attraction, Esther." "That's easy for *you* to say"—I rolled my eyes to make him laugh. He never failed, and in a baritone whose color was mahogany.

Now, almost half a year after losing sight of him, I felt represented by that blinking light out there. He had taught me it pays to advertise. Come one, come all. It's a human right, to name at least what you'd *like* to offer. True, I might not be any motorist's idea of a final destination; but maybe I could pass as just another attraction along a roadside littered with such. —Because, you know what? You never know. And that's a great thing, how they keep us guessing. That comes in second, right after Hope.

Stranger things have happened than life's stopping twice at one convenient off-highway location. Plenty of free parking, God knows. And now, as each headlight played across the slackened front of this, of me—partly ruined yet still far from stupid—I felt I'd maybe outgrown that blue "NO."

Once upon a time in America, a man from nowhere with nothing but shoulders and great teeth, a guy backboned with only one idea—could put up steps to anything that he might make you see as Wonderful. And without bimonthly federal inspections, without any legal charter past a friend or three he called "our Board," that man could shake you down for exactly the number of buckaroos you'd actually part with. And he would send you off glad, with more of your own personal story than you'd had before he took your cash. And all this without exceptional Latin.

Now, through my office plate-glass, I could see the former site of his Attraction. It was lit tonight, salt-white sand, edges of white breakers endlessly uncoiling. All viewed better thanks to sudden commercial flare from here, me. Burning pink, held up against everything, that one word, a proud three feet high. Too rude a come-on for a lone woman of my age and homeliness. Too hardened an admission, even for Florida, right along U.S. 301, even at 2:18 a.m. And yet, leaning back, breathing for one again, my arms folded over a slack chest, I liked going braless beneath a favorite housecoat worn with only "our" bloomers. Who is this woman hidden back of her neon? Why, it's Esther the Impenitent. I would be smoking now, if I smoked.

### VACANCY

Now I knew what it meant.

# ABOUT THE AUTHOR

Allan Gurganus's books include *Oldest Living Confederate Widow Tells All*, *White People*, *Plays Well with Others*, *The Practical Heart*, and *Local Souls*. Gurganus cofounded Writers Against Jesse Helms. He has taught writing and literature at Stanford University, Duke University, Sarah Lawrence, and the Iowa Writers' Workshop. Film adaptations of his work have won four Emmys. Gurganus has been awarded the *Los Angeles Times* Book Prize, the National Magazine Award, a Guggenheim Fellowship, and the Lambda Literary Award. He is a Fellow of the American Academy of Arts and Letters. Gurganus's novel-in-progress is *The Erotic History of a Country Baptist Church*. He lives in his native North Carolina.